WHITE RAVEN

A DEMON'S GUIDE GUIDE TO THE AFTERLIFE
BOOK TWO

AURELIA JANE

KEL CARPENTER

RAGING HIPPO PUBLISHING

White Raven

Kel Carpenter and Aurelia Jane

Published by Raging Hippo LLC

Copyright © 2021, Raging Hippo LLC

Proofread by Dominique Laura

Cover Art by Malice and Mayhem

Discreet PB ISBN: 978-1-957953-53-3

Discreet HB ISBN: 978-1-957953-54-0

 Created with Vellum

About the Authors

Kel Carpenter and Aurelia Jane are the hilarious team behind the international bestselling series, A Demon's Guide to the Afterlife.

They pride themselves in being absolute weirdos, spending hours on the phone coming up with detailed worlds, and laughing about crazy ideas for torturing characters. While they believe they each have the personality of a rabid badger, people still seem to like them okay.

They share a love of coffee, snarky t-shirts, and tacos, and they've made some adorable tiny people with their equally weird husbands. Best friends and work wives, Kel has the audacity to live in Maryland while Aurelia lives in Texas, but they try to see each other as much as possible.

 patreon.com/kelcarpenterandaureliajane

To my husband
For reminding me I'm a motherfucking shark. Or a honey badger, depending on the day. –AJ

To Matt
For keeping me sane and healthy. –KC

I don't care about whose DNA has recombined with whose.
When everything goes to hell, the people who stand by you
without flinching—they are your family.

Jim Butcher, *Proven Guilty, The Dresden Files*

HADES

Didn't expect me, did you?

Well, I'm here for a recap. If you remember what happened, you can move right along. But for those of you that have a shit memory or have just slept since you last saw Fury, this summary is for you.

We start in the Afterlife. It's like it says. It's where you go after your life ends. Your concept of Heaven and Hell? Not a thing. Anyway, Fury is a demon. She reforms bad souls before they get recycled for life again, or just get flat out terminated because they suck too much. Well, she got sent to Earth because she's supposedly good at her job. (I'm not sure about this, but Duke—he runs the Department of Earth Affairs—says she's the best. Upper Management says she's the best. I have some reservations, but I'm just working here.) So, she's sent to stop the end of the world. It's been foreseen that the apocalypse will be brought on by three ultra-powerful supernaturals. Dorian—he's the broody fae, Roman—he's the overprotective and grieving wolf shifter, Ezra—he's the mouthy vampire with an appalling sexual appetite. (No, I didn't mean appealing. I'm not Fury.) These dudes can't die—at least they haven't yet.

In case you need this pointed out, the apocalypse is bad. It's the end of *all* things, the Afterlife included.

Bang, crash, burn, fire, explosion, implosion. Darkness. The end.

Bad. Clear? Okay, moving on.

Stopping them should be an easy task for someone who's "good" at her job, right? Of course not. Because somehow Fury is mated to all three of these guys. That's unheard of. And she's somehow a second-chance mate to all three as well.

It's irritating because I'm stuck as her go-between for the Afterlife and her job on Earth. She can't die—demon, remember?—but the only way for her to go back to the Afterlife is for her vessel to die, dumping her soul right back into Duke's office. It's pretty funny to watch. But the bodies she leaves behind can become a problem. That's where I come in. The go-between. *Not* a pigeon, despite what she tells you. Apparently I'm the go-between here too.

So, she meets all three of these dudes. Lucky for me, she only has a sexfest with one of them. But someone is trying to kill her. They succeed once, killing a vessel. The next time she just suffers injuries. The problem? The assassins have called her Sunny Adams.

Who is Sunny Adams?

That was Fury when she was alive. A twenty-three-year-old girl in the roaring twenties that died at the hands of her abusive husband when he beat her to death.

It's been one hundred and three years since her dick-head husband killed her. So, what the fuck, right? Yeah, we're still trying to figure it out too. Since then, she's been working as a demon. She also drinks to the point of absurdity, and it hasn't gone unnoticed by anyone except her.

Now, add in that Fury has befriended Roxanne. She is Roman's sister. Roxanne gets kidnapped. Wolfnapped? Whatever. It was the kickoff night at the summit—a once every ten years gathering of the fae, shifter, and vampire factions. First night was a fancy banquet. Dinner, dancing, etc. Could that be uneventful? Of course not. This is Fury we're talking about. So that night, Roxanne gets taken by some rogue shifters that Roman pissed off after, well, after branding them rogues. Literally. No, really. He branded it right there on the guy's forehead.

Right. So Fury goes to save Roxanne. Surprise! It's not just shifters. There are some fae and vampires in this group of rogue assassins. Why? Beats me. But they're there. They subdue Fury with some *really* good drugs, stick her on a creepy carousel with creepy clown music, and then cryptically say they know how to kill-kill her. Stop her from existing. Make her for real dead. How? The shifter bites her. See, demons can't be "changed" into supernaturals. The magic from the Afterlife and the supernatural world can't be mixed. The two forms of magic violently collide. In her dying state, she finally exploded in power, killing each and every one of those that hadn't sifted or run far enough away.

Yours truly leads Dorian, Ezra, and Roman to her location. You're fucking welcome. How did they save her? Well, the shifter bit her, the vampire shared his blood with her, and the fae did a thing that's a secret and we don't talk about. Three different supernatural species, each her mate, tying themselves to her indefinitely to save her life—or death. It's complicated when I word it that way. She didn't die-die. But she's changed now, and only because they were, in fact, her mates. Ta-da!

Now you're all caught up.

Oh, and there was some mention of an angel that told the rogue supernaturals how to actually kill Fury's soul and then that angel woke up Lyra in a crypt below Avalon where Dorian lives and Lyra is his daughter that he had to force into stasis because she went crazy and she is fucking dangerous.

And now we're here.

Carry on.

CHAPTER 1

My feet pounded against the ground, sending shots of pain reverberating through my legs. Heart pumping, I sucked in short breaths to keep pushing forward. Another cluster of leaves smacked me in the face as I ran through the trees, cutting my cheek, but I didn't stop. I couldn't.

Roxanne's screams guided me. I had to find her.

Fire raged in the forest surrounding Roman's lake house. *Where the hell was he?*

I turned my head in the direction of another scream as more panicked howls pierced the air.

"Rox! I'm coming!" I called, running once more, pushing myself harder.

I looked around frantically for Roman. Ezra. Dorian. Anyone. Ezra wasn't answering me when I reached out to him mentally. What was happening here?

A malicious cackling in the forest diverted my attention. It echoed, as though it were bouncing off the trees. Seeing the clearing ahead, I pushed myself faster. I had to find them. All of them. I had to save them from this.

Crossing the forest threshold to the lakeshore, I came to an abrupt halt. I couldn't believe my eyes. The lake was no more. The earth had split open, the water drained into the gaping crevice it created. A cliff rose from the once level earth. An eerie orange glow flickered against the rocky sides and suffocating heat rose from the caverns.

I turned my head, searching for Roxanne, but I couldn't get my voice to work when I tried to call her name, choking on the thick, smoky air, coughing and sputtering. That's when I saw them.

Bodies.

Hundreds of them. Thousands. Shifted. Partially shifted. Still in human form. Large. Small. I walked toward them slowly, catching a glimpse of a body with dreadlocks.

The bile rose in my throat, and I couldn't stop it. I fell to my knees, emptying the contents of my stomach as I held myself up on all fours.

"Fury, help me!"

I snapped my head up, searching for Roxanne. She cried out again, and I ran to the edge of the former lake. Holding onto a root, she hung over the side, the river of lava below her mocking her mortality.

I dropped to the ground, reaching out. Tears streamed down her cheeks, carving a path through the blood and ash caked on her face.

"Grab my hand," I told her. "I'll pull you up. I've got you."

She shook her head. "I can't let go."

"You can," I shouted. "You have to. I won't lose you, Rox. I *will* pull you out. You have to trust me. Please, Rox . . . "

She pressed her lips together and nodded. She swung

an arm up and I caught it, starting to pull her up as an earth-shattering scream pierced the sky.

A dragon swooped down, raining fire on the already ravaged forest.

"Roxanne, climb *now*," I urged, grunting as I pulled her up. Her foot found purchase briefly before she slipped, but I didn't let go as her body slammed against the side.

She looked at me with wide eyes, the tears spilling out. "She's here," she whispered. "This is your fault . . ."

I faltered. "No, it's not, I swear."

"See what you've done," she said. "*Look.*"

I choked on a sob as I shook my head.

That same awful laugh echoed, and I saw a petite figure in a white cloak standing on the cliff; long strands of white hair escaped and danced on the wind. Dorian was next to her, resting on his knees. A sword was pressed to his throat, a thin line of red already shining beneath the blade.

"You can't save us," Roxanne said, slipping from my grip.

"No," I grunted, refusing to let her go.

"Sift," Dorian shouted as the woman beside him cackled.

"I can't," I yelled back to him. "I don't know how!" I met his gaze and held it, watching his amber eyes glow with power.

"SIFT," he bellowed before the blade sliced across his throat.

I screamed, the anger and the fear burning inside me, bubbling up in furious rage as explosions detonated beneath my skin.

I looked down to Roxanne, begging her to not let go as her hand slid another fraction through mine. I mentally called for Ezra, pleading for his help.

As she slipped through my fingers, and I cried out to her, Hades flew toward me as though he would crash into my face if he didn't veer away.

"Tick tock."

~

I GASPED.

Then I fell.

My body hit something soft before bouncing. My stomach roiled violently, and I sat up, only intensifying the sudden dizziness. Blinking rapidly, I looked at my surroundings.

No fire. No smoke. The air was cool. The fabric touching my skin was soft. My eyes adjusted to the faint glow in the room.

"Nice of you to drop in," Ezra said sleepily. He lay on his bed next to me, the black sheets pulled up only to mid-torso, his bare chest and tattoos on full display.

I scrambled out of his bed, my body covered in sweat and my breathing ragged.

"What the fuck just happened?" I asked. "I was . . . I was at Roman's. I was . . . dreaming." I let it sink in, thinking about the series of events in my nightmare.

It wasn't real. That meant Roxanne was okay. And Dorian . . . Roman . . . they weren't dead.

A loud pecking on Ezra's window pulled me from my thoughts. I rushed over, pushed the heavy drapes aside, and opened it up to let Hades fly in. Early morning light filtered into the room as downtown Houston began to wake up.

"Now you've done it," he said, landing on a chair. "Every shifter in a fifty-mile radius of Roman's is looking for you."

I sighed. "Not now, asshole. I'm trying to figure some things out."

"Like how you ended up here?"

"Wait." I glared at him. "How did *you* know I was here?"

IIc fluffed his feathers in his version of a bird shrug. "I know a lot of things. If you were nicer to me, I'd probably tell you. Alas . . ."

Ezra chuckled, sitting up and swinging his legs over the bed. He picked up his cell phone. "Incoming," he said. A second later it rang, and he pressed to answer it. "She's fine. She's here," he said.

I could hear commotion and yelling in the background before Roman's voice filtered through. "How?"

"Pretty sure she sifted. Call the fae if you haven't already. This is his area of expertise. We'll head your way shortly." He ended the call and stood up, the sheets falling to the side. He looked at me as he said, "So much for rest before the interrogation."

My eyes raked his naked body, and he winked at me as he walked to his closet. A small laugh escaped me. Only Ezra would be so calm about me unexpectedly dropping out of thin air and into his bed.

"Keep it in your pants," Hades said.

"Ugh, go away." I frowned at him, and he narrowed his little eyes at me. "No one said anything about sex."

"I saw the look on your face," he said. "And he's over there swinging it around—"

"Enough," I said. "Don't you have something else you should be doing right now?"

"Not really, no."

"I find that hard to believe."

"I found you. That was what I needed to do."

"Lucky me," I said. I threw my arm out and pointed

toward the window, away from the building. "Go talk to Duke. I need answers."

He narrowed his little bird eyes at me. "I don't answer to you, you realize that, right?"

"You do, actually. You're the go-between, right? So *go*. I can't exactly go myself right now, and you know damn well we *both* need answers. If you're going to be up in my face telling me to do my job, go do yours. Find me when you know something." I couldn't have suppressed the venom in my voice if I wanted to. Which I didn't. I'd just had the nightmare of all nightmares, which ended with his stupid 'tick tock' bullshit in my face, and then somehow sifted while sleeping.

"You also broke windows and started a small fire before disappearing from Roman's house," Ezra said, clearly having listened in on my thoughts.

My mouth gaped open. "I what?"

Hades snickered in his birdy way. Flapping his wings, he took off without another word.

Ezra came out of the closet dressed in jeans and a black T-shirt. Handing me some clothes, he said, "While I think the underwear and tank top are adorably sexy, you'll want to change."

I took the shorts and shirt from him. "Wait, you said I—"

"You did. Get dressed. Dorian has a lot of questions for you, but this just got more complicated."

CHAPTER 2

I felt the intensity when hundreds of pairs of eyes focused on me as I walked up the steps to the porch in some weird version of a walk of shame. Every shifter in the pack must have been jolted awake by Roman's frantic demands to find me, and here I was. Just fine.

Roman and Dorian stood at the open door, side by side.

"Fancy seeing you here," I said, trying to break the tension.

Ezra snickered behind me, but not a damn thing from Roman or Dorian.

"Tough crowd," I huffed as I walked in between them and into the open living room. I took a seat on the couch, pulling my feet up to tuck them under my legs.

As the guys followed in, they silently sat down and watched me.

I looked around at them, but no one spoke. Ezra seemed bored. Roman appeared conflicted. Dorian was standing by the window overlooking the lake, seeming pissed as always.

I sighed. "Okay, I guess we can keep playing the quiet

game, or one of us can talk. I'll be the bigger person here and go first," I said. "I have no idea what happened this morning. I'm really sorry to have scared everyone, and I didn't mean for everyone out there to spend their time looking for me. Don't know what else to say."

"No one is pissed at you for that," Roman said, taking a seat in a high-back chair.

Roxanne's voice carried from the kitchen. "Speak for yourself, Roman. My favorite comforter was in flames."

"Okay, Roxanne might be pissed at you for burning the bed, but that's not what this is about," he said.

"But it does complicate things," Ezra interjected.

I snorted. "That's an understatement."

Dorian turned around, crossing his arms and resting his shoulder against the glass of the window. "As far as we can tell, you sifted this morning. Have you noticed any other. . . changes?" he asked, leveling me with his signature stare of cool detachment and utter arrogance.

"Other than the slightly pointed ears and permanently yellow eyes?" I deadpanned.

"Yes, other than that," he answered, unflappable despite the undercurrent of annoyance I sensed.

"It's only been, like, what, ten hours?" I shrugged, leaning back. "I can see farther. My canines are a little longer, but I'm not feeling a craving for blood if that's what you're getting at."

"Noted," Dorian said. "But your vampirism isn't the only change you've undergone. You're now a shifter as well. Have you sensed your wolf yet?"

"No."

"Hm." He narrowed his eyes.

"We're still two weeks from the full moon. Not sensing anything right away is normal. The closer we get, the more her wolf will try to surface. She should stay with the pack as much as possible," Roman said. "In case the shift is triggered early for some reason."

"Wait, does that happen sometimes? It just comes out of nowhere?" I asked.

"Fine," Dorian agreed, completely ignoring me.

"As long as sleepovers are allowed." Ezra flashed a cocky smirk. I rolled my eyes. "She is a vampire too, after all. When the time comes, I'll be the one to guide her through it."

Despite his easygoing demeanor, the possessive tone sent a bolt of heat through me. I wanted to shift my weight, feeling my body's aching response between my legs. I tried to ignore it, and I hoped for the love of all that was dead, they'd do the same.

Ezra winked, his psychic hands grazing the inside of my thighs with devious intent. I stiffened, flashing him a glare.

"If you're done with trying to impress her with your *boyish* antics, we can move on," Dorian interrupted. Was that a hint of . . . jealousy?

The corner of my mouth curled upward.

"Just because I'm not old as dirt doesn't mean I don't know my way around the female body, Dorian," Ezra replied without missing a beat. "Or Fury's, for that matter."

"As fun as this is, the summit is starting in two hours, and there are a lot of things we still need to discuss, so if you can both stop swinging your dicks around and save the insults for later, it would be appreciated," Roxanne said pointedly before taking a seat on the arm of Roman's chair.

"Right." I nodded to her, happy to be moving away from the subject of me breaking my own rules and fucking Ezra . . . again. "You said you had questions. Where do you want to start?"

"Why were you sent here?" Dorian asked, point-blank.

"I told you—"

"No," he interrupted. "Why were *you* sent here?"

I sighed, leaning back into the couch and resting my elbow on the arm, propping my chin in my hand.

"There's a group in the Afterlife that I call the risk witches," I started. "They're not really witches. More like the fates from Greek mythology." Namely, speaking in riddles and enjoying the power trip that comes with making everyone in the Afterlife do what they want. "They're basically fortune tellers that predict catastrophic events on Earth, and then they tell the powers that be to go fix it before it comes to pass. Beyond the usual doom and gloom, they predicted you guys would end the world. Like end it for good. And the angels couldn't stop it—"

"The angels?" Roxanne asked.

The question was there on each of their faces, all except Ezra.

"My divine counterpart that deals with things here," I said. "Contrary to legends, demons don't actually come earthside, or at least they didn't . . . ." I trailed off. "Until now."

"What exactly do the angels do?" Dorian asked. He walked away from the window, coming to sit in a chair near the rest of us. He sat back, crossing his legs, his amber eyes narrowed in speculation.

"Same thing I do in Hell," I replied, taking a deep breath. "They fix things. Demons have a longer time frame to work with. Angels work quickly. Their brand of fixing is supposed to be more of the do-gooder variety, but not always." As the words came out, the latter part was spoken quieter than I intended. What I suspected, it was grim. The conversation was treading into dangerous waters, and I was acutely aware of the growing tension in the room.

"How did the angels try to *fix* this 'prediction'?" Roman growled. I swallowed hard, taking in his taut biceps straining against his T-shirt. His eyes were flickering between brown and blue.

"I *believe* they tried to kill you," I said quietly. "Indirectly or not. That's usually how they *fix* this sort of situation."

"My mate . . ." Roman interjected.

I wanted to look away from him, but I didn't as I said, "I'm so sorry."

I meant it, even though it wasn't my fault. Roman's eyes turned wholly blue, and he stormed out of the room. The door slammed behind him. Roxanne got to her feet, giving me a sad smile before following after. I sighed.

"You believe they killed his mate?" Dorian continued without missing a beat.

I pursed my lips and nodded slowly. "The more I've thought about it, I think they killed all your mates."

The silence was deafening. I almost missed that pigeon's incessant blabbing. Just something—anything— to lift the heaviness away from the conversation.

Other than the slight stiffening in his shoulders, Dorian didn't let on how the information affected him. "Let me make sure I have this straight. The 'angels' have been trying to kill us, and when that failed, they killed our mates, all to end some prophecy that suggested we'd end the world?"

I shifted my weight, sitting cross-legged on the couch. I clasped my hands together and cleared my throat. "Correct."

"What did our mates have to do with this?"

I shook my head and took a deep breath. "I don't know the answer to that. This is what I have pieced together as

I've learned more about you three." I huffed, thinking about how little I still knew.

"So I'll say it again. Why were *you* sent here?" He repeated his earlier question with more ferocity.

"You all lived. They failed," I said simply.

I could recognize where his line of questioning was coming from. How did I, someone who happened to be their mate, end up involved in this? After all, I was a demon. By my own admission, we didn't come to Earth.

But here I was.

Not far-off in the distance, I heard things breaking. Wood being ripped apart. Pained growls and angry roars, coupled with soft words as Roxanne tried to coax him down.

It occurred to me that I'd never been able to hear this easily. Advanced senses were not a perk of being a demon—we didn't need it—but it was for fae, vampires, and shifters. The thought made me shift uncomfortably because the current predicament I found myself in made my reasons for being here infinitely more complicated.

Dorian's eyebrows furrowed. "I am rapidly losing my patience with you. You have not answered the question."

"I know what you are getting at." I narrowed my eyes at him. "Despite our bad rap on Earth, a demon's job is to fix people, Dorian. Bad people. Most of my guild has forgotten that over time and a good portion of them prefer to punish blindly. I don't." I shook my head, thinking of Karen the Horrible. "I've dedicated my afterlife to actually rehabili-tating the fucked-up people I get assigned. Souls get recy-cled and sent back. It's up to my guild to send them back so they are better when they live on Earth. My cases have the lowest recidivism rate and I have the best track record they've seen in a very long time. Simply put, I am the best at my job. That's why they sent me—to see if I could succeed where the angels failed."

"Not because you're our mate?" Dorian prodded.

"I don't know," I said honestly, shrugging. "They didn't tell me that. They didn't tell me a lot of shit," I grumbled.

"Upper Management didn't brief her properly before she came down here," Ezra said from his seat, finally choosing to back me up. "She was as surprised as we were to find out we are all mated."

The front door slammed once more, and a booming voice followed it. "You knew about this?" Roman roared.

Rounding the corner, he didn't seem anymore under control than when he'd left. Eyes flickering again between brown and blue, he glared at Ezra with deadly intent.

"Yes, I knew," Ezra replied, meeting his stare. "I was trying to help her."

"That's a bit of a stretch," I said under my breath.

"I didn't tell them why you were here, did I?" he retorted.

I rolled my eyes.

"Your kind killed my mate," Roman yelled, turning to me. Emotional turmoil was eating at him. "Killed my child." My heart hurt for him. It did. But there was a fundamental problem here that I couldn't let go unaddressed.

"No," I said softly. "Angels did." He narrowed his eyes. "I'm a demon. My kind have never been to Earth. You can be pissed at them. I'm angry about it on your behalf. For all of you." I motioned to the three men gathered around me. "If they actually did it . . ." I shook my head. "There are bad eggs in every department. I am truly sorry they killed them. I am. But don't blame me for this. I would never do that."

"Not even to save the world?" Dorian asked darkly; emotionless as he was persistent in his questioning.

"No. I can't—" My hands tightened as I kept them clasped. I straightened in my seat. "There are some lines I will not cross. Children are one of them." I hesitated to say the next part. To give them a piece of truth, of vulnerability, that could very well come back to bite me. I needed them, especially Roman, to understand that this wasn't me or even my kind. That I wasn't lying to them. There was more at play here, and them doubting me now, when the situation was already so far beyond fucked, it just wouldn't do. "I—I know what it's like to lose a child. I would *not* do that to someone."

Roman looked away, a sliver of guilt coloring his expression. Ezra's eyebrows raised slightly as he read my thoughts, learning that new bit of information.

"What is your assignment now?" Dorian asked, leaning forward in his chair.

I took a deep breath and exhaled, trying to ground myself. "The same as it's been since I got here." I shrugged. "Fix you three. Stop the end of the world." The job was supposed to be simple. Then again, maybe it might've been if the stupid poltergeists had done their part and gathered information that would have been useful.

"And how's that going for you?"

"Poorly," I deadpanned. Leaning forward, I put my elbows on my knees. The position brought me and the moody fae bastard eye to eye with only a coffee table in between us. "Seeing as you all know why I'm here, I couldn't imagine how it could get worse. Oh wait, except I'm now changed into some demon-fae-shifter-vamp hybrid thing"—I motioned to myself—"and no closer to figuring out what it is that sets you three off to make everything go *boom*."

His eyebrow twitched. "Interesting choice of words

given your ability to make everything go 'boom'."

I shrugged.

"Is that a demon ability?" he continued.

"No," I said. "It's a Fury one."

He hummed in response, pursing his lips slightly. "Speaking of Fury—that's an interesting name. I can only assume it wasn't given to you as a human."

I stared at him, showing fire and steel in my gaze. "It's the name I chose."

"Sunny Adams—" he said, eliciting a growl from me.

"*Is dead*," I snapped. "You'd do well not to talk about things you don't understand."

His features softened ever-so-slightly. "I'm trying to understand."

"You're trying to pry," I corrected, raising my voice. "There's a difference. I've told you about why I'm here. Why I was chosen. But who I was before all of this—that's my past and I want to keep it that way."

Dorian sighed in frustration. "What if it has something to do with—"

"It doesn't," I said firmly.

"It might," he replied through gritted teeth. "Whoever wanted you dead referred to you as Sunny Adams. That's not an accident."

"And I'm not discussing this," I replied, leaning back and crossing my arms. I needed space from him. From this. From the constant push and pull I felt when I was around him.

Dorian opened his mouth, probably to argue some more, when Ezra interjected. "I wouldn't push it right now if I were you. We have plenty of other issues to focus on for the moment. I think Fury can keep her privacy a little longer."

"Easy to say when you can read her mind," Roman replied, still bitter about that turn of events.

"Yes," Ezra said haughtily. "It means I know when our mate is at her end. Contrary to what you both like to believe, she has a limit, just like us. Who knows what the fae prick is hiding? And you get all pissed off anytime you talk about your mate—"

"Careful with your words," Roman growled. "This is still pack grounds."

"Easy boy. My point is, she is entitled to some secrets."

"When those secrets put her life at stake—"

I was done in. The cold laugh that bubbled in my throat wouldn't be denied. I tilted my head back to let it out. "I need a drink," I said through the chortles.

"What's so funny?" Roman frowned. Ezra sighed.

"This." I motioned to them. "You all. I'm one hundred percent in danger of actually dying because you lot changed me. Something I shouldn't have survived to begin with, mind you." I twisted a lock of my deep red hair, watching it move from near-black to the color of flame depending on where the light caught it. "That's why Taylor Dawson bit me. Whoever wants me dead knew the only surefire way to extinguish me was to try to change me —because the Afterlife and the supernatural don't mix. Our magic is fundamentally incompatible. It's the reason supernaturals that die don't cross over. You know what that means?" I stood and walked over to the liquor cabinet. I plucked a bottle with green liquid from the shelf and read the label. Not recognizing it, I shrugged and took a swig.

I made a face, setting the bottle back. The taste was fruity.

"Odds are if I die now, I'll probably stay dead. No Afterlife for me," I finished. Searching for a bottle of something I recognized, I muttered to myself, "Dead, dead, dead."

Retirement was now a fleeting memory. One I was still coming to grips with. That was easier to take than the rest of it, though. No Afterlife meant no Duke. No jesting with Jake. No strays from the rainbow bridge. Everything I'd known and worked so hard for over the last hundred years was gone . . . unless I somehow found a way back.

"Looks like you get to be all alpha protective over me, after all, Roman," I said, holding up a bottle in cheers and then drinking from it. I winced at the burn as the tequila went down.

Roxanne grimaced at me. "Don't be a dick, Fury. This isn't easy for any of us. I don't know what you are going through and that's fine. If you aren't ready to share that with us, you don't have to. But with the exception of Ezra," she shot him a glare, "this is news to us, and it's not exactly the kind of news you want to hear. It's a hard pill to swallow, okay?"

I softened. She managed to bring out the best in me. She was like Duke in that sense. Logical. Kind. Genuinely caring. I set the bottle down and sighed. "I know," I whispered. "Believe me, I know." I looked at her, meeting her glassy-eyed gaze.

She blinked a few times, pushing back the tears that threatened to fall. Clearing her throat, she said, "Okay, then. Let's move on. We know more now and got some questions answered, right?" She looked at Dorian and he took a moment, but finally dipped his head in agreement. "Good. First things first. You're a super hybrid . . . ish. I don't know what to call it. Do we know anything about that?"

Dorian shook his head. "Two specie hybrids aren't

uncommon. We all know that. But not even the fae knew demons or the Afterlife existed until now."

"The scrolls?" Roman suggested.

"I can search, of course. Even if I find something, it certainly wouldn't include a three-way hybrid with a demon. But it's worth a look to see if any multi-hybrids have ever existed."

"Rava has extensive knowledge of two-way hybrids, and I can send shifters with you if you need help researching—"

"That won't be necessary," Dorian said quickly. "If I find anything, I have no qualms about sharing it with you. I'll bring everything we have to Rava. It would benefit all of us to be informed." He shot a glare at Ezra, who raised a single shoulder in response.

Roxanne frowned. "Fury, if you're a hybrid, that has to give you some level of protection. Fae, shifter, and vampire are the three strongest factions in the supernatural world. On Earth, I mean. And if you have any demon left in you, maybe you aren't as easy to kill as we think."

I took another drink from the bottle, wiping off my lips after I swallowed. "We can try—"

"We are not going to try to kill you," Roman said. Ezra laughed.

I rolled my eyes. "Don't be so dramatic. I'm not suggesting you shoot me. I was going to suggest starting small. We cut my arm and see if it heals."

A buzz on Roxanne's phone interrupted us. She looked down and grunted. "Rava said they're arriving at the summit."

Hades' annoying 'tick tock' seemed appropriate right about now.

I walked back to the couch, setting the bottle down and

taking a seat. I opened my mouth to say something but was cut off when Ezra moved faster than I expected, using a long nail to slice my arm.

"Motherfucker!" I yelled, grabbing the bleeding wound, and pulling away from him. Roman flew out of his chair, and Roxanne slammed her hands on his chest, showing more strength than I knew she had. "What the hell was that for? I wasn't ready, you prick."

"If someone comes for you, you won't be ready then either. Need to test this both ways. You expecting to be injured, and also not. We don't know what your powers are. Maybe you heal differently when you expect it. Maybe you have a way to shield yourself. Best to find out," he said, sitting back in his chair.

"Asshole," I muttered.

Dorian pulled a handkerchief from his pocket, leaned forward, and extended it to me.

"Thanks." I took it, pressing it to my arm.

Ezra picked at some lint on his pants, then looked up. "As Fury said, someone knew how to make her death happen. What do we know about Taylor?"

Roman shook his head. "He wasn't the mastermind. He was too low-level. And stupid. Someone else found him and used him. He never would've known to call her Sun—" Roxanne elbowed him, "—by a different name."

"Exactly," Ezra said. "So whoever is trying to kill her knows they didn't succeed. Again. That's what, three attempts? They all failed. Best to assume they're going to try again, and that this time, she'll die."

"We can't postpone the summit," Roxanne said, frustrated. She looked at me with apologetic eyes. "It's bigger than us. Putting it aside could cause an all-out war between the factions—"

"I'm not offended, Rox. I wouldn't suggest postponing the summit," I said, peeking under the cloth to check the cut on my arm. The burning sensation was still there, but it was starting to heal. That was good news. I held it up for them to see. "Hey, look."

All eyes turned on me, inspecting the handiwork. "That's a good start," Roman said.

Ezra pulled out a small pocketknife. Nothing huge, maybe three inches long. As he approached me, he said, "Do you want to do it, or do you want me to?"

I scrunched my face in disgust. "I don't really like pain, so inflicting it on myself isn't going to go well."

"Suit yourself," he said. "Hold out your other arm."

I groaned, extending it as he requested. Turning my head so I didn't have to watch, I felt him grip under my armpit, then press the blade to the upper muscle. He sliced quickly, and I hissed in pain.

"Calm down, it's superficial," he said quietly, pressing a towel to the wound.

"Tool," I mumbled. I didn't even have much of a reason to be mad. This was my idea. It was a theory that needed to be tested, but knife wounds burned like there was no tomorrow.

I sat there grumbling to myself when Dorian stood up, walking to the window again, staring out at the lake. "There's some healing ability, and that's good to note. Until we know more, she'll need around-the-clock protection."

"This again? I don't need a babysitter, Dorian."

"Clearly you do," he snapped. "Last night, you snuck out of the hotel, damn near got yourself killed—"

"To save Roxanne, you condescending donkey." I stood up as I shouted, throwing my hands out. "Would you rather I had let them kill her? Are you seriously going to chastise me for *saving* her? What the hell is wrong with you? I had one person in my human life—*one*—that gave a shit about me. I am thankful every day that she lived a short, beautiful life before she died. She was that small percentage that moved on to a peaceful resting place. If Roxanne died, she doesn't get the Afterlife. None of you do. Do you get that? Supernaturals don't pass go. They don't collect two-hundred dollars. They just. Fucking. Cease. Existing."

Dorian tried to speak over me, likely answering my rhetorical question, but I didn't let him get a word in edgewise.

"There was absolutely no way I was going to let Roxanne die because of me, so before you go treating me like a child, I knew exactly what my choices were, and I had no problem making the one I did, and I would do it again. Don't stand over there judging me for it, acting as if I'm stupid and can't take care of myself. I'm not as selfish as you think I am, and despite whatever you think of me right now—"

"I'm sorry," Dorian said, cutting me off.

"Don't interrup—wait, what?"

Completely caught off guard in my tangent, I stopped yelling and didn't move. Dorian walked over and stood calmly in front of me. He tilted his head down, lowering his eyes, then looked back up to meet my gaze. "I said I'm sorry. Truly. You're right. Despite all, I know what it's like to have few that care for you, and to have few that you, yourself, care for." He looked over at Roxanne, who had tears running down her face, then back to me. "I am grateful you saved Roxanne. She is very special to me, and of course to Roman. Our lives wouldn't be the same without her. So, thank you."

"I, uh . . . you're welcome." It was all I could manage. I had no idea what else to say.

Dorian took a step back. "With that said, and with all due respect, it is still in your best interest—and ours—that you have one of us with you. For your protection, and for Roxanne's. They used her to get to you once. They won't hesitate to do it again."

I grumbled, wishing I had more time to relish in his apology. Every now and then he'd break through his cold demeanor and show some humanity. Or whatever the equivalent word would be for a fae. More than anything, I hated that he was right too.

Ezra chuckled.

"What's so funny?" Dorian asked him.

"She doesn't disagree with you, much to her chagrin," he answered.

I glared daggers at him. "Rude, much?"

He shrugged.

Anger roiled through me. I just wanted five minutes to think by myself. Was that so much to ask? I checked my upper arm, seeing the cut had healed. It still hurt, though. Of course it would. I couldn't get lucky enough to not feel the pain.

"It doesn't change the fact that I feel imprisoned when someone is watching me and I can't even go to the bathroom without an escort," I said, returning to the conversation. I wouldn't live like that. We had to come to some sort of an agreement. One where I had a choice in the matter.

"You're healing against these minor injuries, but that's not enough for us to go on, Fury. We need to know more, but at this moment, there isn't much time to test further," Dorian argued.

"She knows that," Ezra said. "She's also still feeling the

residual pain even though she's healed."

I swear I could feel flames on the side of my face. My nostrils flared as I breathed deeply and looked at Ezra. "Stop. Doing. That."

"You aren't being honest right now," he said.

"It's not your place to speak for me," I seethed. "No one asked me what I was feeling. I didn't volunteer to give a play-by-play report. Being cut hurts. I'm healing. The end. If this is what it's going to be like, I'm putting my foot down and I'm not going to the summit. I'm not agreeing to any of this. I will walk out that very large door over there and there is nothing you can do to stop me."

A cacophony of loud voices filled the room. Frustration, anger, outrage—welcome to the club, boys. They yelled over each other, arguing with me that I wasn't being reasonable, and that I wasn't making this easy, and blah blah blah. I grabbed the bottle of tequila and walked away while they went on. I tipped it back, taking a big mouthful before swallowing.

This was too overwhelming.

"Stop," I said loudly, feeling a little twinge pound in my head.

Silence. They stared at me, waiting. I inhaled deeply, counting to ten. Don't stab. Stabbing won't help. Breathe out. Count to ten. They mean well. They're just acting stupid, I reminded myself. But some things would need to change.

"I want you out of my head, Ezra."

"I . . . can't do that," he admitted, and his eyes hardened.

Don't do this, he said mentally. *Don't ask this of me.*

I glared at him in our private conversation. *I'm not asking you. I am telling you. Unless I invite you in, get out. I need space. Privacy. You told them I needed it. It's true. But I also need it from you. It's hard enough to wrap my head around what's going on without feeling safe to think.*

He sighed, closing his eyes. To everyone else, we were having a standoff. Maybe it looked like he was giving up, but he opened them, pleading with me. *I can't turn it off. You're my mate. From a distance, it's more manageable, but since we met, the connection is increasingly stronger. When I'm near you, I can't stop. I always hear you in the back of my mind, even if it's only a whisper. I'm sorry. I don't want you to feel unsafe around me.*

I sighed. *It's not that kind of unsafe. It's just . . . I don't know.* I growled in frustration, wishing I could just feel a measure of peace.

I can give you that.

I huffed, knowing he heard my thoughts. He gave me an apologetic look. I gestured for him to go on, seeing Roxanne and Roman look around the room pointlessly in awkward silence. Dorian surprisingly gave us space, having walked back to that window he liked to look out of.

I can give you a measure of peace.

How?

I may not be able to stop hearing your thoughts, but I can stop reacting as I do. I won't speak for you. I won't let you know I'm listening. An ignorance-is-bliss sort of thing. If you don't feel that I'm listening, perhaps that will give you the measure of peace you're looking for. When you invite me in, so to speak, then I'll make my presence known. Within reason. Emergencies don't count.

Deal. I pursed my lips and nodded my head a few times. It was better than nothing. A phantom hand cupped my cheek, a finger grazing my skin affectionately. He smiled, but it didn't reach his eyes.

Ezra cleared his throat, speaking out loud. "I think it's best we figure out who she needs to be with first. We'll all be at the summit intermittently, so we can all escort her during panels."

Dorian's phone buzzed. He reached into the breast pocket and pulled out the device, looking at it with furrowed brows. "To Roman's point earlier, you should stay here to start. We can change things as we go, if needed, but the full moon is in two weeks' time. No matter what, you have to prepare for that, and there is no place safer for it."

Roxanne looked at the time. "We have to get ready, guys. We're pushing it as is."

"I'll meet you there. I have some things to take care of in Avalon," Dorian said. His cold eyes met mine, softening for a fraction of a second before any hint of emotion had escaped. He sifted, disappearing from the living room without any further discussion.

Roman looked pained as he struggled through everything that had just happened. He pinched the bridge of his nose. "Okay. We've got twenty minutes to get ready. Let's move."

Ezra took the bottle I had and silently raised it, putting the rim to his lips, and tilting it back.

My soul felt like it was being crushed. My heart felt like it was being tugged in three different directions. I'd hurt Roman and Roxanne with the truth of their loss. I'd pushed Ezra away, demanding his role as my confidant be silenced. I couldn't read Dorian's emotions, and that bothered me more than I cared to admit.

I wished I could talk to Duke about all of it. My breath caught in my throat, feeling the shattering ache all over again as I thought about my friend I may never see again.

CHAPTER 3

DORIAN

The moment I sifted to Avalon, I felt it. A shift in the frigid air. A buzzing undercurrent of something sinister. The scent of death carried on the wind.

I crashed through the double doors, ready to yell for someone to tell me what had happened. Tristan stood there, waiting. The silence in the foyer was deafening.

"Where is she?" I asked. My voice vibrated with an anger he didn't deserve.

"We don't know, sir." He shook his head, his saddened blue eyes meeting mine. "The island was breached, and the intruder knew where she was. Her coffin was destroyed."

"How many are dead?" I walked past him, taking note of every detail in the castle as I passed through, checking if anything was out of place. A clue. Insight to who had come to my home and done this.

Tristan followed behind me, his footsteps heavy. "Three dozen," he answered.

I stopped short, turning around to look at him. "All of them?" The words were barely audible.

"I'm afraid so. No one had a chance. Had you not called everyone to come to Houston in the search for Fury and kept us all there for her security detail during the summit—I fear they would be dead too. It likely saved their lives."

My brows pressed together, and I closed my eyes, recollecting who I had left there. When Fury had gone after Roxanne, I ordered the search. Roman, Ezra, and I each did the same. Except I chose to keep them there after she'd been located. We'd spent the hours overnight mapping out their security orders to watch Fury from the shadows over the course of the summit. I'd left thirty-six on Avalon. Their lives were my responsibility. They were my people. Dead. Slaughtered. And as I had come to find out, stricken from the universe. No longer existing on any plane. There would be no reunion of any kind with the ones they loved. Extinguished, she'd called it. I inhaled deeply and exhaled, shaking with barely contained rage.

"Everyone's names. What's left of their family line. I want it all." I turned, continuing to my destination.

"I've already started," Tristan said. "The general is waiting for you. You'll want to hear what she has to say."

I moved through the castle with purpose, my mind racing and trying to piece together the timeline of events. I exited the back of the castle, stepping out onto the moor.

Elaine stood in her armor, her blond ponytail high on her head. Hundreds of fae surrounded her as she spoke.

"Strengthen the wards. All of them, including those around the castle. Pull every resource you have into it. Double the number of guards at all points of entry. Sifting is now restricted to the southern entrance, and I want warning triggers on that ward amplified tenfold," she ordered, addressing a group. "You." She pointed at a soldier.

"I want you to oversee the collection and preparation of the fallen. You have a dozen men you can take with you."

The man nodded.

"An extra-tropical cyclone is headed this way. Your time is limited," she said. "Go. I want it done." Her troops dispersed with precision.

Tristan signaled to me he was leaving, and he followed the soldier to gather information on the dead. Elaine turned around, the wind blowing her hair behind her, accentuating her high cheekbones.

"General." It was the best I could do for a greeting.

"Sir," Elaine responded. "I . . ."

"Don't. It wasn't your doing." I held my hand up, stopping her from walking down that path. That was not what we were here for.

Her blue eyes hardened, and she nodded. "Understood."

"Fill me in. What do we know?"

She put her hands on her hips and looked toward the castle. "I sent Markus back to collect some texts from the library. Information we could use during the summit. He came back to the Houston mansion almost immediately. It didn't take him long to find that everyone was dead."

My heart twisted as I prepared to say the next words. "Lyra . . ."

She met my gaze. "Gone. There is no trace of her."

"And the catacombs?"

"Destroyed," she answered. "And the footsteps leading there are the same as last time."

"Did they come from the same location?"

"No." Elaine pursed her lips and her brows furrowed. "They just . . . appeared near a cliff edge."

I narrowed my eyes. "What do you mean 'appeared'?"

"I mean just that. Nothing off the side of the cliff.

Nothing before the footsteps started. No markings of any kind on the shores or the land. Then a set of footprints appeared like they came out of thin air."

"Like someone sifted," I said. Thunder clapped heavily in the distance, warning us of the incoming storm.

"Yes, but not at one of the entry points. They appeared midway through the northern and western entrances." Elaine pointed in the direction she was referring to, a look of frustration on her face.

I could see it. She was thinking the same thing as me. That shouldn't be possible. I had the island warded to prevent trespassing fae. No one could come and go by sifting unless they arrived at one of four entry points. The magic in the wards demanded it.

I ran my fingers through my hair, turning away from my general. My mind was reeling with the possibilities, but nothing was making any sense. I pinched the bridge of my nose and paced, trying to work it out. The cold wind whipped around us, mimicking the turbulent emotions cycling through me.

Elaine's posture slackened, and she stepped forward, dropping all pretenses. "Dorian, whoever did this knew about her." The urgency in her voice was grave. "They knew where to find her, and *worse*, I think they knew how to wake her up. I'm not sure if they knew how uninhabited the island was at the time, or if it was pure luck for us that they came when they did, but they are going to use her as a weapon. There's no other reason to wake her, and I don't think they've done it yet. If she's as bloodthirsty as she was last time, who knows how long we have until she starts leaving a trail of carnage behind her."

I stopped and looked at her. "Are you saying this isn't a trail of fucking carnage, Elaine?"

She looked at me with thinly veiled anger. "I was the second one that arrived here, right after Markus. You haven't seen the bodies yet. I know what this is. I'm saying she didn't do this. Whoever came here killed everyone on the island first, then they took her."

"How do you know she isn't awake? That she didn't do this?" I asked.

She was struggling to keep her composure. Struggling to focus as she looked at me. "I trained my sister to fight. And she's one of the thirty-six that died. I know what Lyra does when she loses her mind. She is like a cat with a mouse. She likes to toy with them. Play games. Give them hope. Then she slaughters her prey. This was not the same. I'm telling you, the intruder killed all of them first. My sister didn't have a chance to pull her sword. None of them did. That's not the Lyra we know."

The crushing loss in her voice jolted me. "My apologies, Elaine," I said, and sighed. "I'm sorry about your sister. Truly. Forgive me. I didn't know Aerinn was one of the fallen."

She straightened her shoulders and dipped her chin, acknowledging my poor excuse for an apology.

"I trust your judgement. I always have," I continued. "When they wake her, they're going to use her as a weapon. Why, or what for, remains to be seen."

"You know what this means, Dorian."

I did. And I hated it. "Only a fae is able to wake Lyra. No other faction has the magic capable of stasis, or its reemergence."

She pursed her lips in response, agreeing with me.

I sighed. "Get a track on her."

Elaine cocked her head and looked at me in question.

"How on earth can we track her? She's disappeared without a trace."

"Find Rya," I answered. No one was going to like it, least of all—

A subtle groan behind me caught my attention. I turned around to find Tristan had returned.

"Do you have something to say, *second*?" I asked, raising an eyebrow.

He schooled his features quickly. "No, just . . . Rya. Surely, we can get—"

"Find Rya," I repeated, harsher, and leaving no room for discussion.

"Consider it done." Elaine and Tristan responded at the same time.

The clouds rolled in ominously, rumbling in warning. I heard the crashing of the waves against the cliffside far off in the distance. Storms were not unusual. It would rage and destroy whatever it could. It would pound against the earth, wreaking havoc as Mother Nature often did. But with nature's destruction, life was born anew.

The tempest was an omen, but it was a cruel reminder that Lyra wasn't of the same force. Nothing good could come of her storm, for she only brought death.

"I'll be in my study," I said, turning on my heel and walking into the castle as raindrops started to fall.

I walked with purpose. I needed to think. Quietly. Alone. The way I preferred it. I needed to work out how to manage the summit, the vampire, and the shifter . . . and Fury. It wasn't something I would bring up to them just yet. This was fae business.

I couldn't help but recall the last time I saw Lyra. The glow of her skin was no longer present. Her eyes didn't shine as they had before but were instead filled with hatred and anger. Her shoulders carried a weight I would never understand. I couldn't save her from whatever monster ate away at her psyche. I couldn't protect her from herself. I couldn't save her mother. I couldn't save those she hurt, just like I couldn't save my people today.

I forced her into a dreamless sleep. Put her in stasis unwillingly until I could find a way to heal her mind, even if it took forever. I needed rest, but I wouldn't take it until I could give her back her life. Now I feared that opportunity was gone. I feared that I'd failed her again. Failed to protect others from her.

Failure . . . an old friend.

I looked up as James came running down the hall, skidding to a halt when he saw me. "Sir, you need to see this. Your study."

I picked up the pace, following after him. It was no use to ask what I needed to see. James was clear. I needed to see it for myself. It would happen soon enough.

The doors to my study were open. I turned the corner, entering, stopping to look around. Not a thing was out of place. Every book was on its shelf. Every paper sat neatly organized, just as I'd left it. The rugs weren't stained or tarnished. The chairs and furniture weren't overturned. It was immaculate.

Except the painted portrait that hung on the wall. It had only faded slightly over the years. Magic had protected it. I looked at it daily. Morvain and I stood beside each other proudly, her black dress a beautiful contrast to her creamy skin. Lyra sat in front of us, angled toward her mother's side, a modest smile on her lips, the blue of her dress matching the color of her eyes.

A jagged rip was torn down the middle of the canvas, now separating me from my family. There was no need to search for the weapon used. The dagger sat embedded in the portrait, centered over my heart.

"Well that answers that question," I said softly.

James scrunched his eyebrows together. "What question was that, sir?"

"She's awake."

CHAPTER 4

I sat in the front row with my legs kicked up on a chair I'd taken, sipping whiskey from a flask I'd refilled before we left. Roxanne kept shooting me not-so-subtle glances from my left. Caitlin sat on my right, and her annoyed glares were a hair more judgmental. Over the course of the past week, my boredom increased while their patience with me dwindled.

On stage, at a rectangular table, my mates sat in a row with microphones and were listening to horribly tedious debates over border disputes, resource allocations, and requests to grow territory. Four days now. If there were a god, I would thank them for this almost being over.

Roman seemed the best at listening to the lot of them and attempting a fair compromise in most cases. Ezra was struggling to give a shit, and I didn't need to read his mind to know that. The flirty, challenging looks he kept sending me followed by yawning when anyone called on him made it easy to see.

Still, the one that left me the most curious was Dorian.

He arrived late that first morning, storming through the

doors and declaring the floor open for discussion. Since then, he'd barely said a word. Unlike Ezra that was pointedly disinterested, Dorian's mind seemed elsewhere. Actively preoccupied by something, and like the nosy demon I'd been for a hundred years—I wanted to know what.

"Does Dorian seem off to you this week?" I whispered to Roxanne, trying to keep it quiet enough so even supernatural ears wouldn't hear me.

Rox tilted her chin back and examined the fae with a touch more interest.

"Not particularly," she said after a moment. "Why?"

"He seems broodier than usual. Not to mention distracted."

"Dorian's never been particularly talkative during the summit," she replied. "I think he views it as a minor inconvenience he has to sit through, much like Ezra in that."

I hummed in response, not completely satisfied. There was more to it. The stiffness in his shoulders and the way his hands kept clenching said something was bothering him, and I'd watched it progress each day.

I took a deep breath and recrossed my ankles for the hundredth time that afternoon, reminded why I never, ever wanted to be in charge. You couldn't pay me enough to do this kind of work. Not here. Not in the Afterlife. Ruling might mean getting to break the rules because you made them, but the responsibility that came with it wasn't my schtick.

I was more of a break-the-rules-now-and-ask-forgiveness-later sort.

Stretching my arms above my head, I casted a glance of the room when a flash of black caught my eye. I frowned, tilting my head at the window when something dropped down into view again.

Hades.

He might be a crow, but he still managed to use his beady eyes to catch my attention across a room full of people. Could it have been another bird? Absolutely not. They didn't usually carry a look of pure exasperation. No, I knew he was my crow, and right now he was trying to get me to notice him.

I dropped my legs to the ground. Beside me, Caitlin huffed, "Finally."

Then I got to my feet.

Despite some whiny vampire lamenting about the big bad wolves that were stopping him from having an all-you-can-eat buffet in bumfuck-nowhere Iowa, almost every pair of eyes shifted my way.

Hades is here. I need to speak with him, I silently sent my message to Ezra. He nodded to me as Roxanne and Caitlin popped up dutifully at my sides.

Judging by the way Roman's eyes flashed in alert, Ezra relayed as much to him. The wolf alpha leaned to his left and whispered something in Dorian's ear. The fae got to his feet, excusing himself without a word to the attendees.

I guess I wasn't the only one wanting answers right now. That or they didn't want to leave me alone with just Rox and Caitlin. It had been uneventful so far, but it didn't surprise me that they wouldn't want to chance it.

So it was going to be a group outing.

Yay for me.

I strode down the aisle toward the stairs and ascended them quickly, my boots stamping against the steps as I exited the auditorium. Rox and Caitlin followed at my heels without question, and Dorian was waiting in the hallway when I stepped out.

"Does this building have a roof? I need to have a word with the pigeon."

"We'll take the stairs. Three doors down to the right," Caitlin said, having memorized the building and every window, door, or stairwell in it five times over.

"Thanks."

I started down the hall and sensed both Rox and Caitlin falling a little behind as Dorian loomed closer. His shadow dwarfed me like a moody cloud that dampened anything he got near. I snorted.

"You think the bird will have answers for you?" he asked, nodding to a fae that stood by the exit.

"He'd better," I answered, wrenching the door open to the stairwell after the guard stepped aside. "You seemed distracted in there," I continued, not subtle in my pushing. "And you were late again."

"Business on Avalon took longer than expected," he said, his voice turning almost brittle.

Something was definitely eating at him. Consider my curiosity officially piqued.

I slowed my pace as we ascended. "So you mentioned the other day. Care to talk about it?"

"No." He sifted to the doorway at the top of the stairs and flashed a keycard that turned the buzzer on it from red to green.

Well then. If he was just going to disappear when I asked a question, I wasn't going to get very far. But it did make me somewhat excited for when I learned to sift. To literally disappear when they were pushing me too hard? Oh I liked the thought of that.

"You know I'll find out eventually, right?" I pointed out

as I stepped onto the roof. Wind whipped my hair back from my face, providing a brief relief from the stifling atmosphere of the summit, then the Houston humidity bore down on me like a heavy blanket. I frowned. A really *damp* blanket.

"For both our sakes, I hope not." The words were murmured so quietly I would have missed them if not for my heightened senses. I pivoted to dig a bit deeper when a loud squawk made me jump.

I ground my teeth together.

"Pigeon," I said, reeling back around, my hair getting in my eyes. I pushed it away and crossed my arms over my chest to properly express my annoyance. "Where have you been?"

"In the Afterlife. Where you told me to *go*, remember?"

Ah, perfect. He was actually being useful for once.

"And?" I asked, dropping all the snark. It was time to get serious. "What did Duke have to say?"

The bird sighed, dropping down onto the ledge of the building to perch. "They're just as confused as you are. No one knows why you didn't die, and no one knows how to get you back."

My lips parted, and I couldn't keep the disappointed expression off my face. Turning quickly, I tried to bury it by swiping the back of my hand over my forehead. This was bad.

"All right, that was not what I was hoping to hear. Anything else?"

"Duke is searching in the Library of Anomalies, but in the meantime, your mission is still on. The clock is still ticking." I turned to give him a sideways glare. Now was not the time for him to say his catchphrase. Strangely, it didn't appear he was going to. He cocked his head to the side, saying nothing more.

I closed my eyes and rubbed my temples with my fingertips.

This is just great. While I was happy Duke was actively looking for a solution, why was I not surprised that the parting line was that there was still work to do? Or that I still *hadn't* succeeded? Of course I hadn't. I still didn't understand what made them collectively lose their cool in the first place. If you can't find the trigger, you can't dismantle the bomb.

"What is the Library of Anomalies?" Dorian asked, interrupting my train of thought.

I ran a hand through my hair and turned to face them. "One of the nine Divine Libraries. It tracks abnormalities and inconsistencies that pop up across history—both in the Afterlife and on Earth. Specifically for cases like this on the off chance it happens again." A thin haze was starting to obscure my vision. I took a wobbly step. Something felt off.

"Who documents them?" Rox asked.

"Scholars department," I murmured, touching my lips. My mouth *ached.* I ran a finger over one of my elongated canines, liking the pressure I felt against them when I did. "They take the case notes from poltergeists and angels, then translate them into the books and then categorize them."

Was this a weird vampire thing? Did I need to eat?

The very idea of drinking blood made my stomach turn.

Nope, definitely not. I swallowed thickly, feeling another throbbing in my head. I'd heard enough about the thirst to know this wasn't it.

I could tell they were still talking. Voices drifted in and

out, but whatever they were saying didn't reach me over the sound of my own heartbeat.

My face felt hot, not warm, but *burning*. Blood rushed to my head, and I took another step. Spots danced in my vision and the shapes around me distorted and warbled like a funhouse mirror.

The humidity was oppressing.

I ran my hand over my upper lip, wiping away the perspiration—

Then I froze.

Red coated my fingers.

Blood.

I realized what it was just as a wave of crimson gushed from my nose, covering my front. It soaked my shirt, dripping wet, sticky drops onto the pavement.

"Ah fuck," I slurred.

Light exploded in my vision.

The world spun in a violent circle.

I felt a tiny measure of relief as everything went dark.

CHAPTER 5

ROMAN

This summit panel was nothing more than a pissing contest. The entire schedule was full of whiny leaders with minor territories, insisting they be given more. Not one of them had earned it. Not one of these groups had put in the work to rise in ranks. They just demanded to be handed more simply because it's what they *wanted*. Like a child. And I had to sit and listen to them complain like I cared.

I did better at it than the other two did. Dorian had been sitting through it with thinly veiled disdain. Ezra was so disengaged he would've been better suited in the audience. The one thing I could at least give him was he didn't discriminate in his apathy. It wasn't just shifters he was bored with in this discussion. He couldn't have cared less about the vampires arguing their points either. The way he saw it—the way we probably all did—was a lot more would get done if they just followed the rules and presented their cases for compromise rather than just trying to get their way.

I picked up my water glass and sipped it, taking in a

breath, and exhaling deeply in a long sigh. I was at the end of my patience. I felt the light throb of a headache coming on.

I turned to glare at Ezra, expecting to see him with his arms crossed and snoring. Instead, his eyebrows were pressed together, and his body was tense. A sharp inhale of breath. A quick flair of his nostrils. His eyes met mine.

Fury.

I stood up abruptly, interrupting the speakers.

"I'm calling a short recess. I think it would be good for all parties to take some time and gather their thoughts. Come up with some practical solutions. We're all here to work together," I said quickly. "Let's break for an hour and then regroup." I looked over to Rava and nodded, knowing she would handle the rest.

Ezra was already out of his seat, walking off the stage and to the side door. Caitlin came rushing through it, her eyes wide and sweat dripping down from her forehead. "You guys need to come upstairs."

Then I saw it.

Blood on her hands.

Splattered on her shirt.

The scent of it was off when it reached my nose, but I knew it was my mate's. A deep growl rumbled low in my chest.

"Easy, Roman," Ezra said, putting his hand on my shoulder. "It's not what you think."

"Then what the hell is it?" I growled, pushing through the door, and heading to the stairwell.

"He's right," Caitlin said, following close behind. "I mean, we don't know what it is, but she's with us. She wasn't attacked. She just started gushing blood out of her nose and ears, then fainted. Dorian has her in the presidential suite."

I took the steps two at a time, Ezra right beside me, climbing to the top floor. When we reached the top of the stairs, a fae guard stood watch, preventing any uninvited guests from entering—and judging by her weapons, preventing anyone with ill intent from getting the chance to try.

"They're expecting you," she said and dipped her head, moving aside to open the door with the swipe of a key card.

I muttered my thanks as we passed through.

Fury's scent and that of her blood washed over me.

She lay on a couch, a red-stained towel being held to her face. Roxanne was next to her, holding Fury's hand. Dorian stood over both of them.

"What happened?" I asked, storming to the couches in the center of the living room.

"Ugh, I'm fine," Fury mumbled. "I just fainted, I think."

Dorian gave her an unamused, sideways glance. "We were on the roof, and she looked disoriented. Nose started to bleed, followed by her ears . . ." He trailed off, and it was no surprise. Bleeding out of the ears was never good, even for supernaturals. "Then she passed out."

"I said I'm fine," she repeated, moving to sit up. She grabbed the edge of the couch and closed her eyes. "Okay, maybe I'm not fine yet." She laid back down, scrunching her eyes shut.

I frowned. Aside from the situation seeming a bit unusual for her, something else was wrong. I came in closer, leaning over her and sniffing.

"You smell it too?" Roxanne asked as she looked up at me.

I nodded. "I do."

"Smell what?" Dorian and Fury asked at the same time.

I sighed. "I don't know. Something about her blood smells off. But I couldn't tell you why."

"Poison?" Dorian asked.

I shook my head. "I don't think so. It doesn't smell like any poison I've ever known. Poison has a sweet scent to it. Subtle and enticing. This is off-putting. Stale."

"Wow. Thanks," Fury grumbled, pinching the bridge of her nose.

Ezra moved around the couch to stand by Dorian. "She hasn't eaten much today. She's mostly been drinking. I can't imagine that's helping her right now."

She glared at him. "You promised you wouldn't—"

He pointed to her flask in her pocket. "You were drinking it in front of everyone. I was stating the obvious out loud, considering the circumstances."

She pursed her lips, and she looked away from him, mumbling to herself about his rudeness. I couldn't say I disagreed, considering his blatant disregard for protocol and showing his boredom during the entire summit.

I made eye contact with Caitlin. "Will you get Fury something to eat? Sugar and carbs. And water." She nodded and went to the kitchen.

I reached down and plucked the flask from her pants as Fury protested. "You've had enough of this today. For fuck's sake, Fury. You've been drinking since this morning. This is already half empty."

"People drink all the time at breakfast, Roman." She tried to sit up again, and this time Roxanne helped her. "You know, mimosas, bloody marys . . ." She trailed off midsentence, looking like she'd thought of something, or maybe just wished she had those drinks.

"This isn't brunch," I said, taking her silence as an

opportunity to respond. I handed it over to Ezra. "Dump it, will you?" Turning my attention back to her, I squatted down and met her at eye level. "Drink some water and eat something. This isn't the cause, but Ezra's right. It's not helping anything."

"Oh, repeat that for me," Ezra drawled as he tucked the flask into his back pocket. "I want to hear those words come from your mouth again."

"No." That pompous fucking vampire. I growled at him in frustration, and he chuckled.

"Enough, you two," Dorian interjected. He looked at a pocket watch, checking the time. "Roman, have you ever smelled blood that was stale before?"

I raised my eyebrows and shook my head, bewildered. "I haven't."

Dorian looked to Roxanne and Ezra and they both confirmed the same as me.

Caitlin came back with some croissants, fruit, and a glass of water, setting it all down on the center coffee table. "I'll be outside if you need me," she said, walking to the double doors that lead into the hallway.

I silently watched Fury with interest as she picked at some food and took sips of her drink. Her hand shook slightly, and she'd squeeze her eyes shut and open them again.

My wolf desperately wanted to protect her. But neither of us knew how. I didn't know what she needed protection from. I just knew that there was more to this than I wanted to admit. We could brush off a nosebleed. But ears? And the smell . . . no, this was something worse.

"What did you feel like before you fainted?" I asked her, sitting on the couch across from her.

She chewed thoughtfully, turning her head side to side

slowly. "Just off, I guess. Kind of fuzzy. A little dizzy. Then I felt really hot. Oh, and my mouth started to hurt. Then the lights went out."

I looked at Ezra and Dorian. "Does any of this happen to vampires when they are made? Or . . ." Dorian cleared his throat, and his eyes flashed a warning. A reminder not to say anything about how he had made Fury in what we perceived were her final moments the first night of the summit. My eyebrows furrowed at being chastised by the fae. "*As I was saying*, have you seen any fae experience symptoms as they grow in their powers?"

Ezra pressed his lips together and shook his head. "No, this doesn't happen to vampires. We don't feel anything in our mouths, and our bodies don't exactly reject blood. We prefer to drink it. We don't expel blood or faint. That's . . ."

"A human trait, though not to this extent," Dorian finished. "And no. As fae mature, they don't experience anything like this."

My senses were on edge. There had to be something more to it. I just didn't know what questions to ask that would lead me to the right answers. "What was happening when it started?" I asked her.

She wiped her mouth with the back of her hand and sighed. "I was talking to that damn bird—wait, where is he?"

"He flew off after you fainted. Said he would be back. Maybe he went to tell your friend Duke about what happened?" Roxanne answered.

"Figures he'd leave. He was giving me news that wasn't that great, to be honest. The Afterlife doesn't know what I am, why I didn't die, and they don't know how to bring me back—"

"You want to go back?" I interrupted before I could

think better of it. Yes, a part of me struggled to accept her as my mate. The truth bomb she'd dropped about how Maya had died—how all of our previous mates had died—didn't help that internal battle. But the other part of me knew I would do anything to keep her here. I could argue with myself all I wanted. At the end of the day, she was my mate. Hearing that she had the desire to leave Earth—had the desire to leave *me*—I felt an ache deep in my chest.

"I want answers," she said. When she met my gaze, something in her reacted. She looked conflicted.

"So do I." My muscles tensed.

"We need a witch," Dorian said. He looked at Roxanne and asked, "Do you mind calling Kelly? Tell me where she is. I'll get her and bring her back here."

She nodded, meeting my glare and shrugging as she stepped into another room to make the call.

"A witch again, Dorian? What the hell?" I asked. I didn't like trusting witches, especially not when Fury was involved. Witches were too unpredictable. They didn't like to make friends, and they often played both sides in a conflict.

"Kelly is different," he said, as if reading my mind. "She protected Fury once already, and then she stitched her back together after that bomb exploded at her shop. She can be trusted."

I looked at Ezra, hoping for some backup. He shook his head at me, but a stiff expression marred his face. He wasn't comfortable with it, but clearly I was on my own in pushing back. I opened my mouth to question more, but Roxanne came back out, putting her phone in her pocket. "She's at her house. She said she's ready to go when you are."

Dorian thanked her, then disappeared.

If we kept bringing others in, it was harder to control

who could get to Fury, and if they had easy access, they could hurt her. We still didn't know enough about her healing. Fuck Dorian and Ezra. I know they wanted what was best for our mate, but so did I.

Rox? If she told me she trusted someone, I believed her. Without question. Aside from the fact she'd never led me wrong before, she had a sixth sense about people. Where I knew my anger and my biases could cloud my judgement—especially when my mate was involved—my sister could see clearly.

"Roxanne, you trust her with this?" I asked.

"I do, Roman. I always have. I know how you feel about witches, but she's one of the good ones. You weren't there. If she wanted Fury dead, believe me, she had the opportunity. Instead, she was ready to die protecting us." She gave me a small smile. I huffed in acknowledgement, leaning back on the couch and crossing my arms.

"Not that anyone asked me, but I thought she was all right too," Fury piped up, crisscrossing her legs and shifting her weight.

Ezra barked a laugh. "Glad you are willing to cooperate."

She shot him a look. "Piss off, Fangs. I want my flask back."

Before he could respond, Dorian and Kelly popped into the room.

She stood there in a flowing royal blue skirt and black blouse. Kelly gave a warm smile and a small wave. When she saw me, she said, "Don't worry, Roman. We will find out what's wrong with her."

I twisted my lips and looked at my sister. When I looked back at the witch, I motioned with my hands for her to get on with it.

"Hey, Kelly. Long time no see. Did you bring me any of those little pastries you had at your shop?" Fury took another drink of her water and smiled.

Kelly and Roxanne laughed. Dorian looked at me in question and I shrugged my shoulders.

"I'm afraid not. But next time I see you, I promise to bring you some. Let's get started, though. The tension in this room is unbearable. I don't know how you manage around all three mates," she said, making sure we all heard her. "That aside, I know they're concerned for you. *That* is evident. I'm going to try a couple of things first. See if I can pinpoint any magic coursing through you. Do you feel better lying down or sitting up?" she asked.

"I'm okay both ways. Sitting up is fine, I guess," she said, leaning to set her water glass on the table. When she sat back, she rested her back against the couch cushions and closed her eyes.

Kelly moved her hands over Fury's head, hovering closely but not quite touching her. I felt zaps of electricity in the air, and my wolf stirred, questioning if that should be happening.

The witch's eyes were closed tight, her eyebrows bunched together as she focused. Her hands traveled over Fury, never touching, but always knowing where she was. She moved over her body once. Twice. Three times.

Kelly stopped, putting her hands in her lap with a huff. Fury cracked an eye open. "Did you find anything?"

Kelly looked unhappy. "No," she muttered. "Not a damn thing."

"How can that be?" I asked, frustration filling my tone.

The look she gave was sympathetic, and it made me angrier than I already felt. "Because there isn't a trace of magic that I can detect. She has no spells on her. No curses, no charms, not even protections." She shook her head. "Roxanne said the blood that came out of her was unusually heavy. And it smelled off. But it's not poison, I can assure you of that." She reached over and grabbed the towel that had been used to clean up Fury's face and staunch the bleeding. She sniffed it, wrinkling her nose. "It *is* stale. Like it's. . . old." She looked at Fury incredulously.

Fury raised her eyebrows, looking around at everyone. "I don't know what you want from me. I have no answers right now, and the one feather-brained jerk I was relying on had nothing useful either."

Kelly looked at me. "Dorian mentioned a wolf called Taylor. What do I need to know about him? He just bit her, right? Was there anything more to this?"

I leaned forward, resting my elbows on my knees, and clasping my hands. "Low level. Branded a rogue. Couldn't even shift anymore. He was a nobody."

Kelly pursed her lips and hummed. "I need to go through some texts. Spell books. I can't detect anything here, but clearly there's something that isn't revealing itself to us."

She stood up, grabbing the towel with blood. "Dorian, do you mind taking me back? I'll call you or Roxanne after I've had some time to research." She turned to Roxanne and kissed her on the cheeks. "Fury, Roman, Ezra, I will see you soon."

She walked to Dorian, and they sifted out of the room just as a knock sounded. Caitlin opened the door and popped her head in. "Twenty minutes till showtime, boss. Rava said tensions are high after you called that unscheduled intermission."

I sighed. If it wasn't one thing . . .

Dorian reappeared. "Well that didn't answer any of our

questions," he grumbled. "However, she's going to keep me posted on whatever she finds."

"Or doesn't," Fury added. She looked around at all of us. "Come on, guys. Do you really think a witch from this world is going to be able to find out what's wrong with me? Even Duke and Hades don't have a clue, and they're from the Afterlife." She looked down at her lap and shook her head. "No. Kelly isn't going to find out what we need to know."

"What are you suggesting?" I said, curious to see where she was taking the conversation. This was Fury. I was learning very quickly that she had several cards she had yet to reveal.

Ezra pointedly looked away to the balcony where Hades had just landed and perched himself on a chair near the window. He had an idea of what she was going to say, but he was clearly giving her the space he'd promised.

"Enlighten us. If Hades and Duke can't help you right now, and you're saying that a supernatural can't help you, then what other options do we have?" Dorian asked, taking a step toward the couch where she sat.

She looked between the three of us before she answered. "I need to talk to someone between our worlds."

Roxanne looked just as confused as the rest of us. "I'm sorry, *between* our worlds?"

Fury nodded. "Yep," she answered, popping the 'p'.

Outside, Hades squawked and flapped his wings in what appeared to be outrage.

"What exactly does that mean?" I asked, voicing the same question we were all thinking.

She took a deep breath and sighed. "Have you ever heard of Bloody Mary?"

CHAPTER 6

"The drink?" Rox asked, confused.

"The queen?" Dorian suggested.

"The legend," Ezra said.

"Bingo," I said, pointing at him. "That one. Although technically the drink plays a role in this too. The legend of Bloody Mary is actually sort of true. 'Sort of' in that chanting her name thirteen times into a bathroom mirror doesn't do jack shit, *but* that there is an entity where that legend came from. She's real, and she exists in a mirror dimension. She's a poltergeist."

"A poltergeist is a ghost?" Roman said.

"Not really. The human idea of ghosts are dead people that linger around for unfinished business. A poltergeist is a job in the Afterlife. It's in the Department of Current Affairs, and they flit between realms to gather information for the Afterlife." It was also an offensive name to some of them, depending on who you said it to.

"What makes you think this poltergeist would have the answers you're looking for if your Divine Library doesn't?" Dorian asked, crossing his arms.

"One," I held up a finger, "we don't know if it does. It's a rather large library. It'll take time for Duke to search. Two," I held up another finger, "I think she might because she's no longer part of the Afterlife."

That got everyone's attention for sure. Furrowed brows and confused looks filled each one of their faces.

"How?"

"She left," I said simply. "Disappeared and never came back. Upper Management considers her a traitor. They sent people after her, but mirror dimension. That's not a poltergeist ability, just like exploding things isn't a demon ability. It was specific to her."

Dorian appeared to be deep in thought. I watched him carefully, looking to see what I could learn about his behavior. I just wanted to be able to read him better.

"If you don't go back, will they send people after you?" Roman asked quietly. The way he asked the question made it clear he was contemplating my future and what punishments Upper Management may send my way.

"I don't know," I said honestly. "If I can't, I suppose that's different. But they may not see it that way."

"If this Bloody Mary was branded a traitor, what makes you think she'll help you? Assuming she can," Dorian said.

"I don't know if she will or not. She's helped a fellow poltergeist here and there over the years, but it's impossible to catch her. All you can do is summon her and ask. She'll either show up, or she won't." I shrugged. It's not like this was supposed to be part of my job. I was supposed to be focusing on the guys. Trying to prevent the apocalypse. Not teaching Afterlife 101 and figuring out what was wrong with me.

I looked over at Hades. He was shaking his head. I knew he was judging me for it.

He wasn't wrong. Asking Bloody Mary for help was desperate. A stretch, really. I had no reason to believe she would listen to me, or help. But if I was supposed to save the entire universe—no pressure—I needed to figure some of my shit out too. I couldn't walk around, fainting and bleeding all the time. I needed to try whatever I could.

I rolled my eyes and waved for him to come inside. Ezra opened the balcony doors, and he flew in, landing on the coffee table in front of me.

"I hope you know what you are doing," Hades said, fluffing his feathers up. "You know what she can do."

I widened my eyes at him, pinning him with my stare. "Yes, thank you, bird. You have any better ideas right now? Tick tock, right?"

He snorted through his beak and scratched at the table with his claws. That was the best he would give me in answer, which suited me just fine.

Dorian glanced at the time again and frowned. "We don't have time to . . . do whatever it is you need to do to summon her. After the summit . . ."

The woozy feeling had dissipated, and I felt more stable. I leaned forward to stand up, and everyone moved to help me.

I waved them off. "I'm fine now. Let's get back so we can get this day over with."

"Not going to happen," Roman said. "You can't go down there. If that happens again, especially in that room—"

"I'll take her to the clan," Ezra said. I looked at him in mock surprise, and he winked. Of course he was fine leaving this boring summit. Roxanne wasn't kidding when she said the first night was meant to be fun and then it got down to business after that. I thought for sure she was downplaying it. Nope. That was a negative. Not that our first night was what I would call fun. Banquet-turned-kidnapping-turned-attempted murder-turned making me a hybrid demon. The turmoil of that night aside, it really was straight and narrow after that kickoff.

"Oh, don't go out of your way for me," I said dryly. "I'd hate to impose on the leadership responsibilities you have to your fellow vampires."

Ezra laughed. "You should be with me if something happens. I am the one that can communicate mentally. I can call for them, but they can't call for me if I'm not listening," he pointed out.

Dorian and Roman looked at each and nodded in agreement. "Go," Dorian said. "We'll handle the rest of the sessions today."

I pointed to my bloody shirt. "Mind giving me something clean to wear?" I asked Dorian. "Pretty sure it's the wrong attire to hang out with vampires. Or the right one, I suppose. Depending on who you ask."

In a second, my soiled clothes were gone, replaced by a simple sundress. Not exactly my type, but it was airy and light. I smiled my thanks at him.

Roman's heated gaze made my skin break out in goose-flesh. I could see it, then. Tiny icy blue flecks flickered in and out. He didn't want me out of his sight. He and that wolf of his wanted to protect me. Wanted to keep hold of me tight and never let go. There was something almost endearing about it. When I really thought about it, I hadn't ever had someone care to actually protect me before.

I felt Ezra's phantom touch skimming up my thigh, pulling me from my thoughts, and I swatted at it. Roxanne looked confused, but then she looked at the amusement on his face and she put it together. She rolled her eyes and huffed.

"All right, then," I said, moving around the table. "I guess that's me out, then." I went to give a little two-finger salute, but Roxanne stuck her foot out slightly and I tripped right over it, stumbling and crashing right into Roman's muscled chest.

His warmth enveloped me as he wrapped his strong arms around my body to stop my fall. The sudden contact and the intensity of his embrace sent electric shots through my veins. I looked up and met his gaze. I swear I could see fire in his eyes, and the flames wanted nothing more than to consume me. A part of me screamed to let him.

He leaned down, his lips grazing my ear as he softly breathed, "Be careful, little one."

"Yes. I would. Will. No, right." I cleared my throat, gathering words and straightening out my scrambled thoughts. "I mean, I will. Thanks for catching me," I mumbled. Glancing at Roxanne, I saw the little smirk on her face.

What. Was. That? The residual tingles of my moment with Roman buzzed over my skin. Stepping aside, I waved at Ezra to go. I needed to get some air. I wasn't so sure that would happen hanging out with a bunch of vampires, but I was about to find out.

STROLLING through Ezra's sex club proved to be more entertaining the second time around. It was strangely crowded for an afternoon. At least it seemed strange to me.

"Aren't vampires supposed to sleep during the day?" I mused as we passed cages of naked men and women on display. They touched themselves for the pleasure of the surrounding crowd that watched them with hungry eyes.

"Some do," Ezra said. "But don't the most delicious acts happen at night?" he questioned, a hint of something warm in his eyes.

I swallowed thickly. "Some do," I mimicked, voice coming out huskier than I'd intended. A fiendish smile stretched across his full lips.

"What is day if not the vampire night?"

I turned my cheek, looking anywhere but at him. It was easy to do in a place like this where there was so much to see. From orgies in one corner to a Dominatrix in another. The sub was spread wide by a St. Andrew's cross, his wrists held taut by suspended chains attached to the cuffs. I hid my flinch when she smacked him with a leather riding crop. The man on display moaned in ecstasy.

Ezra's fingers ghosted a touch over my forearm as he silently urged me on.

"Much as I would love to do some of these things with you," he murmured in my ear, guiding us deeper into his lair of depravity, "I'd want a safer location. Fewer prying eyes and fewer things that might distract you." Like that riding crop.

"Don't like being watched?" I said, easily imagining him in here with the rest of them.

"With you—I'm more particular about the audience," he answered, surprising me. We reached a door I recognized vaguely from my previous visit here. He opened it, motioning for me to go first.

"Particular?" I repeated back, entering the quiet office space.

"People I trust not to attempt to harm you, for one," he

said, right behind me. My breath quickened as my heart sped up a fraction.

"And?" I forced the word from my lips in an attempt to think about something—anything—except the tingling of my skin and heated flush creeping up.

The hair on the back of my neck lifted. A cool breath brushed over the damp skin there, followed by the lightest touch of lips. I groaned, my head tilting back on its own accord as he went from my nape to just below my ear.

"Those that understand 'look, but don't touch'."

The sheer possessiveness of the statement rattled me. I turned around, facing him.

"I thought you didn't mind sharing," I said. Not phrased as a question, but the intent was there.

"The wolf and the fae are also your mates," he said. With surprising gentleness, despite the fierceness in his expression, he reached up to brush a strand of hair from my face. This wasn't the joking, playful Ezra—but the hundred- and seventy-year-old vampire alpha. "You have a connection with them as much as you do with me, and I won't come between you and a mate. That's your business."

"But?" I prompted, hearing it there in the statement, silent but lurking.

"The idea of someone else touching you makes me want to dismember them," he admitted. There was a vulnerability in that honesty that made me tread with caution.

"Ezra," I said his name softly, shaking my head. What happened to just sex? Where did the lack of commitment go?

"Before, you were going to go back," he said quietly. "Now you can't. As far as we know, you're here for good." He took a step forward, and I took one away from him.

"And I'm still trying to find a way to return," I pointed out.

"I know." He nodded. "And if you do, we'll cross that bridge when we come to it. But while you're here—I want to be with you. I'm not asking for forever. Just right now."

I pressed my lips together, feeling caught between a rock and a hard place. On one hand, I had no desire to run off and fuck other guys. It wasn't so much about the exclusivity that bothered me as opposed to *what it meant*. We were a thing. Not just whatever it was we'd already been.

It was scary to take that risk or even consider it when there was still a chance I could somehow find my way back, and then . . . I wasn't sure what came next. For so long I'd worked toward one thing: retirement. But in my plans, it's not like I'd ever accounted for a relationship—or multiple relationships at that, and certainly not while on Earth.

Even if I did return to the Afterlife and somehow this couldn't last, did I really want to miss the opportunity when I had it right here in front of me? My twenty-three short years were all missed opportunities because of the life I'd been pushed into.

But I was not that girl anymore.

I hadn't been her in a long fucking time.

Ezra heard the change in my thoughts before the firm line of my mouth softened and my stance relaxed. He prowled forward, a gleam of victory in his eye.

"Don't make me regret this," I said quickly, taking another step back on instinct. My ass bumped into his desk. I curled my hands around the edge, holding my weight as I slid back onto it.

"Never," he said fervently. His lips came down on mine and I opened my mouth to him. His hands grasped the underside of my knees, using them to push me back further while spreading my legs wide. I groaned into the kiss, and he swallowed it down.

"Truth or dare, kitten," he murmured against my lips.

Uhhhh. . .

He grazed his fingers across my skin, then skated up the outside of my thighs, pushing back the thin material of my sundress.

"Dare?" It was an answer, but it came out like a question. He could read my mind. Truth wasn't really an option, anyway. I felt his smile against my lips, right as his fingers slipped under the edge of my thong. I started to lift my hips for him to pull it off when a loud rip made me jolt.

Ezra tore it off me and then pocketed it with a devilish grin.

The door to the office opened behind him. I jumped on instinct, but Ezra knelt between my legs with his hands clamped around my thighs, holding them there.

"What do you ne—" Kendrick, Ezra's second, broke off.

"Take a seat," Ezra said quietly. But his voice was a boom in my ears. My heart started to race, a thrill working its way up my spine as my eyes flashed between the two.

Ezra stared at me purposefully. Then I understood.

Truth or Dare.

"For your pleasure, I asked him to join us. Kendrick is going to watch me eat this pretty pussy." At my vampire's words, Kendrick slowly started toward the couch and took a seat, bracing his hands behind his head and legs sprawled out—at ease.

My breath caught in my chest as Ezra waited, silently, for any inkling of consent.

I bit my lip and spread my legs wider.

Ezra's gaze turned dark with hunger as he crooned, "Good girl."

He trailed light kisses and small nips up my inner thigh, making my back arch. Reaching the sensitive skin just a few inches from where I really wanted him, he sucked on a patch of flesh that made my legs jerk.

After the last few days I'd had, my body was wound *very, very* tight, and I needed this more than I cared to admit.

My hands tangled in his dark locks, I pulled tight as I tried to guide him where I wanted him to be. Ezra huffed a laugh against my center, a cool breath of air hitting my clit and making me stiffen.

I looked up to see Kendrick staring unabashedly. His dark brown eyes burned with lust, all the more inflamed when Ezra took my clit between his lips and my mouth dropped open in a silent moan.

I bucked up, urging him on. Ezra rewarded me by pushing two fingers inside and using the flat of his tongue to scrape along that sensitive nerve bundle. I fisted his hair even tighter, using my sheer demonic strength to pull myself to him. He punished my clit in the best way possible, driving those fingers home with only the strength a supernatural could have.

It. Was. Heaven.

Heaven may not have been real, but this was as close to it as it got.

My legs shook, and my grip slackened. My eyes closed as I raced toward that edge of release. The feel of his teeth pinching my clit followed, but a soothing suck sent me careening over the edge.

"Ezra," I moaned his name, throwing my head back as I lost all control. My body flashed hot, then cold as my orgasm soldiered through me, taking no prisoners. He lapped at me, sending shock waves on the heels of the best oral I'd experienced in my long life. I writhed against him until the last of my pleasure died off, leaving me sated, but greedy for more.

Ezra stood up, pressing two fingers to my lips. I opened up without preempt and tasted myself on his skin. His green eyes smoldered with barely restrained heat as he said, "So fucking sweet."

I reached for his belt to return the favor, but he placed his hand on mine. "Next time."

I frowned and decided to mentally prod. *Why?*

Because the first time I take this cherry-red mouth, I don't want an audience.

My cheeks flamed a little as I realized how utterly serious he was being about why he brought Kendrick here. It really was for my pleasure, and perhaps, his way of showing me that being his mate didn't mean he would run around banging his chest like a fucking idiot every time another man looked at me.

Ezra smiled, his way of telling me I was right on the mark.

"Now, you had another reason for coming to see me?" he said, tugging my sundress down to cover my glistening center. I arched an eyebrow at him, and he held up my torn underwear, then turned as he not so subtly adjusted his pants.

"Right," Kendrick said, coughing once to clear the hoarseness in his voice. "There's been some accusations brought against one of the clan enforcers."

"Accusations?" Ezra asked, walking over to the bar to pour himself a drink. I noticed that he pointedly didn't offer me one.

"A dozen or so vampires claimed he took advantage of his position and raped them during their sentencing. Male and female," Kendrick supplied.

A shiver ran through me, and I slid myself off the edge of the desk, letting my dress fold naturally around me. "Do any of them have proof?" I asked.

Kendrick looked from Ezra to me, and instead of questioning it, he didn't miss a beat. "No," he said, "unfortunately not. Their stories all have one thing in common, though, and none of the victims have any record of knowing each other—which gave me pause."

"Oh?" Ezra chimed in.

"He only anally raped them."

I cringed. "Do you have the vampire in question in custody?"

"Yes," he answered. "He's being held in the dungeon. Ezra's ability to read thoughts should tell us for certain, but I suspect that he's guilty."

I lifted my eyebrows. "You're keeping him in a sex dungeon?"

Kendrick tried to hide his smile at my confusion. "Not *that* dungeon."

"It's below the club," Ezra said. "It's mostly used as a holding cell until judgement is passed. I actually have a specific den set aside for clan enforcers to do their punishing. It's a nice place. You'd like it." I snorted, amused by his assumption.

"My methods might surprise you," I said.

"My dear, I'd be disappointed if they didn't. You are *The Fury*, after all." I preened a little under his compliment.

"You said this dude is in the dungeons right now, yeah?"

Kendrick nodded. "I picked him up this morning during

the summit meetings when he was blowing off some steam in the club. Haven't told him what for just yet, but I imagine he has an idea if my gut is right."

"It usually is," Ezra said, downing the rest of his drink.

"Then I say we pay him a visit."

CHAPTER 7

The dungeon was aptly named.

Gone was the sexy glow of the dim lights and the leisurely atmosphere of the club. In its place was a cracked concrete floor, cinder block walls, and metal bars. "What are the bars made of that it keeps them inside?" I asked as we walked along a row of cells, mostly empty, but not all. Kendrick followed silently, several paces behind us.

"Tungsten," Ezra said. "One of the hardest metals on Earth. Just in case they are able to bend it, though, they'd have to break through it first. They're also chained to the floor."

I looked through a gap in the bars to see chains the same color as the metal attached to the concrete floors. Hm.

As a demon, I could most likely break those, but I'd never tried to bend anything that was Tungsten before. It was a long-standing tradition of my guild to test our strength and flaunt it at parties. I was the strongest in my age bracket, but not the strongest amongst all demons. The more one aged, the more their Afterlife abilities grew.

For demons, that skill was our strength. For angels,

their ability was to manipulate minds. The rainbow bridge attendants could communicate with animals. Poltergeists were interesting in that their abilities largely showed on Earth. The older they got, the more physical they could become. It was rumored that if left to time, and their own devices, one could eventually flip back and forth between human and phantom. It wasn't exactly a secret that Upper Management tended to pull them from Earth before they were actually able to achieve that, though. Something about the temptation of life again being too great.

Before, I might have wrinkled my nose at the prospect. But now . . . my eyes ventured to Ezra's back. His proud shoulders and lush dark hair. I had something with him. Even if I couldn't feel the mate bond as he did, I felt something, and when I thought about it, staying on Earth didn't seem so bad.

"Robert Waters," Ezra remarked as we approached a figure at the end of the long row. He stood against the wall, smoking a cigar. His honeyed hair was gelled back, and his pinstripe suit was reminiscent of a time closer to my own.

"Finally," the guy huffed, blowing out a stream of smoke. "Boss, I knew you'd come clear this mess up," he said, stepping forward. The chain attached to his ankle dragged across the floor, scraping as he walked.

"Actually," Ezra hummed, "we have some questions for you first."

The easy demeanor he wore froze, a mask settling over as Robert repeated, "Questions?"

Ezra nodded, not seeming in any particular hurry. I wasn't sure if it was intentional or not, but I knew from experience the lack of a rush tended to freak people out.

"How long have you been working for me, Robert?" Ezra started, hands in his pockets, the picture of utter calm.

Robert sucked the air between his teeth, eyes darting toward the ceiling.

"Since the seventies. I wanna say 72', right at the end of my first decade after being turned." He scratched the back of his head.

"Do you know why I make the newly-turned wait a decade before they can become an enforcer?"

Robert licked his lips, a hint of anxiety creeping into his expression. He started to shift his feet. "So we know the rules and have the bloodlust under control."

Ezra nodded. "Partially, but not completely." He paused, taking a look around his dungeon, as if admiring the view. "I make the newly-turned wait so they have plenty of opportunities to see what happens when someone breaks my rules. Enough time to understand that any delusions of power they might have are simply that. To understand their place in this world. *My* world." He looked back at the man behind the bars, eyes hard. "Do you understand your place, Robert?"

He swallowed. "Yes, sir."

"Hmm," Ezra replied, as if he were doubtful. "And what is that?"

"A-as your enforcer, sir." He was already pale by nature, but his face seemed to go white as a sheet under Ezra's scrutiny.

"And what is your job as my enforcer?" Ezra continued.

"To enforce your rules. Give out punishments." He licked his lips again, something I figured out was a nervous habit.

"Tell me, what happens to enforcers who break the rules?"

Robert went silent, his mouth opening, then closing. "I'm not sure—"

"You're not?" Ezra asked, his voice sharp as a blade. "Well, let me remind you, then. I am hardest on those that have chosen to abuse their power when I have allowed them to enforce my law."

Robert swallowed, but stayed quiet. As I watched him, I assumed he sensed the end of the conversation and what it would mean for him.

"Have you abused your power, Robert?"

A pause.

"N-no."

Ezra hissed. "I don't like liars, Robert."

The cigar dropped from his fingers, and while I'd suspected partway through the conversation, I knew in that moment he was guilty.

"I didn't—I swear!" He jumped forward, fingers coming within inches of the bars when the chains around his ankles stopped him short.

"How many?" Ezra asked quietly.

Despite his attempts to look confused by the question, I saw recognition behind his dark brown eyes.

"Don't make me ask again, Robert. How many vampires entrusted to your care have you raped?" Ezra said, the first signs of his anger actually showing.

"I—you—I don't—"

"Seventeen," Ezra said quietly. "Kendrick, pull the files for every vampire he's had to deliver punishment to for more than a month. That seems to be when he starts up. They need to be aware their abuser is in custody and that I'm willing to provide every service available to help them move on from their mistreatment."

Kendrick stepped out of the shadows and nodded. "Understood."

"Fury," Ezra said as his second started down the hall,

leaving us with the piece of shit. "What punishment would you give him if he were assigned to you?"

I blinked, not expecting the question. Instantly, my mind started turning with possibilities. I stepped forward, toward the cage, and I stroked the cold metal bars with my fingers. "I'd need his history to say for certain, but usually rapists are a combination of punishment and rehabilitation. Punishment, because they actually did it. But you need rehabilitation because the urge came from somewhere. It's long-term reconditioning, essentially."

"Such as?" Ezra prompted, less angry and more curious.

"I start with the punishment. Rapists have distorted views on sex. Power trips. They enjoy taking something from their victim; hurting them and watching them suffer. So I take that and turn it on them. I simulate the beginnings of a rape over and over again, where their victim becomes the abuser. This teaches him that trying to force someone won't go the way he expects, and he should fear raping someone. The entire time they are powerless. They hate it in the beginning, of course." I smiled. "Once they're broken down enough, I start giving them choices again, little by little. Recondition the way they view everything. So rehabilitation comes with finding power, control, and sexual gratification in consensual ways. Finding a new outlook that isn't distorted anymore takes time. Overall, I condition them to reject every notion of what they once were. Provided I had enough time and did my job well enough, when they're reborn, they break the mold."

"Interesting," Ezra said, as if considering. "How long does this process take?"

"It depends on the person. Between twenty-five to sixty years is about average. I imagine it would be at the higher end for this one because of his already longer life. Not to mention there's no being reborn, so I'd need to be confident in the level of conditioning that he could possibly re-enter society without relapse or being unable to function. It's a fine line and if I broke him too much . . ." I shook my head. "Unless my job is to torture and kill, that's not the way to go and it doesn't fix anything anyway."

"Do you think you could change him?" Ezra asked. The tone of his voice made me turn.

"Are you asking me to?" I replied. His green eyes stayed fixed on me, us both ignoring the man quietly freaking out in his cell trying to process what was happening.

"You're bored here, and you enjoyed having a purpose as a demon. You still can." He thrust his chin toward Robert Waters.

"I may not be here long enough to finish the job," I started.

"Then write down how. Create a guide for someone to finish the job, if for some reason you can't," Ezra said, taking a step closer. His scent was intoxicating to me.

"You won't like all my methods," I said quietly.

"You don't fuck your assigned cases. You told me that." My eyebrows lifted at the crassness in his tone.

"I have to put myself in compromising positions to do this job, and I'm not just talking sex." I crossed my arms, leaning my shoulder against one of the bars.

"Would you let him hurt you?" he asked.

"No."

"Then I trust you," Ezra said simply.

"I'll need his history," I started slowly, my mind considering the very real possibility and what it would take. "And a secure location, but not like this. It needs to be normal. Like a house or an apartment."

"The enforcer den has suites for the prisoners. I can

have one assigned to you, just for him, without any others present," Ezra said with a dip of his head. "Is that all?"

"I have to be able to do this multiple times a week," I said after a moment. "While it's not a set schedule, a certain amount of frequency is needed to condition properly. I don't know how Roman or Dorian will take it, though, so I may need a ride if I'm not staying with you."

He nodded once. "Consider it done, and if either of them give you grief—let me know."

I cocked an eyebrow in question. He flashed a mischievous smile at me before extending his hand. "Come," Ezra said, taking my own. "Roman will be here to pick you up soon and I'm not done with you just yet."

CHAPTER 8
EZRA

I rubbed my temples in slow circles. I didn't even bother to listen to Roman as he spoke, closing out after the last speaker. One much-needed recess, then one more grueling, but thankfully short, gathering to send farewells, and the summit would be over.

Finally.

I was focused on more important things. Like Fury. I kept my promise and gave her as much privacy as I could offer, but I still heard her all the time. I heard the questions and the worry. The conflict . . . and the desires. She was trying to solve so many problems, and she was still trying to do it by herself.

I saw in her mind what Upper Management told her we would do. End the world. I scoffed. A bunch of soothsayers in the Afterlife. What a fucking joke.

I had once told her that I would help her complete her mission. That I would not get in the way. That was still true, but things were different after the night we changed her. I had changed.

Her internal struggles with the mission and the lack of

understanding it had been steadily increasing with each passing day. So was my attachment to her.

"Ezra," Roman said impatiently, breaking through my train of thoughts.

"Hm?" I looked up to see him standing next to me, the crowd clearing out. "What?"

"I've said your name three times. It's time to go. Fury and Roxanne are upstairs waiting."

"Right." I slid the chair back and stood, reaching my arms up to stretch.

"I need to check something in Avalon. I'll be back in time for the final closing," Dorian said, looking at his phone. "Call if you need me."

He sifted without another word.

I cocked an eyebrow and stared at the spot where he had just stood.

Roman grunted. "It's bad enough that you're so disengaged. Now he is too."

I shook my head. "No, we're nothing alike. My lack of caring is pure apathy. He's preoccupied. Maybe distracted. You know Dorian. He stares out the window and just thinks or drifts off. I don't know. He's old as shit. Nothing he ever does surprises me."

Roman smirked. "I can honestly say the same about you," he said, crossing his arms. "Which brings up an excellent question. Would you care to tell me why Fury spent most of last night drawing up what she called 'a torture outline' and mapping a dungeon for punishment?"

I barked a laugh. A torture outline. How organized.

"I've enlisted her help as an enforcer, of sorts. We had a vampire abusing his power. Raping. I asked Fury what she would do and how she would handle it. She told me, and I liked what she had to say. I said it was her case to take." I shrugged, wondering what kind of pushback I would get from the shifter.

Roman looked unconvinced. "Do you think that's wise?"

"Why wouldn't it be?" I asked, leaning on the edge of the long table that sat on the stage, curling my hands over its side. The room was entirely empty. "It doesn't put her in danger. This was her job when she was in the Afterlife, and the place where she'll be doing the work is safe."

"I question that considering everything that has already happened to her," he said. Roman reached into his pocket for a rubber band. He pulled his dreads back, away from his face, and tied them off. "What's the purpose? There's something you aren't saying, so spit it out. We're in this together now, much as we don't want to be."

I crossed my arms. He was right about us being in it together. More than I wanted him to be, especially considering what he was to Fury. But that was part of it. I wouldn't come between her and a mate. Ever. I didn't want them to come between us either.

"I want to get her involved in something she finds useful. She's been gone from this world for a long time. She was important there. Respected. Good at what she did. She valued that more than you know. This may come as a shock to you, but I want her to stay here."

His brows shot up. "The vampire has feelings. Color me surprised."

I glared at him, and I could feel a rush of angry adrenaline push through my veins. "I didn't reject my mate if you recall. She rejected me. I can't claim to know your loss. Don't claim to understand mine."

While I silently cursed that I had allowed that to slip—

showing more of myself than I cared to admit—my words had an effect on him. He nodded, a look of sympathy and regret shone in his eyes. He cleared his throat. "I'm listening."

"Let me ask you something, shifter," I started, my temper rising as I tried to maintain a measure of control. "What will make her *want* to stay, hmm? What about you is worth sticking around for? Yeah, she might like fucking me, but that won't keep her here long term." He narrowed his eyes, a bit of his jealousy peeking through. I had his full attention. "What are you—we—doing to make her feel like this is her home too? Now she may or may not get stuck here, unable to return, but what if Fury and that bird find a way for her to go back? We can't make her stay. She leaves. We all lose. Forget the end-of-the-world bullshit. She's *gone.*"

A threatening rumble came from Roman's throat. The icy blue in his eyes flashed as he and his wolf heard the words I'd said. They knew I was right.

Some of my anger dissipated. I couldn't believe I was trying to side with a shifter, but I went on. "She has to belong here. This needs to be her home, and that's what I'm trying to give her. Where she comes from, mates aren't a thing. This isn't her world. It's ours. And her human life before . . ." I trailed off, knowing it was territory I shouldn't cross. "Well, it's not my place to say. It's her story to tell when she's ready."

Roman's jaw was clenched as he understood a small fraction of what I wouldn't say. He nodded slowly. "It's why she drinks, isn't it?"

I pressed my lips together in acknowledgement. I didn't need to say anything. He already knew the answer.

He sighed. "I figured."

"She still hasn't dealt with that yet, so she drinks to cope."

"That's a piss-poor way to cope. Doesn't fix anything. To make it worse, she's not a demon anymore," Roman said. "Whatever she is, the liquor has an effect on her. She's getting hangovers, even if she won't admit to that yet."

"I know."

"I don't want that for her. And I . . . agree with you. Given the possibility she could leave, we need to give her reasons to stay. Beyond the mate bond. She needs to make the choice," he said quietly. "I want her to stay too."

"Then we would do better working with her, not against her," I said. I considered my next words carefully. "And we would do better working together, the three of us. This goes beyond protecting her. If you don't want her to go back to the Afterlife if she finds a way, then you and I at least have the same goal in mind here. I'll have to ask the fae what he wants."

He huffed a humorless laugh. "I'm not sure Dorian even knows what he wants anymore." He sighed, sticking his hands in his pockets, and staring at the floor in thought. "If we give her more of a reason to stay, help her feel valued and part of this world—our world—then that's what we do. We give her what she needs. And I can support her doing whatever it is she has planned on that torture outline of hers."

I twisted my lips in a smile and reached out to shake his hand. Here we were. Alpha vampire and alpha shifter, teaming up to keep our demon hybrid mate on Earth. What was the world coming to . . .

CHAPTER 9

"What is taking them so long?" I asked, laying on the couch with my head hanging over the edge. "They recessed like fifteen minutes ago, yeah?"

Roxanne picked up a strawberry from a fruit tray on the coffee table and popped it into her mouth. "Yeah. We can go downstairs and get them," she said while she chewed.

"Finally. I'm starving up here. I want real food." Standing up, I readjusted my shirt, pulling a small gray feather off me. I groaned. "Ugh, is Hades molting and leaving shit on my shirt now?"

Roxanne glanced up and laughed as I tried to flick the feather off my fingers. "Hades has gray feathers under the black? Or is there some other bird you're hanging out with now and you don't have the heart to tell him?"

"Don't even joke about that. It's hard enough dealing with the one. He's driving me crazy," I said. "He's off searching for some answers with Duke, supposedly. But when he's here, I think he's sleeping in my clothes."

"Perhaps," Roxanne said, tucking her phone in her back pocket and grabbing another piece of fruit. "Maybe it would help if you made him a bed and didn't leave your clothes on the floor," she added with a know-it-all shrug.

I considered my response, then thought better of it. I was hangry, and when the hanger wanted to talk, it wasn't nice. I needed to be fed more often. Instead, I grumbled incoherently.

"You need a purse." Roxanne walked to the door and opened it. "That will help some of this."

I scrunched my eyebrows in confusion. "What? What does a purse have to do with anything?"

"A place for you to put snacks. You're a grouch when you're hungry. I can see it in your eyes. I don't need to be Ezra to know that," she said, waving her hand for me to exit first.

The guard at the door turned to us. "Shall I escort you and Fury down?"

"No, we'll just meet the guys downstairs, Frances. Thank you," she answered.

I followed her out and gave the fae a forced smile. She was right. I was grouchy. I was over this summit. It was days on end of doing what felt like nothing. I still hadn't figured out what would trigger the guys. I was no closer to getting answers on what the hell I was. I'd sifted into Ezra's bed, and bled like a stuck pig from my nose and ears, and we still had no clue what that was. Nothing else had happened yet, but it had only been a day since the last episode. Small victories, and all. I hadn't been alone long enough to summon Bloody Mary, and if I had, I wasn't sure what to ask her just yet, anyway. I didn't know if she would show up, and if she only gave me one question, I wanted to make it good. I didn't want to play that card just yet. It was pretty much the only one I had. If Duke and Hades didn't find what we needed, then I would take the risk.

I missed talking to Duke. I missed conversation and bantering with him. He was the closest thing I had to family, and more than anything, I missed that connection. I wanted his advice. I wanted to ask him questions I wasn't ready to even voice out loud to myself just yet, but it would be different with him. All I could do was hope he found some answers soon. In all my years in the Afterlife, I had inadvertently come to hate the unknown even more. I liked being in control.

I liked having a plan—even if that plan was winging it, it was still my choice to have that chaos as my strategy. I didn't feel like I was given a choice in what was happening now. At this point, any plan I might've had was shot to shit. I was truly flying by the seat of my pants, and I had zero control over it.

As soon as we entered the stairwell, I heard a cacophony of crashes and screaming. That was when I realized our other fae guard was not at the top stairwell post. Roxanne looked at me wide-eyed and I pushed past her to run down the stairs.

"Damn it, Fury, stop!" she shouted behind me as she followed. "Get back to the room—" She grabbed my arm, and I whirled around to face her.

"Fuck the room, what if they need us?" I said between clenched teeth.

"They want you safe. I can't let you run down there into whatever that is," she answered. She kept her grip on my arm tight.

I could have pulled away. Tossed her aside. It wouldn't take much effort. She was strong, and I knew that, but she wasn't as strong as I was. Every day I felt an increase in power, even if it was only a tingle. A tiny measure. I could hear just a little bit more in the distance. I could see just a little further or with a touch more clarity. My strength was there before the change. I could tear away from her, and she couldn't hold me back.

But this was Roxanne. I wouldn't do that to her if I could talk to her first.

"Why haven't the guys come to us? Why hasn't Ezra reached out to me? Where are they, Rox? Now let me go. Something is very wrong, and you know it. I wouldn't let Ezra stop me from getting to you the night of the banquet. I won't let you stop me from getting to them. I won't lose any of you."

Her grip loosened as she contemplated what I'd said, a slight flicker of her wolf flashing in her eyes so similar to her brother that it sent a chill down my spine.

She nodded. "Go."

I turned back and raced down the steps with Roxanne at my heels. The closer we got, the louder each shout and scream became. Reaching the bottom, I stilled, putting my hand on the doorknob and turning to Rox. She pulled off the purse she wore across her body and tossed it behind the stairs. She nodded silently, and I did the same.

I cracked open the door and saw supes running past us. They were all headed in one direction. Cool. That meant I needed to go the opposite way.

I flung it open and took off down the hallway toward the room where we'd held the panels.

I came to a screeching halt and Roxanne almost crashed into me.

It looked like the biggest bar fight I'd ever seen.

Countless supernaturals fought each other. Fists pounded into faces. Blood sprayed and bones crunched. Bodies were picked up and tossed into overturned furniture. Not a single table was upright. Chairs had been thrown across the room, some were still in the hands of those using the seats as weapons. Glass was shattered and broken everywhere, the light filtering in from the windows catching the shards and making them sparkle like jewels. Surveying the room, I saw there were entirely too many that lay unmoving, bleeding from gaping wounds or missing limbs.

"What in the hell?" Roxanne breathed behind me.

My mouth hung open before I could find the words.

"I don't know, but this was not what I expected to find."

"Where are the guys?" she asked, taking a step forward and standing next to me. "What happened here?"

I shook my head as I looked around. No one even seemed to notice us.

I saw a shifter stand up from behind a table she'd used for cover. Her green fatigue pants were covered in blood spatters, and her tight black shirt was torn in places. Whatever brief feelings of confusion I'd had dissipated quickly when I met her gaze. She walked slowly amongst the chaos, not paying attention to anyone or anything around her.

Something was wrong with her. I looked her in the eyes and what I saw was not a shifter. I didn't know what she was. Her eyes looked blank and hollow, but she was alive. There was no question.

Roxanne gasped when she saw her, coming to the same conclusion, throwing her arm in front of me like a mother would her child.

"Fury, go," she whispered harshly.

I looked over at her incredulously. "And leave you here? Fuck that."

Roxanne and I stood shoulder to shoulder, and she refused to take her eyes off the approaching imposter.

I turned my head a fraction, looking to see if we were

going to be ambushed from behind, trying to formulate a way out. But where?

Ezra, now's the time to be prying in my head. Where the hell are you?

Slightly busy. A fight broke out. Roman and I are handling it.

Where is Dorian?

Avalon.

I placed my hand on Rox's arm. She shook her head slightly, never breaking eye contact. Don't speak. The shifter would hear us.

Ezra, this isn't just a random fight . . . main room . . .

Before I could finish, the shifter strode forward, cocking an eyebrow as her lip curled on one side in a cruel smile. I watched her fingers twitching at her side like she was eager to get her hands on something. I realized why. She moved lightning fast, reaching for a knife she'd kept at her side, and she threw it.

Everything happened so quickly, yet it felt like I watched it in slow motion.

The dagger sailed through the air, aimed directly at Roxanne's chest. Shoving my shoulder toward her and putting all my weight behind it, I pushed into her body, moving her out of the knife's path.

And into mine.

The blade sliced through my deltoid, and I felt the intense fiery burning that only comes with an open wound. The knife landed behind me, clattering to the floor. I screamed in anger and pain, grabbing my arm in reflex. Blood squeezed through my fingers and gushed down my arm.

That fucking bitch just cut me.

Oh hell no.

I heard Ezra's panic in my head as the events unfolded.

The shifter laughed, and she ran toward us, transforming into a wolf as she approached. I reached down to pick up the knife as Roxanne roared in response. Her brown eyes went so icy blue they turned white. Her canines grew, and she exploded into a monstrous wolf with black oak fur. She bolted forward with a deep growl, her jaws open as she lunged and met the attacker head on.

Were it not for the life-and-death situation playing out before me, I would have marveled at Roxanne's beauty. The shine of her coat and the powerful yet graceful way she moved. But it wasn't the time.

The wolves clashed together in a frenzy, snapping and biting. I ran toward them, watching as the unknown shifter pushed up on her back legs, pushing Rox with her front paws. I dropped to my knees, sliding across the wood floors. I leaned back as far as I could, slashing the legs of the wolf as I glided right behind her. She collapsed, a distinct canine whine piercing the air. Roxanne jumped on top of her, jaws clamping down on her throat.

Ezra shouted my name through our connection as he saw what was happening, no doubt sharing it with Roman. It was then I heard Roman's bellowing reverberating through the walls.

My mates burst through a side door, knocking the fighting supernaturals aside with brute strength as they ran toward us. The fighting factions scattered, taking cover, or running off in fear as their enraged alphas tore them apart in an effort to get to us.

Ezra's strong, lean arms wrapped around me, pulling me away from Roxanne. "Let me go."

He held tight. "Just wait. He needs to calm her. Roxanne as a wolf is dangerous." I stopped fighting his hold and watched as Roman placed a hand on her shoulder, stroking the fur gently while he shushed softly. She growled in response, baring her teeth even more as they held the imposter. Then she looked at her brother from the corner of her eye.

Roman nodded in some sort of understanding as he looked at his sister. I realized he could communicate with her when she was a wolf. Would he be able to do that with me once I shifted? He pulled back his muscled arm, fist closed, then punched the subdued wolf in the head with a loud crack. The light left her eyes, and her breathing ceased. He'd killed her, taking the weight of that responsibility off his sister's shoulders. Roxanne let go, shaking out her body and rapidly shifting back into her human form.

"What in the world is going on here?" Roxanne asked her brother.

"I don't have a fucking clue." He ran both hands over the top of his head. "What did you mean Carly was like a zombie?"

"That one?" Ezra asked, pointing to the body as I pulled away from him. He took the knife from me, inspecting it.

Roxanne nodded. "Her name was Carly. She was a mid-level ranger in our pack."

I scoffed. "Well, *Carly* looked blank. Possessed. Like she didn't know what she was doing, but she was laughing after she threw the knife."

Roman looked down at my bleeding arm and he grabbed it, looking at the wound. "It's not closed yet." He took off his shirt and ripped it, tying a piece of the cloth around the cut to staunch the bleeding. He cupped my face, stroking my cheekbone as he leaned down and touched my forehead with his own.

The serene moment was interrupted by a melodious

laugh, echoing in the giant conference room like the peal of wind chimes.

We all jerked our heads in surprise, looking to see who it was. I turned my head around, not seeing anyone. Until I looked up at a chandelier. A woman in a red dress and white cloak sat on the curve of an arc. She rocked her legs forward and back, swinging like a child on a playground. She kept her head ducked down, the fabric obscuring her face from view.

"Come play with me," she purred, curling her finger and beckoning me. "You're mine, pretty girl."

I crossed my arms. "I am not."

She stopped her childlike movements, a low hiss escaping her lips.

I felt a tingling sensation on the tip of my nose, and I rubbed it. Then I sneezed.

"No," she breathed. It was barely a whisper, but my enhanced hearing picked up on it.

Ezra—

I can't read her. She's blocked.

Of course she is.

I sneezed again.

"Stop making me sneeze, asshole," I said to her, annoyance filling my tone. She growled at me in response.

Roman looked at me confused before recognition flashed across his face. "She's trying to control you. A spell."

"Fucking witches," Ezra said through clenched teeth.

The woman jumped down from the candelabra, almost floating gracefully to the ground. She landed on one knee, her head down, looking at the floor. She picked up a shard of glass in one hand and squeezed it. Blood oozed from her hand, seeping between her fingers.

"Mortem. Exitum," she whispered as she started to look up. "Venit."

Crazy person speaking Latin about death and destruction was a bad sign. My mouth fell open as Ezra's voice drowned out my own thoughts.

She's after you. Go with Roxanne. We'll take her out.

Ezra flipped the knife in his hand, catching it blade side in preparation to throw it at our mystery witch. Roman's skin vibrated, his wolf itching to come out and fight.

The cloak fell from her head, settling on her shoulders, as Ezra's arm came down to throw, but I grabbed his wrist, stopping him from releasing the blade when her face came into view.

"Stop," I shouted. "Don't kill her!" My words came out quickly as I panicked, and I stared into her haunted blue eyes. A single tear ran down her bloodstained skin, leaving a clean path of white amongst the crimson splatters.

Ezra and Roman looked at me incredulously.

"That's Dorian's daughter."

CHAPTER 10

"What?" Roman and Ezra said in unison.

"Impossible," Roxanne breathed, shifting her weight. She shook her head in disbelief, but her wide eyes said she knew I was right.

A million questions ran through my head. I tried to recall what Dorian had told me about her. We were in Avalon. I saw her portrait in the green room. Lyra. That was her name. He said she had been forced into a sleep to stop her from hurting herself. And others. What that meant, he never told me, and I didn't ask. As I looked at her bleeding hand, her tear-streaked face, and the crazy look in her eye, I now regretted suppressing those questions.

Dorian said she was in something called stasis. She couldn't just wake up on her own. Yet, here she was, standing before us, surrounded by destruction.

"You knew about this?" Roman asked his sister, turning his head a fraction in her direction. Anger rippled through his voice.

"Not the time," she answered through gritted teeth, her fists clenched at her sides.

I decided to take a chance. See if I could talk to her, or at the very least, get some answers.

"Your name is Lyra," I said cautiously as she approached us.

Her steps were slow, and her blue eyes flashed with an emotion I couldn't place. She masked whatever it was she felt, then drew her brows together in anger. That one I could read well.

I held my hands up in a peaceful gesture, and I hoped she would accept it. "I don't want to hurt you. I won't. I just want to know why you're here."

Her lips curled upward in a vicious smile. "Why, I'm here for you," she answered. "I was sent for *you.*"

A thunderous growl emitted from Roman, shaking the ground beneath us. I didn't know he was capable of shaking the very earth in his rage, but it was something I needed to note for later.

"Ignore him," I said, waving off the alpha wolf, trying to keep her attention on me. I couldn't risk taking my eyes off Lyra. "Okay, you were sent to kill me. Got it. Who sent you?"

She shook her head, the white-blond hair moving around gently. Her pointed ears peeked through the strands. A humorless laugh escaped her lips. "I'm not here to kill you. I just want to play." She dragged out the last word, running her tongue over the tip of her slightly pointed canine.

A chill worked its way down my spine, but I didn't want to give away how her words affected me. The way Roman, Roxanne, and Ezra were frozen, I only imagined they were experiencing something similar. This fae wanted to do damage. She didn't want me dead. Whatever it was she wanted to do with me was worse than the simplicity of death. I didn't need to ask more questions to know that. But why?

Can you read anything about her yet? I asked Ezra. He stood in a defensive position, ready for the attack.

Nothing.

We need to get away from her. I don't know her powers, but I know she's dangerous. Tell Roman and Roxanne I want them out of here. They can call Dorian. Just be careful, and please don't kill her.

You're fucking kidding me, right?

Ezra, please. I hoped pleading with him would be enough. There was no way for me to explain it. I didn't even have all the information, but I knew she was Dorian's child. I knew she was ill. I knew he loved her more than anything. I heard the longing in his voice when he told me about her. I saw the sadness in his eyes. We couldn't do that to him. We couldn't kill his daughter. Roman was struggling to survive after the loss of his mate and child. I didn't want Dorian to go through it too. *I know you can hear me. She lives, do you understand? Promise me.*

Nothing but silence in return. Not once had she changed her speed as she approached, but she was too close, and I was out of time to argue with him.

"Here to play? I'm not much for games, Lyra. I'm more of a straight shooter."

She shrugged. "Suit yourself. Everyone breaks eventually," she said and lunged forward.

That Earth phrase about all hell breaking loose—it was an appropriate description.

I dove out of Lyra's reach as she took a swipe at me. I hit the ground, rolling with intent until I bumped into an overturned table. I groaned, quickly getting to my feet.

I had no idea how to subdue her. We couldn't kill her.

We'd have to play her game until Dorian came, or until she was sated. I just hoped she wasn't planning on satisfaction via murdering us the time around. Maybe I could knock her out? That seemed unlikely, but I didn't have much to go on.

Ezra heard my thoughts and shook his head vehemently as he moved his position, circling her location with the knife still in his hand.

The floor rumbled and a furious roar filled the room. Roman and Roxanne shifted, exploding into their wolf forms in a matter of seconds. They stood side by side, hackles raised and baring their teeth as they growled in warning.

Lyra grinned in response. Looking above her, she reached a hand up, closing her fists, then pulling down hard. Her eyes darkened, flaring indigo in color, and I saw her intent. The chandelier she'd sat on earlier came crashing down. Both wolves jumped out of the way in opposite directions as it crashed on the floor, sending glass flying in all directions.

A piece of shrapnel flew outwards and embedded in Roman's shoulder. He shook his body hard, trying to dislodge it as blood coated the fur around it. All I could see in his blue eyes was rage.

A childlike laugh bubbled up and Lyra reveled in it. She spun around, looking for her next target.

Roxanne was by my side, but we had no way to reciprocate communication. I grabbed her giant muzzle, turning her to look at me, speaking harshly while I told her what I needed. "Go. Call him. We need him here. The longer we drag this out, the worse it could get. We don't know what we're dealing with."

She growled softly as we stared at each other. Several tense moments passed before she dipped her head and closed her eyes in an extended blink. She nudged me with her nose, pushing me toward an area of furniture. She wanted me to hide.

"Go," I whispered, pushing her away. "I'll be fine."

She grunted, turning away from me to run toward an exit, keeping close to the wall, her great paws thudding as they hit the wooden floors.

I scanned the room, catching Ezra's form as he circled behind Lyra while Roman prowled in front of her and snapped his jaws, his shoulder wound already healed.

"I know what you're doing, vampire," she said in a singsong voice, picking up her skirt and twirling it like she was dancing around a Maypole. She'd completely turned her back on Roman.

She was incredibly confident or overly stupid, and I was betting on the former. The little that I knew about her didn't suggest she was easy to take down.

Roman hunched close to the ground, but I held my hand up to him, shaking my head. He growled deeply, not liking my command.

Lyra held her hand out, turning it over front and back, admiring it. She grinned, then her claws extended slowly, long, pointy, and from the looks of it, sharp. "I have knives too," she said to Ezra quietly. "I bet mine are sharper. Would you like to see?"

Keep your distance, Ezra. Bide our time. I worked my way toward him slowly, circling the way he had.

Ezra flicked his gaze to me, then back to her. I saw the slightest twitch in his arm. I faltered, realizing what he was going to do. I burst into a sprint, hoping this weird supernatural hybrid magic would allow me to be faster than all of them.

I wasn't.

Ezra darted at an impressive speed, only to have her sift away from him. She landed four feet in front of me, and I tried to stop before slamming into her. A cruel smirk lit up her face when she turned and looked at Ezra over her shoulder. She tutted, then swiped her hand out, slashing across my stomach and digging into the corded muscle before she disappeared and moved to another location in the middle of the room.

Pain and burning ripped through me and I fell to the ground, crying out. I pressed my hands to wounds, pretty much hoping my insides were not on my outsides because the intensity of the fire I felt around it said maybe they were. Red oozed around my fingers, and I looked down, not seeing anything I shouldn't. Well, except the torn skin and pouring blood.

Roman roared, running toward Lyra as Ezra screamed a curse and ran to me in a flash. I rolled over to my knees, and pushed myself up, feeling every bit of the strain in my abdomen, and it freakin' hurt. He held on to me, trying to help me, but I pushed his chest away, yelling, "I fucking told you not to kill her. Don't engage."

He ignored me, reaching for my stomach, and pulling up the shirt to see the wounds knitting themselves back together. "It's healing," he said and breathed out in a sigh of relief.

Back in her human form, Roxanne burst through the side entry, shouting for Roman to stop, but he was too focused as he advanced on Lyra. He aimed low, looking to take out her legs, but she jumped in the air effortlessly, landing with an undeserved grace, her dress billowing in the air around her. Roman skidded, then turned to face her again, pissed he hadn't made contact with her.

There was a mischievous gleam in her eye as she smiled

—then all her movements stopped. Her sapphire eyes flashed a deep indigo, then back to blue. The almost joyous look she had on her face disappeared and a single tear fell from her eye again. Her harsh gaze held mine as she opened and closed her fists.

"WE'LL SEE each other again soon. The angel calls to me."

My blood ran cold.

I knocked Ezra away from me and rushed toward her, shouting, "What angel? Lyra!"

In a split second, she sifted, leaving me running toward nothing. The angels. This was about me. All of it. Again. I dropped to my knees and screamed in frustration as I pounded my fists into the ground over and over. A crack splintered across the room as I took out my emotions on the floor.

Roman shifted back, and I felt his and Roxanne's warmth next to my body. She knelt down beside me, wrapping her arm around my shoulders. Roman's strong hands stroked my hair. They were attempting to comfort me in the only way they knew how. Ezra was smart enough to stay away from me at the moment.

"You said to come back now. What the hell happened here?" Dorian's voice boomed in the expansive room.

I snapped my head up, and so did everyone else. He walked with authority and confidence, taking in the destruction surrounding us.

"Lyra happened," Ezra said, crossing his arms and cracking his neck from side to side. "Care to explain that one, *Dorian*?"

The fae alpha halted. His steps were no longer steady.

His normally unshakeable poise wavered. Something troubled passed over his glowing amber eyes.

"No . . ."

Roxanne stood up beside me and stormed over to Dorian with purpose. Tears filled her eyes, threatening to spill over the moment she'd blink. She stopped in front of him, saying nothing. He said nothing in return. Then she slapped him across the face, the smack echoing in the silence. His head whipped in the direction she'd hit him, and still he said nothing.

"You said Lyra was dead," she said, her voice an angry whisper. "Don't you ever fucking lie to me again. *Ever.*"

I pushed myself up, wiping off my knees. Blood dripped down my knuckles from hitting the floor. "When Dorian? When did she wake up?"

He brushed his hand over his face where Roxanne had hit him, then ran his hand through his hair. "The same night the summit started. The night of the banquet."

His words played on repeat in my ears.

The same night Roxanne was kidnapped.

The same night I was bitten.

Lyra woke up that night. Every part of my senses were on edge, vibrating with barely contained rage. Even though Ezra wasn't pushing into my thoughts, I felt his presence. I shot him a look. It said 'back the fuck off.'

"When were you going to tell me?" I asked him. I gritted my teeth. The muscle in my jaw hurt. I knew what he was going to tell me. I needed to hear him say it. He was pushing me to be honest with them. Asking me question after question. Demanding answers. He chastised me for keeping my secrets, and my secrets weren't even all my own to tell. He judged me for the truth of who and what I was. And for a brief moment, I had felt badly for it. Now he was going to tell me what he was. And that was a goddamned fucking liar.

Dorian's features were cold and guarded. He narrowed his eyes a fraction but didn't answer me.

I closed my eyes and counted. Counted and breathed. When I opened them again, I met his stare. "When?"

Silence.

The anger inside me couldn't hold much longer. I clenched my fists and felt the prick of my claws extend into my hand. It pierced the skin, and I could smell the copper tang settle around me. My vision clouded in a foggy haze. "WHEN?" I screamed, drawing it out. My body shook as I allowed the violence I so badly wanted to unleash come out in my voice instead. It was better than the alternative.

Still. The windows shattered, and another chandelier shook precariously. The upturned tables and toppled chairs rattled against the once gleaming antique wood floors.

When the last of my echoing demands had abated, I stared at him.

"I wasn't going to tell you."

CHAPTER 11
DORIAN

The tension in the room was palpable. Roxanne's hurt was undeniable. I had lied to her. Probably my dearest friend in my long life, and I hadn't shared the truth of my loss. I had no doubt she was questioning my reasons for not trusting her.

Roman and Ezra were furious. I didn't care. They could go fuck themselves. I owed them nothing. I surely didn't know their most closely guarded secrets, and why should I? It wasn't my business.

But Fury. She looked at me with stormy eyes, seething. Her red hair clung to her neck and face with sweat. Her nostrils flared as she breathed in and out. I refused to look away.

"Why?" she asked, breaking the silent standoff.

I thought for a moment. It didn't matter how I worded what would come next. The anger she felt toward me would not be easily forgiven.

"Because I didn't want to," I said finally.

She huffed, "No, that isn't a good enough answer."

"I'm sorry you feel that way."

"Fuck you," she spat. "You aren't sorry for anything. Why didn't you want to tell me? To tell any of us?"

I straightened my posture, lifting my head up to look at the ceiling. The exhaustion of the week's events was taking its toll. My shoulders always felt heavy with the weight of time and knowledge. Mentally I was drained. I wanted to rest. I had wanted to rest for a thousand years, but I couldn't. It was my responsibility to take care of Lyra. To take care of those she had hurt all those years ago. To protect the living fae and honor the memory of the dead. I had no successor. It was my burden. My punishment for not being enough when I was needed the most. With that thought, I simply said, "It isn't anyone's business."

"Like hell it isn't," Roman roared. "You have some nerve saying it wasn't anyone's business. Look around you, Dorian." Roman threw his arms out as if I couldn't see the dead bodies and the room in complete disarray. "Tell me how she can destroy all of this, kill people, and come after Fury—come after *our mate*—and then claim it's somehow not our business."

Bringing my gaze to the shifter, I looked into the icy blue eyes of his unstable wolf. "She wasn't here for Fury. She came looking for me."

"That's not what she said." Fury's voice was quiet. Level. I considered, at that moment, that she may be a bit like me. The quiet in me was dangerous. It was when I was thinking. Strategizing. But it was also when the wrath was fed. When the tempest of anger in me grew. The quiet before the storm. Perhaps we were alike in that. Time would tell.

I glanced at Fury, taking my eyes off her face for the first time. Her arm was covered in blood. It coated her hands and clung to her clothes. Three slashes in her shirt exposed the bloody skin of her stomach. A deeper part of my instinct responded. The need to be near her. Heal whatever wounds she had. Protect her. It felt feral. Almost uncontrollable. Almost. I took a step forward, my hand reaching out. I pointed to her midsection. "You're hurt."

She followed my gaze and wiped her hand over it. "It's healing. I'm fine. No thanks to you."

"Did Lyra do that?" I asked. The muscles in my back tensed further. I knew the answer. My daughter had harmed my mate.

"Some of it," she said, wiping at the ripped shirt over her abdomen. "There was a huge brawl. Everyone was fighting. Like something out of a bad western movie. Nothing made any sense. When Lyra made her appearance, she said she was here for me. Not to kill me. To play with me."

A harrowing cold descended on me. I felt it run the length of my body. Snapshots of haunted memories flashed in my mind. They never went away. Even when I slept, I saw the past. The bloodstained fields she'd left in her wake. I could see the trail of bodies. I could hear the screams of those dying, and agonizing wails of those clinging to their loved ones when we found her victims. The images would never leave me. Nor should they. It was my fault. "What else did she say?"

"She said she was *sent* for me. And right before you came, she said the angel calls to her." Fury watched me closely, no doubt looking for my reaction. "What does that mean?"

"I don't know." A truth I hated to admit. A second mention of an angel was only complicated by Fury's disclosure about our mates' deaths. I searched my mind for what it could mean, or why Lyra would say it, but it was a world I didn't know. That was her territory. Angels were unknown to us. Their lore was nothing more to us than a fairytale until Fury told us otherwise.

"Bullshit," Ezra said. "That crazy bitch showed up talking nonsense and speaking in riddles. We find out she's your daughter—something Fury managed to keep from me,"—he shot an incensed glance her way—"and you kept it a secret when she 'woke up', whatever that is supposed to mean. Why the actual fuck would we believe you now?"

"I had no idea she would come after Fury. She doesn't even know her—"

"But she did," Roxanne interrupted. "What is she capable of? And you better not lie to me. You owe me the truth."

"I think you owe us more than that," Roman said. "You told Roxanne she was dead. Fury recognized her, but seemed shocked at her presence. What's the real story here? Why did you keep this a secret?"

The vampire had looked over that detail in his tantrum. At the moment, he was too emotional. He had yet to look at my reasoning, only focusing on my action. Somehow, the shifter had. He surprised me at times, especially for one so young. His wolf was riding him, demanding answers. He barely had him under control, but his wolf and his strength were not the only reason he was an alpha, and whether or not he knew it, it was showing.

I had to decide how much to tell them. I found it curious that Ezra hadn't gleaned that little bit of information from her with all the mind games he played. I wasn't sure how she'd done it, but I wanted to know.

Fury kept quiet as she watched the exchange, and her silence did not go unnoticed. She raised a single eyebrow, challenging me to tell them before she did.

"Lyra is my daughter. My mate was her mother. Lyra saw what happened to her mother when she died, though I didn't. I found them afterward. After that day, she was broken. It sent her into a dangerous spiral of self-destruction. We tried to help her. Over time, the pain morphed into something worse. She became . . . not herself. I put her in stasis to keep her safe. To stop her from harming others."

I heard the questions forming in their minds. I suspected they were piecing it together. I knew what was coming.

"What does that mean?" Roxanne asked. The tears on her face had dried, leaving marks crusted on her warm brown skin. She'd never even bothered to wipe them away.

I tilted my chin up. "It means I forced her into a dreamless sleep until I could find a way to heal her."

"How long?" Roman asked. I met his judgmental gaze.

I inhaled deeply through my nose before speaking. "A thousand years, next winter."

Their curses and sounds of shock weren't hard to discern in the quiet of the expansive room. The high ceilings pushed the noise in circles, making sure I heard just how much they judged my actions.

"How is she out of stasis now?" Fury asked, crossing her arms.

I pressed my lips together and leveled her with a stare. "I . . . don't know. The magic and strength it took to put her in stasis was more than you could imagine. To wake her is . . . there are few in the world that could come close to having that kind of power."

"But someone did," she pressed. "And it wasn't you."

She hadn't asked a question, so I chose not to respond.

A realization sparked in her eyes. "The footsteps."

I inclined my head. "Yes, the footsteps. Whoever that was came back. Whoever that was woke her."

"Which brings me back to my question, Dorian," Roxanne interjected. "What is she capable of?"

I studied each of their faces, gauging how they would react to what I was about to say. They had no idea the havoc she could wreak. She fed on violence and bathed in blood. No matter how much I tried, I never understood why. I had spent a millennium seeking answers, but I came up short every time. I had tried to find a way to heal her mind without knowing what was wrong to begin with.

Roman, Roxanne, Ezra, and fae all over the world thought they knew the reasons for my intelligence and power. They were only partially correct. Yes, it was my job as protector and alpha to look after those placed in my care.

Without knowledge, there was no power. I'd spent centuries upon centuries pouring through scrolls, seeking wielders of old magic and new, learning legend and lore, accessing the secrets hidden within artifacts in mythology and religion—anything to give me a clue where to look next.

I still came up with nothing.

"Annihilation," I answered, my voice quiet. "And if for one moment you aren't fearful of what that means, you should be."

"You should have told me," Fury said.

"I had no way to know she would come after you," I admitted. "Nothing indicated a connection."

She rolled her eyes at me. "You're not as smart as you think you are if you actually believed this isn't connected. After everything I've told you—"

"Your arrogance almost got her killed," Roman said, his wolf sending a warning growl in his words. His eyes were a crystalline blue. The way his shoulders twitched told me he was on the brink of shifting. I met his gaze.

"I won't fight you, Roman, nor will I fight your wolf. Certainly not over this." I clasped my hands behind my back. "Take her with you, back to the compound. Keep her safe. Lyra is on the hunt now, and if she wants to find Fury, we need to be prepared to find her first."

"I thought that was what you were already doing," Ezra snapped. "Trying to find her and keep your dirty secrets safe?"

I quirked an eyebrow at his outburst. Mouthy vampire. Still . . .

"I could use your help. Roman and Rox can stay with Fury. You can come with me in the meantime. If I'm not mistaken, all Fury needs to do is reach out to you in the event they need us."

He squinted at my offer then gave a single nod. He briefly looked at Roman and they shared a moment, some unspoken understanding passing from one to the other. Curious that the vampire and the shifter were in on something together. It was not something I would have expected from them. I would take the opportunity with Ezra to learn more about what that meant.

I walked over to Fury and stood before her. Reaching up, I brushed my knuckles down her cheek. "I'm sorry Lyra hurt you. I *will* find a way to stop her."

She closed her eyes and leaned into my touch, if only for a second. "You should be apologizing for lying to me. To all of us." She pulled away, pushing past me, and heading for the exit. Roman huffed angrily, following at her heels. Roxanne passed me silently, looking at me from the corner of her eye before leaving.

I sighed. "It's you and me, Ezra."

"A thrill, I'm sure," he mumbled.

I hummed, pulling out my phone and hitting the speed dial. Tristan answered on the other line.

"What's your location?" I asked, motioning for Ezra to come stand next to me. "I have one stop to make, then we are coming to you. Lyra has been sighted, and it would appear she is back to playing her old games."

CHAPTER 12

I fidgeted with the stray locks of red hair that escaped my messy bun. Tonight was the ceremony for the shifters that died at the summit. Everyone from Roman's pack would be there, but it wasn't them that occupied my thoughts, but how they died.

Lyra was awake, and she was hunting. For me. Not to kill, but to play. The thought sent a trail of goosebumps up my bare arms. The Bruce Springsteen T-shirt had cutoff sleeves and a ripped midsection, putting both my demon brand and stomach on display. The three cuts I'd suffered earlier would have been fatal to a non-supernatural. Now all that remained were three very faint pink lines that would be gone by morning.

I tentatively reached down and brushed my fingers over the slightly uneven skin. This was what Lyra's version of play looked like. And to think, an angel sent her after me.

I knew one was behind the supernaturals before they kidnapped Roxanne and tried to kill me. But to wake Lyra . . . my hand dropped away. I couldn't understand this endgame. Before they wanted me dead, now they wanted to fuck with me? It didn't make any sense. If this were about the prophecy and the end of the world, I suppose killing me would have made sense if they wanted me to fail. But this . . . this felt personal.

Which was all the more confusing because I didn't know any angels. Not as anything more than an acquaintance, and no one in my human life would have been made one. That wasn't an option on the job roster. Angels were old. They'd been there since, well, forever.

So why come after me? And furthermore, I didn't know why the Afterlife hadn't stepped in to intervene yet. It's not like this was sanctioned. They'd sent me here for a purpose. Whoever was doing this had clearly gone rogue. But they hadn't been stopped yet, which made it all the more bewildering.

"Fury?" Roxanne called out before knocking softly on the door. "You ready?"

"Yeah," I said. "Coming." I took one last troubled look at the long mirror before heading downstairs. The house was eerily quiet compared to the usual chatter of people milling about. Rox must have seen the confusion on my face.

"Most everyone is already there. A lot of them had families that wanted to say goodbye before the burning." I followed behind her as we stepped out onto the front porch. The smoke from the fire hit me instantly, even though the plume rising in the sky was almost half a mile away.

"Did you know any of them?" I asked her as we started walking. The humidity still sucked, but without the sunlight, it wasn't quite as bad at ten o'clock at night.

"All of them," Roxanne answered quietly. "Carly and I went to school together. I dated her older brother for a while. He was supposed to be at the summit, but he got called away for work last minute." She walked at a gentle pace with her thumbs casually hooked in her pockets. She appeared at ease, despite the grief in her voice. "Most of the others I knew in passing. A few of them I was friends with. We're a pack. One way or another, I know everyone."

"Saying I'm sorry feels inadequate, but offering condolences just feels fake," I replied, kicking a rock out of the way with my boot. "I'm sorry I can't make it better."

"You're here," she said simply. "That's enough. I probably seem cold to some of the others because I'm not sobbing on the outside, but after watching my parents die and then what they did to Roman; Maya . . ." She shook her head. "I don't have it in me to cry right now. I'm so sick of watching people I care about die, I can't even react to it anymore."

"There's a point where pain and suffering become too much. That you become so used to it, you grow numb," I said quietly. "I can understand if that's what you've had to do to handle it." I knew it from my own experience. Not grief in the same way she was dealing with, but a grief all the same. I mourned the loss of myself before I even died. I turned numb because it was the only way to survive, until one hit too many took me.

Dying was the best thing that ever happened to me. But it wouldn't be that way for her friends and family. There were no promises or silver linings that I could offer her, knowing what I knew. And I'd shared that information with her, so there was no doubt in my mind that she wasn't thinking about it too.

"I need you to promise me something," she said as the funeral pyre loomed nearby. I could hear others easily at this range, which meant if they were listening, they could hear us too.

"Hm?"

A cool hand grabbed my own as she pulled me up short. "Don't go to them. Don't let that bastard win."

"Who—"

"The angel," she whispered. A flicker of blue ran through her desperate eyes, telling me all I needed to know. "Today happened because of them. Maya happened because of one of them. I need you to promise me that you won't run into danger again, not even for me. Roman, Ezra, even Dorian—much as I'm pissed at him right now—I don't think they could survive losing another mate, and I don't think the world will survive them."

My mouth opened then closed. Her words clicked together the missing piece.

All this time, I'd questioned why.

What makes them lose it?

What could do that to all three of them that hadn't before?

The answer was so fucking simple, but I needed Roxanne to see it.

I was the piece that connected them. *I* was the only person that did.

Which meant I was the reason.

My death.

"Motherfucker," I muttered under my breath. Roxanne narrowed her eyes at me. "Sorry, I just had an epiphany." She lifted her eyebrows, urging me to continue. I shook my head. Now wasn't the time, not when she literally just begged me not to die. Didn't seem like a great time to tell her my end was inevitable. Probably.

"What is it?" she said, dropping my hand to cross her arms over her chest.

"Noth—" I started to lie, then stopped. Judging by her

expression, she wouldn't have bought it anyway. "I figured out part of my case, but it's not important right now. What is—is that I won't promise you that." Her eyes flickered blue again, not liking that answer. "Not just because I care about you, but because it's not in my nature. Everything that's happening right now surrounds me, and I can't run away from that. I need to figure out what's going on and why an angel turned against the Afterlife. That doesn't mean I'll go to them or give up, though. We're playing with someone from my turf, and I need to be more careful than I have been because of that."

Roxanne let out a tight breath. Her shoulders sagged a little before she uncrossed her arms. "I suppose that's the best I'm going to get from you."

"It is." I smiled wryly. "Besides, the one sure fire way to kill me before won't work anymore. Given we don't know what will work, I can't imagine they do either."

She pursed her lips. "That's supposed to make me feel better?"

I shrugged. "I'm just being honest with you. Given I'm more likely to die-die this time, I won't hold back from using all the weapons I have at my disposal. People tend to back the fuck off when I can blow them up with my mind."

"I forget that, even though I shouldn't. It was scary as shit when you did it that night."

"It's a last resort. I prefer not to because of casualties. Demon strength also tends to be way more fun when it comes to handing people their ass." I smirked, and she rolled her eyes.

"You enjoy fucking with people too much," she huffed. I chuckled.

"I believe you meant to say I picked my job well, and yes, I did. That aside though, I think they're waiting for us."

I thrust my chin toward the fire where a huge group of shifters were gathered. It was relatively quiet considering the number of people, and more than a few were staring at us.

Roxanne sighed; the ease we'd found began slipping away as grief took hold again. "Come on." My smile dropped away as soon as she turned around. It wasn't just burning the dead or what it meant to these people, but the realization that this really, truly might be me soon.

Despite dying once, and almost dying again, I never really thought it would happen. The Afterlife takes away all anxieties surrounding it and I'd been living in some existence for so long now that having to comprehend the finality I might have to face . . . it was deep. Thought-provoking.

The ceremony went by quickly for me. They burned the bodies of their dead while Roman talked about each of them. He shared stories about their lives, what they meant to him, and others. I could tell the shifters were moved by it. I had to keep myself from cringing every time someone said a prayer, believing they'd see their lost loved ones again in the end.

At some point when the mood was high, the atmosphere changed. Roman stepped down and people took their turns going up to the fire, then retreating back to their spots. Most people brought blankets and towels to lay out. A few trucks pulled up and dropped their tailgates open to reveal coolers of beer and soda, mini-grills for hotdogs and hamburgers, and a projector that they aimed at the side of the barn closest to us.

"What's going on?" I whispered to Roxanne.

"A celebration of life. When a shifter dies, we burn their body and then throw a party until dawn. We spend that time honoring them," she said. "I'm going to go grab a blanket for us. You want something to drink?"

"A beer sounds good," I said. "Wouldn't say no to a hotdog either if you were feeling nice. Ketchup and mustard if they have it."

"You got it," Rox said. She sauntered over to the group forming around the trucks. I stood there watching her for a moment. It was easy to see myself making a life here. Where Ezra offered me an escape from the ordinary, Roman offered a home. Safety.

I liked how down to earth they were. Their customs. The way they treated each other. It was so foreign to me. At the turn of the century, the portrait of the American dream hadn't even been painted yet. I was born into an authoritarian family that didn't share love, feeling, or emotion; that was our home. My father, the banker, my mother, the housewife. Support the household, raise the children. Those were their roles. My role was simple. Listen and learn. I was schooled on how to behave like a lady. To know my place in the world. It was the way of our social class in the early 1900s.

I scoffed internally at the absurdity of it all.

Everything about that life was hollow inside. Big empty houses filled with sad, empty people.

Here they lived and laughed and loved. There was no silence. No empty houses hiding secrets. They celebrated together, and they mourned together. They shared their grief and their happiness. They respected and protected one another. I loved that, though I'd never known it.

"I've never seen hair that shade of red before. Is it a demon trait?" The new voice that greeted me was high, feminine, flirtatious even—and completely unknown. I turned my cheek to a shifter with lilac hair and eyes to match who couldn't have been more than five feet tall. I might've questioned if she dyed it, if not for the faint purple sheen of hairs on her arms.

"Purple hair and eyes aren't a shifter trait, either," I said, tilting my chin to study her better. A wry smile flitted across her lips. She wore a red and black long-sleeved T-shirt and jean shorts that were fraying at the ends.

"I'm special," she said and smirked.

"Me too," I replied. "How do you know I'm a demon?" While my mates and those close to them did, it wasn't exactly common knowledge yet. Not in the least because the living weren't supposed to know.

"I'm Caitlin's mate," she answered. "Name's Rava." She stuck her hand out. I noted her nails painted with black nail polish, and the black lines of a tattoo peeking out of her cuff. I shook her hand, surprised by the strength. Nothing trumped a demon, but she was stronger than the average supe. That much was obvious.

"Fury," I supplied, taking my hand back.

"I know."

"I gotta say, I prefer being on the other side of this conversation." Her eyebrows drew together before lifting in silent question. "The side where I know everything, and the other person is stumped. This side isn't as much fun." Rava chuckled, pushing a strand of violet hair back from her damp forehead to behind her ear.

"I wouldn't say everything. Just more than most of the pack. I get perks from being her mate, but she told me I might be able to help you some too."

"Oh yeah?" I questioned.

"Because I'm also an oddity. Half-shifter, half-fae." My eyes flicked to her ears, now noticing their subtle points. Less than a full fae, but more than any other supernatural.

"I didn't know there were any hybrids in the pack," I murmured.

"Hybrids are everywhere, nothing quite like you—obviously—but those of us that were either born to mixed lineage or turned a vampire at some point have some experience with the in-between. Because of my heritage, I'm not the same as most wolves or fae. I exist in the middle, like you."

I nodded slowly, taking her in again. "They say I should shift in the next week, by the full moon, but I'm still not feeling my wolf."

Rava nodded. "I didn't feel mine at all until *after* my first shift—which was much later than most of the shifters. For a while they thought I might not be able to."

"Does it hurt?" I asked, not psyched on the prospect of pain but curious what her experience was, given I might be more like her than anyone else I knew.

"For me it didn't, but my shift wasn't conventional. Many need the full moon to shift the first time. It helps them cross that last little barrier. In my case"—she hesitated for a moment, debating how much to say. I narrowed my eyes a fraction before she continued. "I lost control. My anger and adrenaline powered it, which carried me through the pain."

"Ah," I said, because I wasn't sure what else to say. On one hand, I was curious what caused her to have that much anger and adrenaline. On the other, it was usually considered rude to ask if someone didn't volunteer the information. Might be good to ask Roxanne about it later. I could be nosy without being a jerk.

"Yours may not. You likely have greater healing properties being part vampire. They recover from wounds better than any other species." She offered the information half-heartedly as if it might make it better.

"I'm also part demon as you pointed out, and they don't heal for shit when in a human body."

That wry smile she wore when she first spoke to me was back.

"Half the fun of being so different is learning all the ways you truly are," she mused.

"For someone considered different, that's an odd opinion to have," I said. "Most people don't like their differences. I can't imagine growing up in a pack was easy when you didn't shift with others your age."

She lifted a brow, either amused by my observation or questioning my audacity. I wasn't sure which. "It wasn't, but as I got older, my perspective changed. My mother is a shifter, and my father was fae. While I was born from a one-night stand during a previous summit, they both took responsibility and co-raised me. I got to have a pack, but also see places like Avalon. And because of my fae tutor, I can now sift anywhere in the world. Differences aren't bad when you learn to appreciate them."

I hummed, tucking the information away as Caitlin and Roxanne walked up to us.

"I see you've met Rava," Rox said, handing over my hotdog and beer.

"I hope she hasn't interrogated you too much," Caitlin said jokingly, even if there was a serious note in her eyes when she looked at her mate.

Rava raised both hands as if in surrender. "We were just talking."

"Mhmm." Caitlin smirked. "You'll have to forgive my skepticism. Rava is a counselor that helps hybrids cope with the accompanying challenges. She's been very eager to meet you ever since I told her what you were."

Things clicked into place when she said that, and the bubbly yet straightforward personality made a bit more sense. "You fix people."

"Correction; I help people fix themselves—although fix isn't the right word. Learn to appreciate and be okay with themselves is more accurate."

Roxanne grinned like she'd seen this conversation before. "That's fair, I suppose. Fix usually implies that it was broken, and I don't think being a hybrid counts as that. You'll have to forgive my terminology some. I'm a bit of a fixer myself."

"Oh really?" she asked, her eyes lighting up. "In what way?"

"Just the usual shitbags of the world. Rapists. Murderers. Abusive people that need some modifying." I shrugged, not noticing how Rava's face paled. She sent a semi-alarming look at Caitlin, who grimaced. "I take it they didn't tell you what I did in the Afterlife?"

Rava shook her head slowly. "I knew you were a demon, but I assumed that human preconceptions were likely far from reality."

AKA she didn't want to believe I was a soulless monster.

"Yes and no, I'm afraid. In the Afterlife, the bottom forty percent of people are reconditioned and punished in an attempt to fix their souls at the fundamental level before they're sent back. Demons have the job of doing that."

"Well, that's just *fascinating*," Rava said, utterly serious. "You'll have to tell me more when there are fewer sensitive ears around." She flicked her unnatural eyes to the shifters around us. While no one seemed to be paying attention, she had a good point about subtlety.

"Anytime," I offered with a smile. I took a swig of my beer and sighed happily into the frothy, foamy goodness. It'd been a solid twelve hours since my last drink and I was dying. A small voice in the back of my head said keeping track like that wasn't a positive thing, but it was easy enough to shut it out with the sounds of a crackling bonfire and easy chatting around me.

"Have you guys seen Roman?" Roxanne asked as she spread the blanket out. "I haven't seen him since the burning ritual." Both Rava and Caitlin shook their heads. A worried expression crossed her face before she scanned the woods. "Maybe I should go look for him."

"I'll do it," I volunteered. "I need another beer, anyway." Roxanne looked from me to the half-full red solo cup that I promptly emptied to make a point. Her expression turned annoyed, but she didn't call me out on it. I had a feeling Caitlin and Rava were the reasons. More Rava than Caitlin since Roman had no problem bitching at me about my liquor intake when she was around.

Rox tipped her chin. "Let him know I saved him a spot if he wants to watch the slideshow with us."

"Will do," I called, starting for the trucks. After a pit stop to fill up my cup, I took a walk around the whole of the fire, not spotting him anywhere. That seemed a bit odd since he was the leader of this pack, but perhaps he ventured off somewhere. Maybe back to the house to use the bathroom?

I walked around for a few more minutes, seeing if I just missed him the first time, but when he couldn't be found anywhere—and wasn't on the half-mile-long dirt road that led to here—I started to question myself. Logically I knew nothing could happen to Roman. He was unkillable. But that didn't mean he wasn't in a different sort of trouble.

Standing at the edge of the forest, I squinted my eyes to peer into the murky shadows. While I didn't see anyone, a glint of silver caught my eye before disappearing. I took one last look over my shoulder, still not seeing him, before starting toward it.

The mating call of cicadas quickly drowned out the party behind me while tiny flashes of yellow light from fireflies illuminated the forest floor. I was thankful to be wearing Doc Martens while stepping over fallen and rotting logs, not knowing what might be in the underbrush beneath. The last thing I needed was a frickin' snake to bite me. Watch my ass not be immune to poison, even if I could survive getting stabbed.

My gravestone would read:

Here lies *The* Fury
Demon
taken out by motherfucking snake

Talk about lame. If I were going to go out, I'd hoped my exit would be far more dramatic this time around. Considering it might be the key to bringing on the end of the world, I had high hopes.

At least Lyra offered that, though my heart hurt for Dorian if I died by his daughter's hands. Talk about a complicated relationship. He loved her unconditionally, as he should, even if he was an unrepentant asshole to me. I can't imagine killing one's mate would make it any better, though. Or that Roman and Ezra wouldn't hold back from trying to end her afterwards.

A shiver worked its way up my spine.

Definitely need to avoid that one.

A sharp thud drew my attention. While there was no

glint of metal this time, it came from the same direction. Slowly, I crept forward, my heart racing at the prospect of what I might find.

Please don't be a dead body. More dead shifters were the last thing I needed tonight.

When a second thud followed up, my heart skipped. I quickened my pace.

"You might be a good interrogator, but you'd make a terrible spy," Roman's rumbling voice greeted me.

I stepped out from behind a bush and through the tall ferns, into a small clearing with tree stumps littered throughout. I looked from the forest floor to the hulk of a man standing shirtless with his back to me. His muscles rippled as he lifted an axe over his head and split the log in front of him cleanly in two.

"I wasn't spying," I murmured, walking around the edge of the circle.

"Could have fooled me."

"How'd you know it was me behind you?" I asked, crossing my arms over my chest. Roman reached down with two hands and grabbed either side of the split long, ripping it down the middle another time. His muscles bulged, making me want to run my nails down them.

"Your pace," he grunted, leaning down to rip the other in half as well. "You're heavy with your lead foot and walk with a sort of rhythm because you sway your hips."

I lifted my eyebrows dubiously. "That's very specific."

Roman shrugged, picking up another log and setting it on the stump. Without saying anything more, he went back to splitting them and ignoring me to his best ability.

"Do you pay attention to how everyone else walks?"

"No."

My cheeks warmed a little. "Anything else you notice about me you'd like to share?"

Roman swung the axe. It split with a loud thud, cutting clean through, and planting itself in the stump below. He looked up at me and lifted an eyebrow.

"What are you doing out here, Fury?"

My lips twisted at the tired note in his voice. "I could ask you the same thing." He looked down at the wood and back to me. I suppose it was fairly obvious.

Roman sighed. "If Rox sent you—"

"I volunteered," I interrupted. "What gives? Why are you out here splitting wood instead of with your pack, mourning and celebrating?"

His expression turned frigid, a hint of blue peeking through his gaze. "Can't say I feel much like celebrating," he answered quietly before going back to his pile. I grit my teeth in frustration.

"If you're upset about the shifters that died, I understand that, but are you sure that isolating yourself out here is the best course of action?"

Roman gave me a hard look. I wasn't used to this part of him. This cold. Roman was all hot blooded and wore his emotions on his sleeves. This . . . it wasn't right. "I think I'll take advice from you about how to cope with grief when you admit you're an alcoholic and you do something about it."

My lips parted. I would have been equally shocked if he slapped me.

Overtly conscious of the half a beer still in my hand, I said, "Now we're onto leveling me so you feel better about you?"

He closed his eyes and looked away, muscles tense. "I'm sorry. I shouldn't have thrown that in your face like that, even if it's true. You should go. I'm not . . . my wolf is close to the surface, and it's better if I'm away from everyone right now."

"No," I said, standing my ground.

Roman's jaw hardened. "I wasn't asking."

"I don't care."

The muscles around his mouth tightened. "You don't want to do this with me right now."

"Maybe I do," I replied. Dumping my drink out, I wrinkled the cup and let it fall to the ground, freeing my hands. "I can handle your wolf. Stop avoiding the question. Why is it better that you're away? Why do you think you should isolate yourself when your entire life is built on a pack mentality? This seems backwards to me, and your piss-poor mood has me inclined to think I'm right."

"Because I don't want to be around them." His fists clenched, and he took a step away from me. I followed, not letting up.

"Why?"

"I don't need a fucking reason—"

"Why?" I repeated harder, pushing him.

The dam burst as he towered over me, snarling under his breath. "Because every time I see them I'm reminded why I'm a failure as an alpha and a mate. Because I couldn't protect them any more than I could protect Maya. Because a fucking angel is hell bent on ruining me and I'm fucking terrified he'll find a way to take you away."

My lips parted. I'd anticipated some of that, but not all.

"Roman," I whispered.

"I keep hoping that if I put enough distance between you and me that it won't hurt so bad. It's tearing my wolf apart, making us crazy. I dream about fucking you like a savage and then I have nightmares about you being taken.

I'm so hyper aware of your every move it borders obsession. I'm not . . ." He turned away, putting his back to me. "I'm not in my right mind, Fury—and you're not ready to take things where we need them to go."

I stepped forward without thinking. My hand grazed his back and Roman stopped, freezing against my touch.

"You don't know that," I said quietly.

He tilted his chin, permitting me a side view of his sharp cut jaw and ice-blue eyes.

"Don't give me hope unless you mean it. I can't play the games you and Ezra do."

I lifted my chin. "I'm not playing with you."

"Then you're ignorant."

He started to walk away again, and my own frustration bubbled over. I stomped after him and grabbed his forearm. Before Roman could respond, I forcibly turned him and then shoved his chest. He stumbled back into a massive oak tree. It shook on impact, branches swapping heavily above us.

Without wasting time, I gripped either side of his face and wrenched it down toward me as I jumped up, locking my legs around his hips. Roman caught me, hands grasping my ass.

"Does this look ignorant to you?" I snapped. Our teeth clanked as we came together in a kiss so vicious there was no stopping it. My tongue thrust into his mouth, and his was ready. In a battle of wills, Roman squeezed my ass with one hand and lifted the other to knot through my hair. He pulled on it, directing my head to the way he liked to give him the advantage as our tongues twined together. He tasted like whiskey, smoke, and regret. Not regret that we were finally doing this. Regret that we'd waited.

My hips rocked into him, feeling the hardness of his

cock. Roman groaned, breaking off our kiss. He yanked on my hair, pulling my head back enough to look at him clearly.

"There will be no friends with benefits. This isn't just fucking. If I take you, you're mine, and you accept that claim for as long as you're here."

My throat felt thick. Commitment. That's what he needed. Not long ago I would have walked away. But after my chat with Ezra, and then figuring out my death may or may not be imminent, I wasn't wasting any of the time I potentially had left.

I had feelings for Roman. Maybe not love. I wasn't sure if I was truly capable of that anymore. Not after so long. But something more than lust or the pull of the bond. In him I saw a safe place. Shelter. Maybe even a home. I didn't have to be Fury the demon with him. I could just be me, as I was, whatever and whoever that meant.

I nodded slowly, swallowing hard.

"Say it," he growled, not a hint of give in his voice.

"I accept your claim."

CHAPTER 13

ROMAN

My head fell forward, touching her for a brief moment, eyes closing in sweet victory.

She accepted my claim. She accepted her place. By my side. As my mate.

I flipped around, pinning her back to the tree with her thighs spread wide for me. The tiny jean shorts she'd worn at the ceremony were bringing havoc down on me and my wolf through the burning. I had to catch myself several times from letting my mind drift to her and the way I wanted to bend her ass over the back of my truck. Better yet, have her ride my cock on top of my bike. One fantasy after the next played over, and I'd had many of them since the first time I saw her—but only now would I act.

Her breasts rose and fell, tight against my chest, I could feel her heat through the thin fabric of her T-shirt. My hips rocked inward, grinding into her delectable warmth, eliciting a shiver from my mate. Her head started to loll to the side, and I angled it with my hand in her hair. My lips skimmed up her cheek and down her throat in little nibbling sucks. My fangs sharpened at the taste of her. So fresh and sweet, like ripe fruit for the taking.

"You'll have to forgive me if I'm not gentle enough the first time," I rumbled against her skin. "It'll be impossible for me to rein it in."

"I can handle rough," she breathed. "Just no hitting or slapping. And no daddy kink."

"Noted," I hummed. That wouldn't be difficult for me, seeing as neither inflicting pain nor 'daddy' was a kink of mine. I let my hand slip free from her hair to grab a handful of her thigh. I loved that she was soft yet toned there. Her skin was supple and flushed.

"Shirt off," I grunted, not wanting to put her down. Fury arched up, grabbing the hem of the ripped T-shirt, and pulled it over her head. "No bra," I commented as she dropped it on the ground.

"Are you complaining?" she murmured, toying with me. I leaned down to skim the top of her breast with my lips. I lapped at her nipple and then sucked it softly, letting my front teeth scrape over the sensitive flesh. Fury's head hit the tree trunk as she let out a moan.

"You shouldn't sass me," I said, moving to her other nipple and repeating my actions again. I alternated back and forth every few moments, grinding my erection into her as I did. Fury's hands dropped from my face to my shoulders, nails digging into my skin.

"Fuck me," she demanded.

"No," I breathed, blowing a cold breath against her taut nipple. "I fuck you when I choose. Not the other way around, cherub."

A grin flitted across her perfectly fuckable lips. "Cherub?" she commented.

"Mm?" I hummed, debating how difficult it would be to

get her home unnoticed if I ripped those tiny fucking shorts off her.

"Last I checked, I'm a demon, not an angel."

"Cherubs are cute and innocent looking. The opposite of an angel. You look like hell on wheels, but dig a little deeper and there's a heart of gold beneath that demonic aura," I said.

She lifted an eyebrow at me, but now wasn't the time to debate my name for her. The only name I wanted to hear was mine while I fucked her into the next morning. "Keep questioning me and you'll be doing the walk of shame in my T-shirt tomorrow."

"It's only shameful if you think it is. I couldn't care less what your shifters think of me." Her answer was music to my ears. My hand skated up her thigh to the waistband of her jean shorts. I pulled sharply, and the material ripped straight down the side.

Fury gasped, clearly not taking me seriously enough. I rearranged her weight, using that hand to hold her up so my other could do the same. With both the sides split wide on her shorts, all I had to do was reach between to pull the bunched-up material away.

Naked and bare to me, Fury trembled. She reached for my jeans with steady hands and quickly unbuttoned my fly, yanking the zipper down. She reached inside my boxers and ran her palm up and down my hard shaft.

"What happened to no games?" I hissed between my teeth.

She flashed me a coy look as she took my cock out of my boxers, but continued stroking me. Her thumb pressed against my head, wiping at the drop of pre-cum and using it to circle around again and again. "I'm just giving a little payback for how you treated the girls," she said, lifting her hand. She licked the pad of her thumb, then pushed it between her lips to suck.

I lifted her hips above me, positioning her over my cock. I let the tip rub between her slick folds, back and forth, eliciting small sounds of pleasure from her. Fury rolled her hips, trying to pull me in, and I let her, roughly pulling her down on top of me.

A groan escaped me as she took me to the hilt, then wrapped her legs around me.

"Be careful what you ask for." Not giving her a chance to reply, I pulled all the way out and thrust back in. Her warm heat enveloped me, her pussy clenching me tighter than a fist. Unable to help myself, I started pistoning in and out between her legs, fucking her so hard against the oak tree that its branches shook.

She arched back on her own accord, creating better friction between us for her clit. I didn't slow as I kissed her roughly before breaking away to lick the skin between her shoulder and neck. Fury's moans encouraged me, driving both me and my wolf wild with lust and need. I had to claim her in all ways. With my cock and my teeth.

I sucked at the patch of skin I picked to bear my mark. It occurred to me when I marked Maya, I chose her inner thigh. Somewhere away from prying eyes. It felt close. Personal. Much of my love for my past mate I treated that way. Something to be expressed when we were alone, and that was all.

But with Fury, my feelings were different. Complicated and messy and utterly unique. Wolves were possessive by nature, and with Maya I wanted to hide her away. I kept that possessiveness to a minimum. With Fury, I wanted to bend her over and fuck her in front of my pack for all to see. I wanted them and everyone else to know she was mine, and that I'd rip apart any man or angel that tried to take her from me.

That's why I chose her neck, for all to see, and if she'd let me—it wouldn't be the only place I marked her. Even thinking about it had my cock stiffening further as I took her bare. I could feel her legs shaking hard as she approached the edge of her own climax.

My hand skimmed up the curve of her ass. I ran my index finger down the crack, feeling her reaction as the balls of her feet pushed into my lower back, guiding me onward. I pressed my index finger to her opening there, applying just a touch of pressure as I pushed it in knuckle deep. Fury moaned her approval.

"Roman," she whimpered, eyes closed and sweat coating her body. "I need to come."

Just what I wanted to hear.

I let my fangs fully extend before pricking her skin, then sinking them to the root.

Her body tightened like a vice. Her inner walls clenched, providing delicious pressure as I thrust into her furiously. The animal in me roared with dominance. Fury screamed bloody murder, a sound that I might have confused with pain if not for the way she clawed at my back, trying to pull me closer. Blood scented the air, mine and hers, as she broke skin.

It was a savage coupling, just as I dreamed it would be. But it was everything.

The aftershocks of her orgasm fluttered around me as I came. I stilled, and it was only when we were both sated that I retracted my fangs from her flesh.

The look on her face right then was something I'd never forget.

Sheer bliss. Sexy as all hell. It amazed me how this

redheaded demoness came into my life, uprooted every-thing I knew, and somehow managed to realign my world surrounding her. When I fell asleep at night, it was her I was aching for. When I succumbed to thoughts of lust, it was her name on my lips. When I searched the crowd, it was her red hair that I was seeking.

Somehow, someway, she was eclipsing Maya. While she wasn't forgotten, nor loved any less, Fury was filling the space she'd once occupied. In losing my first mate, I learned how precious having a partner was—and how much I would do to hold on to it and never lose that again.

Maya might have been my past, but Fury was my future.

The guilt of that still ate at me, and I turned my cheek to press it against her shoulder as I sighed.

Her body tightened, but this time she squirmed to get away.

"What did you say?"

"Hm?" I murmured.

"You—I—ugh!" She shoved against my shoulders, and I let her go on reflex. She dropped to the ground in a crouch, lethal in her elegance, yellow eyes narrowed at me.

"What's wrong?" I said, looking around the clearing, but there was no one here, save the cicadas that likely kept most of our fucking from my packs' ears. Probably not that climax, though.

"*You*. What the fuck, Roman? I can't believe you right now." She stood up with her jean shorts, eyes flicking to them for a short inspection before discarding them again. She cast a glance around the clearing, zeroing in on my button-down shirt I'd left hanging on a tree branch. Without asking permission, she marched over and took it, pushing her arms through the sleeves and haphazardly buttoning it up, albeit unevenly.

"What are you talking ab—"

"You said her name," Fury tossed out in an angry huff. "You called me Maya."

Fuck.

It wasn't what she thought. I opened my mouth to tell her as much, but she wasn't hearing any of it.

"I understand you still miss her and love her. I wouldn't expect any different, but I'm not a stand-in for her, Roman. I can't do this with you if I'm playing second fiddle to a dead woman—"

"Fury," I growled. "I wasn't calling you by her name—"

"But you did," she said. "And it's not fair to any of us. Me. Her. You. I fucked you and let you mark me because I thought you wanted something between *us*. But for that to happen, you need to accept that I'm not her and be okay with that. I don't need you to love me more or some bullshit like that, but if I'm always less than, I'm always in her shadow—and I won't be with someone that doesn't want to be with *me*."

"I do," I argued, frustrated that she wouldn't listen for even two seconds.

"Then find a way to show it because right now I feel used."

With that, she walked away, and the chilled tone of her voice told me I'd be an idiot to follow.

CHAPTER 14

I paced by the window in my room, tired but restless. The moon had risen high in the sky, shining a pretty beam of light through the glass. The groups by the bonfires in the distance had quieted down. Nature's soft voice surrounded me; only the sounds of insect calls and nocturnal animals scurrying about filled the air.

It was almost maddening.

My mind raced. I was wound up, both emotionally frustrated with what had happened and simultaneously longing to be back with the one who sent me to this place to begin with. I traced the spot on my neck where he'd bit me, eliciting a shiver that made my skin tingle.

Stupid, traitorous body.

Like I would give in and sleep in Roman's room tonight.

He said her name. He held me, fucked me, marked me . . . but it wasn't me he had been thinking about.

I wasn't jealous of Maya. There was absolutely no reason to be. The poor girl had died. Killed by someone in the Afterlife. No, I would never be jealous of Roman's love for his first mate. I just wouldn't pretend to be her ghost for him either.

I was hurt that even if it were only for a second, he wanted me to be her instead. That he couldn't be with just me. I hated to admit it. I hated to feel it. I hated all of it.

Something festered inside me, and it felt an awful lot like human emotions.

Ew. No. There would be none of that.

I walked over to the bed and stuck my hand under the pillow. Pulling out the flask, I unscrewed the top and tipped my head back, swallowing a mouthful of whiskey.

My head and my heart had collided over many things in my past, and it finally felt like they were on the same page for once. I knew what I wanted. Maybe once, long ago, it was simply love that I had sought, but in all my long years, I'd finally realized I wanted something more.

Up until recently, I had only craved stability. Freedom. Independence. But never love. Never *more*. That was what my head said.

Now my head and my heart said belonging somewhere could also be good. My heart reminded me that what I saw tonight, and what I felt—watching the pack and the families come together in love and support—that was something I truly did want. My heart said I deserved it. Was worthy of it. Would it be so bad to be a part of something special? What would life be like to be loved that way?

I wouldn't know. Never truly experienced it. I had a baby sister once. She was beautiful and perfect in every way. I adored her, and every time she looked at me, I saw nothing but pure and unconditional love. A piece of me died when Spanish Flu took her from me.

It was the last time I had felt what it was like to be loved.

I only realized later that her death spared her a future like mine. Given away by our shitty parents to a man I hardly knew when I was barely seventeen, all for the sake of our family's good name. I took a backhand to the face the day my father told me my purpose, and I'd told him I'd rather die. Joke was on him, the bastard. I died anyway.

It was a hard pill to swallow when you realize you have no autonomy. That you are a tool used for closing business deals. That your ambitions are meaningless. You have a uterus, so your purpose is less than a man's. What was that old saying? Something about being pregnant and barefoot in the kitchen? That was supposed to be my future.

My family handed me over to John. He was handsome. Incredible lapis blue eyes and stark white-blond hair. His smile could light up a room, and he was extraordinarily charming. His work in real estate was demanding, often sending him travelling for weeks on end. It started off okay, but time changed him. I never knew who would walk through the door. Jekyll or Hyde.

Jekyll, who seemed as though he was trying to love me, but he was still a little distant all the same. He didn't know me any better than I knew him. He was kind, though. Thoughtful. He'd bring me flowers, shower me with generic affection, and thank me for keeping our home nice. I may have been miserable being forced into a life I didn't want, but those days were easier when it was that husband. Then he'd leave again, buying land and building his brand.

But sometimes Hyde came home instead.

He was the same charming husband. Kind and thought-ful, until he wasn't. Something sinister would flash in his eyes, and everything would change. His cruelty knew no bounds. I could still hear the way he'd laugh as he stood over my bruised and broken body while I gasped for air and coughed up blood. Reminding me that I was his, and no one else's. Telling me it was my fault he'd had to beat it into me. Blaming me for his anger. Swearing he wouldn't do it again, if only I understood how much I meant to him. How much he loved me . . .

I scoffed. *Love.* I wanted no part of that love.

I'd felt an inkling of bliss in my short, married life. Once. A flicker of life growing inside me. That was love. It was instant. It was eternal. And he'd made damn sure to beat that out of me too. He would not share me, he'd said.

I skimmed my fingers over my flat lower abdomen, resting my hand there absentmindedly.

I lifted the flask to my lips, taking another drink.

And another.

And another.

I sighed when it was empty, and I wiped my mouth with the back of my hand.

How had I gone from being with Roman to wallowing in my misery and thinking about my past? My stomach churned slightly. I shook my head and laughed a little. Roman had essentially done the same thing. He was tangled up with me, and for some reason he thought about Maya. No, I didn't think about my baggage while we were together, but I went there all the same.

The only difference was that he was crushed and lost when Maya had died. I, on the other hand, did a happy dance when that monster was exterminated.

I didn't want my ex back.

Roman did.

We were both damaged goods in the end.

A blurry figure swooped from the tree line and headed for me. Hades flew toward the window and I opened it, letting him in. He landed on a chair, pulled in his wings, and then hopped onto the windowsill.

"Had enough to drink yet? Or are you still trying to disinfect your internal organs?"

"You know what? Come here. I'm in no mood for your bullshit." I grabbed for him, and he jumped away as I kept swiping my hands at him. "Go sleep outside with the fucking mutant mosquitos—"

"I saw you," he interrupted. His eyes lowered, looking at my midsection, before he returned his gaze to me. "I know why you're drinking. I just don't know why you're thinking about it right now."

My mouth fell slightly open, shocked at what he'd said. "How'd you," I paused, stumbling for words. "How do you know about that?"

"I told you it was my job to know things." He settled, content that I wouldn't snatch his little body and chunk him out. He turned his head and looked out the window, bouncing on his little feet to move closer to me. Almost as if he were trying to comfort a friend. "We all have our secrets, Fury. I'm not telling anyone about yours. But you aren't going to find any answers or comfort in the bottom of your flask."

I bristled. "That's not what I'm doing."

He looked back at me and gave me a deadpan look. "Well, whatever it is you *are* doing, it's not good for you."

"Friendly advice, or is this a message from work?" I asked in an irritated tone.

Hades made an undignified sound. "We are not friends, so it can't be friendly advice, can it? It's just an observation."

I hummed in response, not believing him. "Sounded an

awful lot like you cared about me there for a second," I trailed off, waiting to see if he would respond. When he didn't, I let it go. "All right, pigeon, have it your way." I turned away, watching the breeze as it rustled the treetops. "Any news?"

"None yet." He shook his head.

I grumbled in frustration.

"There's eons of history in those libraries, and not the watered-down version men write down."

"I know. I'm just . . . tired." I sighed. So bloody tired.

"What about the alphas?"

I glanced at him and twisted my lips to the side. "I had a small revelation tonight. Nothing so far has fit together to say they are going to lose their shit and destroy the world. There are fractions and pieces of their lives that are intense, but they've all been through some hellish experiences that should have triggered whatever it is inside them by now." I ran my fingers through my hair, tugging on some tangles while I combed it. "They don't even like each other in the end. They have nothing in common except the summit . . . and me."

"And you," Hades echoed, coming to the same conclusion as me.

I tapped my temple. "Exactly. I'm the key piece here. They've all lost their mates once already. If something happens to me, could they handle it? What would they destroy in their grief?"

He stretched, then tilted his head, thinking. "It's quite plausible. You do have a tendency to bring out the worst in people." He snickered, making a sound through his nostrils that sounded remarkably like a kazoo.

I barked a laugh. For a brief moment, I felt the flicker of

a kinship. It felt good to laugh and forget for one second the weight of everything in my life. Afterlife-life. Whatever I was in now.

My smile faded, though. "What really confuses me is that the risk witches didn't say I was in the picture. They've been seeing versions of this for a long time. I've never been in the prophecy. Not once."

"I know." Hades nodded in agreement. "But it does make sense that you'd be the key to all this. Maybe they've been wrong all along and you're the one that ends it all. Maybe you are the one that explodes. Alcohol is flammable, right?"

This time I snorted. "You are literally the worst," I said through my laugh. "Here I am talking about the end of the world, and you're making jokes."

He did his little bird shrug. "What can I say? I have a sense of humor. It was hilarious for me when you got hit by a bus."

I glared at him, trying to be as serious as I could. A tiny smile crept up on one side. "Maybe it was a little funny. I might have laughed if it happened to someone else. Like you, perhaps."

I walked to the bed and stripped off Roman's shirt, replacing it with my own. The back of my head throbbed a little as I sat on the edge of the mattress, pulled my legs up, and stuck them under the covers.

"I made a bed for you," I said, pointing to the top of the dresser. I'd piled together some soft T-shirts and moved them around in a circle, making the best impression of a nest that I could.

Hades looked surprised. He flapped his wings a few times, gathering air to lift himself up there. He stepped inside my makeshift nest, scratched around, then settled down, wiggling his body to situate himself. "Thank you," he said. "That was . . . nice of you."

"What can I say? I can be nice sometimes," I said softly, laying on my side and curling up on the pillow.

My head wasn't entirely settled, but Hades coming and pulling me from the downward spiral of my thoughts helped quiet things just a bit. I closed my eyes and tried to fall asleep. I was tired. Sleep would have to come soon.

A CHILLING LAUGH ECHOED in my mind. I squinted my eyes and looked around, but there was nothing except fog settling over an open field. Dew formed on the blades of grass, and all of nature had fallen quiet. The moon was descending for its daily slumber, and the sun had not yet awoken on the horizon.

I turned, searching in all directions, trying to find where the laugh was coming from. It increased in intensity, the shrillness making my skin crawl.

I slapped my hands over my ears and screamed, trying to block it out.

"What do you want?" I shouted into the nothingness.

"Hybrid," the voice hissed.

The hairs on my neck stood on end. Goosebumps burst along my skin. Cold sweat dripped down my face and onto my chest.

I took off in a sprint, running toward the tree line in the distance. I needed to find cover. I pumped my legs and pushed off the ground as hard as I could.

Was this déjà vu? Had I been here before?

I checked my progress, gauging how much further I had before I reached my destination, but it looked no different.

A sense of dread washed over me as I felt an unfamiliar presence nearby. I turned my head over my shoulder to find what brought it.

A lone figure stood, tall and foreboding. A white cloak lined in shimmering gold obscured its face. An aura of light surrounded it, pulsing in time with my racing heartbeat.

"Fuck!" I yelled, trying to move faster, but it was useless.

The angel laughed and gave chase, catching up to me.

Spindly gray fingers with pointed talons gripped my shoulder, crushing down on the bone and drawing blood when it pricked my skin.

I screamed again, and the angel laughed. "Oh, Sunny, you are making this too easy."

My screams echoed in the room as I shot up to a sitting position.

I heaved deep breaths in and out, my hands curled into a death grip on the bed. Early morning light filtered in from the window. White and gray feathers were strewn about, some floating in the air. Feathers? I looked down to my claws, taking in the shredded bed and pillow.

Roxanne and Roman came bursting through the door, disheveled and clearly pulled from sleep. Roman's eyes were blue and alert, ready to let his wolf out at the first sign of danger. Roxanne held a fire extinguisher in one hand, and used her other to wave around, knocking the floating fluffies out of her face.

I frowned at the red canister, and she shrugged. I gave

her an apologetic look in return. I felt bad that she expected another fire.

"What happened?" Roman said, his jaw clenched.

His voice washed over me, equal parts comforting me and annoying me.

"Bad dream," I answered. "I'm fine. Go back to bed." I turned away from him. I wasn't ready to confront anything. I felt like I'd been asleep for all of five minutes.

I glanced at the clock, unsure of what I wanted to see there. I felt exhausted. I wanted more time to rest, but if my sleep was going to be filled with nightmares, I'd rather push right past it and start the day.

"Fury," Roman said, his tone getting softer. "If you want—"

"I said I'm fine." I waved my hand around. "No danger. Just feathers. I'm *safe*."

A crease formed between his brows, the line deepening as he struggled with what to say. He straightened his shoulders, and with a grunt, he gave a dip of his chin. Turning on his heel, he stormed out of the room.

Roxanne whistled low. "Well, if that's not tension, I don't know what is."

I threw my legs over the bed, knocking feathers around. "Leave it alone, Rox. I'm not . . . I can't right now."

The voice in the nightmare rang in my ears. It called me a hybrid. The angel called me Sunny. Were they the same entities?

She sat down beside me and put her hand on my back. "You okay?"

Not even a little bit.

"I'm okay," I answered. Looking at Hades on the dresser, I met his calculating gaze. "What did you see? What happened?"

"Not a damn clue. I woke up because you screamed. I opened my eyes, and all I saw was an explosion of feathers filling the room. Wasn't sure what to think." He stood up in his T-shirt nest. "Worried something had happened to me, to be honest," he mumbled, lifting his wings and peeking underneath.

I grinned. "Hope you didn't shit yourself."

He turned around and looked down. I couldn't help but smirk at his expression.

Roxanne pressed her lips together in a firm line, trying hard to not laugh. She shook her head and stood up. "Can I get you anything? Like a new bed?"

There was no way I'd be able to get back to sleep. I had questions about Lyra and where she was. Who she was with. I wanted to know what I had been turned into. Were there others from the Afterlife like me? What it meant for my future. Would I ever make it back to the Afterlife? So many questions. I needed to talk to someone about all the things running through my mind, but no one would be able to give me answers. And that was what I needed more than anything.

Dorian's lying by omission made my blood boil, even if I partially understood it. Ezra's disregard for my pleading to spare Lyra made me want to hit him if I even looked at his face. Roman, well, I had already soaked in that emotional hell all night. It didn't matter, anyway. None of them had the answers, but each one of them wanted to be a part of finding them.

But their actions said they didn't trust me, and they certainly didn't trust each other.

Fuck them. I would do it on my own. I always did.

"I need a favor," I started. Roxanne looked at me dubiously, her eyes flicking to the door and then back to me. "I need you to make me a drink."

She groaned. "Fury, it's—"

"It's not for me, I promise." She looked at me in confusion, waiting for me to give her more information. "I need you to make a bloody mary."

CHAPTER 15

With the signature drink in hand and Hades perched on my shoulder, I walked into the bathroom and shut the door.

"You're sure about this?" my crow asked as I offered him my hand. He stepped onto it, and I moved him to the counter.

I looked at the lock on the door before I reached to twist it, and then nodded. "I am. What's the worst that could happen, right?"

"Um . . ."

I sighed. A lot. A lot was the worst that could happen. That was the answer. We'd all heard the stories, but I'd never met her. She had bolted from the Afterlife long before my time. Even there she was a legend. A legend I had only read about.

Bloody Mary's narrative on Earth was sparse, and her supposed history was muddled and had changed over time. No one really knew enough about her, so her origin story was made up. I at least knew the truth in that. Still, so often children and drunk teenagers tried to summon her. What they were hoping to gain, I wasn't sure. Since the legends said she would come and possess you, try to kill you, or just scare the living daylights out of you, I didn't understand the appeal.

I just needed her to show up and talk to me.

"Aren't you supposed to light a candle?" Hades asked.

"I just need to be able to see, that's all," I said. I clicked on my phone flashlight and turned it upside down, facing the beam upward before flicking off the lights. I looked at Hades. "Ready?"

He fluffed his feathers in response.

Standing at the sink, I moved the drink and held it in front of me. Taking a breath, I blew out, skimming across the top of it, pushing the scent of herbs, tomatoes, and vodka into the direction of the mirror. To anyone else, I would look like I'd absolutely lost my marbles. Maybe I had.

"A bloody mary for Bloody Mary," I said to my reflection. "I have a request."

The mirror warbled, and I heard a faint sound just as Hades mumbled, "She is going to be so pissed when she sees me."

"Wait, what?" I whisper-shouted.

"Too late," he said, tiptoeing to the side out of view.

An image finally appeared. A teenage girl with chestnut brown hair, rosy cheeks, and a heart-shaped face greeted me. She looked so young, but her soulful hazel eyes gave away her age. She'd been around for a long time. Much longer than most people thought.

"If it isn't *The* infamous Fury," she drawled, reaching out of her mirror dimension to swipe the drink in my hand. My skin tingled at the brief paranormal contact. She sniffed it deeply and smiled, taking a sip, and letting out a long sigh. "Oh, this is a good one."

I was quite curious to know how she'd heard about me considering she had left the Afterlife before I'd arrived. A question I would most definitely ask if I were given the chance in the future. For now, I needed to know something just a tad more pressing. "I'm glad it exceeds your expecta-tions," I said.

She stirred it with the celery, and without looking up, she said, "I see you, Hades. You can't hide for shit."

"Hey, Dottie, how goes it?" Hades asked, cautiously moving back toward me.

I shot him a dirty look. He did not just say that. I would pluck out his feathers one by one if he'd just screwed me. Calling her by her living nickname was a surefire way to send her back into her world, never to return.

Her expression deadpanned. "I changed my name after I died, just like you did."

I couldn't say I blamed her. I didn't want the memories that came with my name either. Dottie, or Dorothy, was the youngest to be accused and jailed during the Salem Witch Trials. Her baby sister was born while her mom was impris-oned and later hung, found guilty for being a witch. It was a load of crap back then. None of the puritans were witches, but that didn't stop a bunch of lying shitbags from accusing innocent women and a few men of consorting with 'the devil'. I'd read up on those people and what happened to them when they came to the Afterlife. A few of those accusers were extinguished due to so many failed attempts at changing them. The remaining were rehabilitated and recycled. Their souls had come back a few times over, but I hadn't ever had one assigned to me. By the time I became a demon, those souls weren't in the worst-of-the-worst case files.

"I, uh, I didn't know you two had a history. Had I

known," I narrowed my eyes at him, then met her gaze again, "I would have stuck him somewhere else."

"A cage, perhaps?" She waved it off, taking another drink. "It's fine. A story for another time."

I twisted my lips. "While he's annoyingly rude, he unfortunately brings up a good question. What would you like to be called? I know you don't like to be called Mary anymore—"

"You wouldn't either if you spent decades with people repeating your name over and over and over. It's like having someone open your windows and randomly shout into your house. It's very disturbing."

"So . . ."

"Juliet. Like from the Shakespearean play," she said, her voice a little dreamy.

"Wow. That's—"

"Romantic?"

"No, I was going to say tragic, honestly."

Hades shot me a look that said, 'now who's screwing this up?'

She furrowed her eyebrows. "I didn't insult your name."

"You could if you wanted. I was a little angry when I showed up. Duke says it's like the Jessica of the Afterlife," I grumbled.

She barked a laugh. "I suppose it is. But Juliet *isn't*."

In for a penny, in a for a pound, right?

I smirked. "It's not. But you picked the name of a thirteen-year-old girl that knew a guy for five seconds, claimed she loved him, and their so-called romance caused the death of six people, and brought down two prominent houses. That's a tragedy—the way he wrote it—not a romance," I pointed out. "I mean, if you wanted romance,

Rosalind or Beatrice would have worked. You're headstrong and witty, or so I've heard."

I hoped my attempted recovery worked, and I waited silently while she considered my rebuttal.

"You make a good case." She looked at me and frowned. "You didn't strike me as a Shakespeare fan."

I shrugged. "I'm full of surprises. You should see me blow up." I waggled my eyebrows.

The corner of her lips curled up on one side. "I did, actually. It was quite impressive."

Hades stepped forward. "You were there?" he asked, dubious.

She waved a finger at him. "Enough about me. I concede your argument. Call me Jules."

I tilted my head to the side and crossed my arms over my chest. "That was an awfully quick change."

She grinned. "Someone I know convinced me to change it a while back. Same reasons you presented, actually. So you have my attention now if you'd like to make your request." She brought the glass to her mouth and took another drink, leaving a small line of red above her lip that looked remarkably like blood. She wiped it off with her fingertips. "I assume you have a question and that's why you summoned me."

I hadn't missed that tiny breadcrumb there. She said someone she knew. Who that someone was, I didn't know. No one could enter the mirror dimension, and she'd disappeared from the Afterlife over two hundred years ago. She had other people she visited, and I wanted to know who.

"I do." I nodded my head, contemplating which question was the most important. If all she gave me was one, I had to make it good. "You've seen a lot happen in the world. Been around for a while, right? Something happened to me, and I need help figuring it out." I lifted my top lip and ran my tongue over my elongated canine.

"You have my attention." The look on her face was filled with curiosity.

I hummed. "I'm sure I do."

I went through the basic parts of the story, omitting some of the heavier details. This was a need-to-know basis. She didn't need to know about the end of the world. She just needed to know I was on a special mission on Earth. Unorthodox for a demon, sure. But I was here, nonetheless. She'd already made it clear she saw me go boom, and I planned on bringing that one up in the future, so I picked it up from there.

"To save me, they changed me. I don't know what this means. No one in the Afterlife does either. But some strange things are happening to me, and none of it is related to what shifters, vampires, or fae experience in their youth, during the change, or while maturing."

She stirred the drink again with her celery and took a bite out of it, speaking with some still in her mouth while she chewed. "What is it you're asking of me?"

"I want to know if you have seen anything like this. If you know of anyone who is a multi-species hybrid. Or a demon hybrid. You have access to mirrors all over the world. If anyone knows, it's you." I gave her a twisted smile. "I was told demons don't come to Earth, but at this point, there's a lot that just doesn't make sense. The other poltergeists have done an absolute shit job at recon for this case, so I honestly don't trust anything they say or report to the Afterlife either."

She narrowed her eyes. "Wankers, all of them. They were a disgrace then, and they are a disgrace now."

Hades snorted, which still sounded more like a wheezing burp through a beak.

I side-eyed him. "I won't argue."

She sighed. "I don't have any answers for you. I haven't seen this before."

And there it was. I was shit out of luck. The one big card I had to play and—

"But I haven't been actively looking for it either. That doesn't mean I can't start now."

"Really?" Hades and I asked at the same time.

She shot a glare at my crow and narrowed her eyes before she looked back at me. "I'll help you. Bring me more of these tasty delights," she shook her almost empty glass, "and I will look around and see what I can find. It's a big world. Might take some time."

She looked happy as she drained the rest of her drink, clinking the ice in the bottom. She was far more pleasant than I expected, and I needed her more than she knew. It was a gamble, but one I was willing to chance. "There is another question I have for you."

She raised an eyebrow in surprise, the arch creating a striking angle. "Toeing the line, I see."

I raised my hands in a peaceful gesture. "I'm happy to keep bringing you whatever you need. Just say the word."

"Go on," she said. She listened as I told her about Lyra's awakening and the mysterious angel that she'd referenced in our encounter. Her features darkened as she muttered something in a language I couldn't understand.

"Does that mean anything to you?" I asked.

She shook her head. "Not specifically, no, but if angels are involved, it's seriously classified. We won't be able to find answers. They don't stay earthside. This one might, but there won't be others. Angels are more strategic than people think. That stupid image of halos and pretty wings is so far from the truth, it's laughable."

"It sounds like maybe you've had some rough encounters with our divine counterparts," I said, probing more than I probably should have.

She shrugged. "I have a tendency to break and bend the rules. They don't like that."

I didn't disagree. Clearly they had it out for me. Jules defecting from the Afterlife earned her a mark that would never go away. If they could find a way to rip her from her mirror dimension, they would do it in a heartbeat. "I don't know what they want with me, but something about the situation feels personal. I just don't know why. I'm hoping you can find Lyra. She may have answers."

She considered me for a moment. Eventually, she said, "I will think about it. First things first. Let's find out what you are. I'm intensely curious to know."

"The full moon is a week away. I don't want to put pressure on you, but I am on a bit of a time crunch. I haven't sensed my wolf just yet, but it's likely to happen any day now. The sooner I know more, the better off everyone will be. We'll have an idea of what to expect."

"Sure thing," she said.

"Wait, do you want me to um, summon you again?" I asked, not entirely sure what to call it. I couldn't exactly send her a text.

"Don't worry. I'll find you," she answered with a wink. The mirror warbled again, looking almost liquid in nature. Her voice sounded far away as she left, and the glass stopped shifting, looking as if it were solid once more.

"Oh, *now* you're paying attention to the clock," Hades mumbled.

"Tick tock, pigeon."

CHAPTER 16

DORIAN

"Monte Carlo?" Ezra asked me, confusion filling his tone while he walked beside me in dress slacks and a white shirt he kept unbuttoned at the top. We'd sifted to a copse of trees across the street from a famous hotel overlooking the Mediterranean Sea. We'd arrived to meet my second and find out his progress.

"Indeed." I straightened my tie and adjusted my collar, smoothing the vest of my three-piece suit. "It's the next location on his quest to find someone I need. A witch."

Ezra halted. "Why?"

I exhaled deeply through my nose, turning my head to look at the vampire I'd asked to come along. I was beginning to regret it.

"Because we need her to help us find Lyra," I answered. "Whatever it is with you and witches, let it go. It's not exactly like vampires have a good reputation, yet here you are."

He grunted, running a hand through his black hair. "Witches are different."

"They are. Especially the witches I know." Our footsteps

echoed on the floor as we entered the lobby and headed to the elevator. I dipped my chin at the staff that made note of our presence and dress. Money always talked. "When we find this one, be careful. She's quite flirtatious, and she's incredibly powerful."

I pressed the button and the sliding doors opened. We stood in silence, side by side, waiting for our floor. I could tell he was concerned, just as Roman had been. I didn't know his history with witches, but he was hesitant to trust them. Even with his gift, he didn't trust them. When Fury was in the explosion at the dress shop, he'd read Kelly's mind and knew she was pure. Still, he was wary. Rya would be a treat for him. She teetered on the edge of madness, and he would have a difficult time trusting her. We needed her powers. She was the only one that could help me. Even Kelly's magic couldn't find Lyra. I'd already tried.

Arriving at the suite, we walked down the hallway and knocked on Tristan's door.

He opened it, greeting us, and moving aside so we could enter. The suite was large and had expansive windows, giving a panoramic view of the bright blue water. It almost looked teal the way it glittered in the sun. The living room was spacious, with two couches facing each other and two chairs facing the glass to overlook the sea. It was a stark contrast to the scenery in Avalon. Or Houston.

"Tristan, what news?" I said, moving to a chair and taking a seat as though it were the head of the table.

"I've been to London, Singapore, Bali, Hong Kong, Paris, Bermuda, and Rome. Nothing yet. She isn't responding to my . . . ads." He glanced at Ezra, unsure of how much he wanted to share.

Tristan was quite powerful in his own right, and I'd shared with him that the vampire's ability was reading people's minds. I couldn't leave my second without protection. He'd increased the barrier on his mind, guarding himself from the mental probing.

Ezra raised his eyebrows, realizing he couldn't get the information he wanted. He would be forced to use his words to get answers like the rest of us. "What do you mean ads?" he asked, clearly displeased by the discovery.

"Rya and Tristan have a long tumultuous history," I started. I knew Tristan wouldn't want to go into detail, and I would spare the aspects that weren't necessary. "When we have needed to reach her over the ages, Tristan uses creative ways to call her out of hiding."

"Such as?" he asked.

"Right now? Craigslist and Tinder," Tristan said.

"You're putting ads out for a fucking booty call, is that it?" He huffed a laugh and shook his head. Looking at me, he said, "Your daughter is trying to kill our mate, and some invisible clock is ticking for the end of the world, and your grand plan is finding a witch using hookup apps? Jesus Christ."

"Doesn't exist," I said. "He'll be of no help here."

He gave a deadpan look. "It's an expression and you know it. Don't be a condescending prick, Dorian. Basically, don't be you."

"Then don't question the methods we're using when you know nothing of which you speak," I countered. "Now, if you are done *whining*, we can move on."

He narrowed his eyes, considering me for a moment. I often wondered what went through his head. It had to drive him crazy that he didn't hold the upper hand when he was around me. "Fine. Tell me why those locations. What can I do to help?"

Moving to sit in a chair, I checked my watch. "Rya likes

the finer things in life. Extravagance. She also likes to flirt and play hard to get. The ways to contact her have generally involved going to luxurious locations. Tristan then puts himself out in the open, both physically and via some type of announcement, so she knows it's him."

"Right." Ezra moved to the couch, taking a seat. "Because you two are ex-lovers," he said, looking at Tristan.

"Something like that," he mumbled. "It's complicated."

That was an understatement. Rya was complex. At her core, I believed she was a decent witch, but it was never safe to let your guard down. For Tristan, it became more personal. She had a flare for being dramatic. Relished in it. When it came down to it, she liked mind games, and Tristan grew tired of it. He'd never fully shared the details of their on-again off-again courtship, and I didn't push it. Their struggle was their own.

For me, it was business. Over the years we had need of each other's abilities. I would hear rumors of her dealings as centuries passed by. I knew what she was capable of. If I didn't know her as well as I did, it would be difficult to tell which side she was on. Rya would do what was best for Rya. The trick was figuring out what that was so we could entice her and benefit from her power. Lyra was a different case. Lyra was *always* different.

"And what exactly do we need her for?" Ezra asked.

Tristan's gaze shifted to meet mine.

I sighed. "Rya is the only witch capable of helping me put Lyra in stasis. We did it together once. We'll have to do it again."

He cursed under his breath. "This goes far beyond just tracking her down. You're telling me you can't stop her on your own?"

I pressed my lips into a firm line, drawing in a deep breath. "No."

A truth I absolutely loathed to admit.

We had little time. We had to work fast. We had one option. I always had a backup plan. Lived by the notion that one should always plan for the risks involved. When it came to Lyra, there were no backup plans.

"Lyra's power is unmatched. Not only does she carry magic similar to my own, but she also has hers as well. Lyra and I essentially cancel each other out. I battled her for years, trying to tame the monster inside her. Trying to cure whatever disease was eating away at her mind. I never succeeded. That was when I knew she needed to be put into stasis," I said. I interlocked my fingers and placed my hands in my lap. "When I tried, the outcome was worse than I had expected."

"I can't imagine why. You were trying to chain her, right?"

I sniffed and adjusted my posture. "The process binds her powers first, yes. Then she would enter stasis. It has always been a state we choose for rest or re-energizing. We live such long lives . . ." I trailed off, lost in thought. Tristan cleared his throat, bringing me back to my senses. "No one has ever been forced into stasis before. Not until Lyra."

"And she lost her shit, I assume."

Tristan snorted, crossing his arms, and looking away, clearly perturbed by Ezra's tactlessness.

"Yes, Ezra, she lost her shit. She slaughtered thousands in cold blood." I closed my eyes, wishing the mental image that had been burned into my memory would fade. A millennium and it still felt as clear as day. As though it had just happened. Every detail, every blood splatter . . . every single body. And equally worse, the picture of my once kind child standing in the middle of it, her hands dripping in red. I inhaled deeply and opened my eyes. "She didn't discriminate in who she played with before killing them. A family of prominent and powerful witches were amongst her final victims. Rya and her sister were able to escape, finding me when they were refugees seeking safety. It was upon meeting Rya that I realized she had the powers I needed to help me stop my daughter."

"So Lyra is unstoppable, and we can't do anything about it except sit here and wait for this all-powerful witch to answer Tristan's personal ads?" He glared at me wide-eyed, waiting for a response. I met his stare, unyielding. He scoffed. "Great. Just fucking great."

I rolled my eyes, wishing Ezra would just listen for a moment. This was the problem with him and Roman. They were so young and emotionally charged, whether the former was willing to admit it or not. His bias with witches was clouding his judgement and his ability to think logically about the situation.

A loud pop in the room stopped me from responding further. A giant plume of lavender smoke exploded, sparkling specs spewing in the air. I wafted a hand in front of my face trying to clear the debris. In the middle of the purple haze stood a tall figure, lean in stature, draped in a green cloak.

Ezra jumped off the couch, pulling a knife while he wheezed.

"Don't," I said, coughing and waving my hand at him to settle down.

Tristan didn't move a muscle. Except he rolled his eyes so far back in his head he likely saw the back of his skull.

"Why yes, vampire, I am fucking great," the witch said, twisting her arms and taking a bow.

I stood up, adjusting my coat, and running a palm over my clothes to wipe off the dust. I went toward her, reached out, and grasped the hood, tilting it back. Clever brown eyes twinkled with mischief when they met mine. Her plum-painted lips curled into a smirk, and she turned her head slightly.

I leaned down, lightly kissing her cheek. "Rya. It's nice to see you again."

She untied her cloak, letting it fall to the floor.

"Of course it is," she said, dusting off her white sundress.

"See, Ezra? Penchant for theatrics, like we said," Tristan muttered.

Ezra's brows furrowed, and he watched Rya cautiously. She noticed the way he looked at her. "Oh, calm down, bloodsucker. You and I have no quarrel."

She clapped her hands together and looked at my second. "Well, Tristan, my love, you've been just screaming to get ahold of me. And you brought Dorian and a friend." She winked at Ezra, then walked toward Tristan, reaching up to graze her fingernail down his jawline softly. "What could be *so* important that you had to speak to me, especially after everything you said to me last time we saw each other?"

Tristan's internal struggle was put aside. He didn't vibrate in anger, and he didn't crumble under her gaze. "Lyra is awake."

Rya's flirtatious games halted, and she froze. "What?" she whispered, and he nodded in response.

She dropped her hands to her side, and turned around to face me, a questioning look on her face. "It's true, Rya. We have a lot to fill you in on, but not much time," I told her.

She threw her hands up in the air in exasperation. "Why didn't you just bloody say that, Tristan?"

He scoffed. "I can't exactly put that out in the open, now can I? Some Craigslist ad or making a Tinder profile saying Lyra woke up? Be serious. Supernaturals read those too, and some of them know who she is."

She gave him a deadpan look. "Next time it involves someone else, just say looking for a threesome with an old friend, eh?"

Tristan looked stumped. It wasn't a bad idea. Maybe not naming her directly, but still adding that third party for urgency. I shook my head, clearing my thoughts. "Let's hope we don't run into this situation again. Should there be a next time, we'll remember to do just that."

"Good. Now what do you need? Tell me where we're at," she said.

I filled her in on Fury, discovering we were mates, and the attempted assassination of Fury when she saved Roxanne. All about the footsteps on Avalon, the awakening and disappearance of Lyra, and then her appearance at the summit.

Rya blew out a harsh breath. "An angel? What in the hell is an angel doing involved in this?"

I shrugged, noting her demeanor upon supposedly learning about the Afterlife. She seemed shaken, but not as much as I would have expected. "None of us know that just yet."

"Well, let's see if we can start by finding her." She held her hand out to me in expectation. I reached into the breast pocket of my jacket and pulled out a small piece of white satin cloth.

"From Lyra's pillow," I said, answering the unspoken question. She nodded.

She grasped it, running her fingers over the fabric, and muttering some words softly as she closed her eyes. A crease formed between her brows and her lips pursed. An unnatural wind swirled in the room, tossing her jet black hair all around her face. What felt like minutes passed. Her sun-kissed olive skin glistened when she started to break out into a sweat, a small bead dripping from her forehead.

She let out a loud gasp, and the wind stopped. Opening her eyes, I saw the worry and the fear. "She's being blocked, Dorian. That's impossible," she whispered.

Tristan cursed, and I rubbed my temples, trying to think. Ezra looked at each of us, confused. "Has this never happened before?"

I raised my eyebrows. "No. We've always been able to track her with Rya."

"There's no one I can't find. I am the best at what I do. Even a thousand years ago, we were able to always track her. We always knew where she was. Stopping her was a different story, but I never couldn't find her," she said softly. Looking at me, she changed course. "This is magic beyond Earth if she is being blocked. I need to know *everything*. What more do you know of angels?"

"Nothing." I sniffed and looked out the window, taking in the beauty of the sun beginning to descend over the sea. "But I know someone that does. Brace yourself. It's morning in Houston, and Fury isn't exactly pleasant when she wakes up."

CHAPTER 17

I stood in the bathroom with my hands pressed against the counter's edge. My phone flashlight still illuminated the space, and the mirror only showed my reflection. I took some deep breaths. I didn't know what to do next, but I needed to sort that out.

My stomach rumbled loudly, reminding me that I hadn't eaten since the bonfire the night before. I grimaced and looked at Hades. "I'm going to get something to eat from downstairs. We need to troubleshoot some of this while we wait for Jules to get back with us. I'll bring you something. I read that crows will eat trash and cat food. Do you have a preference?"

He scoffed and flapped his wings at me in anger. "I will not eat either, you twat."

I laughed. "Fine, if you aren't willing to entertain me that way, then I guess I'll just bring you something normal to eat."

He huffed in response, but I didn't get the chance to speak. The air changed, and I stayed quiet. A tiny charge of electricity felt like it sizzled lightly over my skin. My mate was here. Dorian had come back.

I was equally intrigued and irritated at his presence here. I wasn't ready to talk to him, but time wasn't exactly on our side right now.

"The fae is back," I said to Hades as I reached for the knob to open the door and go into my room. "Stay here a minute, will you?"

The moment I stepped out of the bathroom, I heard a knock.

I knew it was him. I didn't want to see him. I reminded myself why. Lying sack of shit. Manipulative asshole fairy. Cold, guarded, moody jerk.

Stomping over to the door, I repeated the mantra in my head.

When I opened it, a burst of cool air rushed over my skin. Dorian's amber eyes took me in, perusing the length of my body. Having moved so quickly from my dream to summoning Jules, I didn't even bother putting on pants.

When his gaze met mine, his pupils dilated, and his nostrils flared.

"May I come in?" Without waiting for me to answer, he began to step forward, walking into my room.

"Apparently you may," I grumbled as he passed me, and I closed the door. "What do you want, Dorian? I really don't want to see you right now."

He stopped, taking in the feathered mess. Turning in a circle, he looked around. "What happened in here?" he asked, reaching down to pick up a feather and inspect it.

"I had a dream. Clawed the bed and pillows in my sleep, apparently. Now answer the question," I said, crossing my arms and jutting out my hip.

"At least you didn't sift and set something on fire. Small

blessings, I suppose," he said, dropping the feather from his hand.

I rolled my eyes. "Everyone's got jokes. Final time. What do you want?"

"I came to talk to you."

I scoffed. "Oh, now you feel like talking to me? Sure didn't feel like that when you were keeping me in the dark about Lyra." I cocked an eyebrow at him, daring him to lie about his reasoning.

Dorian inspected his fingernails, not taking my bait. "You smell like the shifter."

"Maybe that's because we fucked last night." His eyes flashed when he looked at me, and his jaw tightened slightly. "Does that bother you, Dorian? It's hard to tell if you have feelings or not, so you'll actually have to use words to tell me." I heard the sarcasm and venom come out in my voice, but a tiny whisper in my head told me to ease up.

Still, he ignored me, not rising to the occasion. How did he do that? He grabbed the vanity chair and took a seat, crossing his leg over the other. He clasped his hands and stared me down for what felt like several agonizing minutes.

I wouldn't give in and speak first.

Tick.

Tick.

Tick.

I huffed in annoyance, sat on the edge of my mutilated mattress, and crisscrossed my legs while I waited in silence.

Tick.

Tick.

Tick.

"For fuck's sake, will one of you just talk already? It's boring in here," Hades griped from the bathroom.

"No, I will not, thank you very much," I responded to the crow while looking directly at Dorian. "He came here to talk to me, so I think this one is on him."

He raised his eyebrows in surprise. "Why is Hades in the bathroom?"

"Because we were calling Bloody Mary. Hung up just before you arrived," he answered.

I whipped my head around. "Shut up!" I hissed at him.

He flew out of the bathroom and landed in his nest. "Well, crow is out of the bag now, so I'm just gonna hang out here and watch the show, if you don't mind." I squinted my eyes and glared at him.

"Why did you call Bloody Mary? You were supposed to wait for us," Dorian said quietly. I could hear the irritation in his voice.

Returning my attention to Dorian, I said, "Are you serious right now? You aren't entitled to answers, fae. You have a lot to explain to me, and truthfully, I don't owe you anything. I guess you thought the same of me, otherwise I can't imagine why you didn't share what was going on with Lyra."

I looked out the window for a while, thinking about the way his lies made me feel. I hated it. It was lying by omission, but it was still concealing the truth. I didn't blame him for the death of those at the summit. That was not his fault. Lyra was going to show up whether we liked it or not. She was going to cause chaos and try to toy with me regardless. It wasn't Lyra's actions that were the issue. It was that none of us knew she was a potential problem. I don't know what that knowledge would have accomplished since she appeared to have an angel on her side, but at least we wouldn't have been in the dark.

That little voice in my head whispered again, reminding me of everything I thought about the night before. About all that I'd felt, and the realizations that had come to me.

I was here, and for however long that was going to be, I wanted to belong with them. I wanted to try. I couldn't very well make that happen while I sat here and gave him the cold shoulder. Nothing was ever solved this way.

I sighed. "It's hurtful, Dorian. You didn't trust us. You didn't trust me. You should've told me," I said, a soft anger in my tone. "I'm not asking for much, but I do ask that you don't lie to me. I already lived a life filled with secrets. I'm not willing to do it again."

He looked down at his lap and closed his eyes, taking a deep breath and exhaling. When he looked back up, I saw conflict. "My intention wasn't to hurt you, Fury. I would never do that on purpose. I kept it to myself for reasons I'm not ready to explain just yet. However, on the subject of trust, you were the only one that knew about her. Consider that."

"True." I tilted my head. "Why not Rox? You didn't tell her, and I thought you two were close."

"We are, but she isn't my mate," he said, his amber eyes flashing with a brilliant light.

I felt that tingle over my skin again, and a strange warmth spread through my body. Trying to ignore it, I pressed on. "But she is your friend. Friends trust each other."

He dipped his chin in agreement. "I suppose they do. It's something I'll address with Rox, though. Just as I wouldn't have this conversation with anyone else about you and me."

Fair enough. He respected boundaries with relationships, and that I could appreciate. It spoke a lot to his character. I admired it, even if I was still pissed at him.

"Trust goes both ways. You came here to ask me questions, but you still won't answer mine." I picked at a feather that was on my leg, trying to flick it off my finger when it stuck. "I'd also like to point out that you demanded I answer everything when you interrogated me after you found out what I was."

Uncrossing his legs, he leaned back in the chair and looked at the ceiling. "I did. For the same reasons I expect answers now."

"You're unreal," I scoffed loudly. "How does that make any sense?"

Rolling his neck for a stretch, he took his time while I started to stew in anger again. When he finished, he sighed. "It's different." I opened my mouth to argue, but he held a hand up to silence me. I pressed my lips together and narrowed my eyes. "The questions I had then pertained to our safety, your safety, and to the safety of our people. Yes, you shared information you never had any intention of telling us, for reasons that were originally beyond your control. You had a job to do. I understood it, whether I liked it or not. The questions I have now also pertain to your safety, and the safety of others. If what you've said continues to be true, and it is prophesied that we'll end the world, then it would stand to reason that the protection of everyone overrides the desire to keep secrets. That being said, my reason for keeping Lyra a secret was purely emotional. There was no malicious intent. I acknowledge that I should've shared with you that she had been awakened. I'm sorry for that. I like to handle things on my own. I've been around a long time and that's how I've always been. I know that isn't an excuse; it is my reasoning, which I believe you deserve to hear. I don't think anyone knowing about her would have stopped her that day, but I know I'd be pissed beyond reason were I in your place. And perhaps theirs." He titled his forehead toward the direction of the living room downstairs, telling me all I needed to know. Everyone was here. I wondered for a moment if they could hear us or if they were minding their own business.

My mouth hung open for a bit. That may have been the most he'd ever spoken to me in one sitting.

"Okay," I said lamely. I waved my hand at him, motioning for him to carry on. "What do you want to know?"

A small smile graced his lips in response to my acceptance of his pseudo-apology. It faded quickly, and a more serious look washed over his features.

"I need to know more about angels," he said.

"Could you be more specific, or are you asking for a history lesson?" I asked him, quirking an eyebrow. "That's a lot of ground to cover. It'd be easier if you just asked me what you want to know."

Leaning forward and resting his elbows on his knees, he began to fill me in on Rya, and I listened to what I assumed was the CliffsNotes version of their time together, both past and present.

I learned she'd helped him bind Lyra and force her into stasis. That she was the best tracker in the world. And that she was Kelly's sister. That was definitely a conversation I wanted to have at a later time. But most importantly, I learned that Rya couldn't reach her. Never in all her years— which were apparently as long as Dorian's, yet another question for later—had she been unable to track someone, especially Lyra. She'd had a brush with death by her hands, her parents instead sacrificing themselves to save their daughters. Whatever spell her parents used sent Rya and Kelly to safety, but in doing so, it created an invisible marker between their girls and their killer. With the strength of Rya's tracking magic added to that obscure tie, she'd always been able to find her anywhere in the world, at any time. Rya had said she was being blocked. More importantly, she'd said it shouldn't be possible.

I cursed under my breath and stood up. I started pacing the room, feeling the feathers as they stuck to my bare feet.

I looked at Hades, asking a silent question. He knew. He knew as well as I did that this almost certainly confirmed the angel was with Lyra. He nodded his head.

"What does that mean to you, Fury?" Dorian asked. A tiny crease appeared between his brows as he looked at me with concern.

I exhaled loudly. "It means the angel is *with* her. He's cloaked her."

"What kind of magic is that? Do you know?" he asked. "If we know what kind of spell or charm or protection has been placed on her, Rya and Kelly can—"

I shook my head, cutting him off. "It's not as simple as a magic spell. It's an object. It's a talisman that angels use on Earth."

He considered my answer before asking why.

"It protects them from supernatural magic in this realm. Over the ages, religions have believed in all sorts of entities. Gods, angels, spirits, saints, devils, demons . . . furies." I smirked. "Anyway, man has tried time and time again to call on what they believe will help them. Call on their patron saints or ask for their god to give them a sign. Those sorts of things. Not like Ouija boards and stuff like that. Poltergeists always had fun with those, but they aren't meant to do anything real. But humans are foolish, and they always keep trying to reach the other side one way or another. It happened once. A drunken accident when a supernatural actually summoned an angel, ripping him into existence from wherever he was earthside to right in front of this moron. Wrong place, wrong time kind of thing, but it happened all the same. After that, angels carried a talisman to protect them from supernatural magic when they left the Afterlife. If Lyra is being blocked, that's why. She's most certainly wearing one. I just don't know how."

Dorian stood up and ran his hands through his hair. "How do we break through it?"

I pursed my lips and shrugged. "We can't. Not that I am aware of. But that doesn't mean we can't try to find out." I looked at Hades as he got out of his little T-shirt nest. "Will you go to Duke? Keep this as quiet as you can. Trust no one. If she has an amulet, you know there's some shady shit going on. I just don't know why. None of this adds up yet."

He snapped his beak in response as he stretched out his wings, preparing for flight. "Mind opening the window for me?"

Dorian was closest, and he slid the glass up for him.

"Be careful," I said.

He cocked his head. "Friendly advice?" he asked, mirroring my comment the night before.

I huffed a laugh. "Can't be. We aren't friends," I said with a wink.

"Talk to Jules. She'll be happier to see you without me around," he said, a small fleck of sadness briefly flickered in his eyes before it was gone. "I'll be back soon." With a loud caw, he took off, flying through the opening and heading back to the Afterlife.

Dorian closed it, and asked, "Who is Jules?"

I smiled. "Bloody Mary isn't her real name."

His mood darkened again. I was going to get whiplash. This damn fae.

"About that. You were supposed to wait." He walked toward me slowly, but I stood my ground, unmoving. When he stopped in front of me, I craned my neck to look up at him while he towered over me.

"About that," I mocked, "you aren't the only one that likes to handle things by yourself. I needed answers, so I asked her for them. I didn't need you, Ezra, or Roman there to do it," I said.

"What did you ask her?"

I jutted my chin out. "I asked her what I am and if there are any others in the world like me. She doesn't know, but that's only because she's never looked before." I paused, waiting for that to set in when I caught the slight disappointment in his eyes. "And then I asked if she could track Lyra for me. Find out where she is."

He raised his brows in surprise, completely caught off guard that I would've been a step ahead of him. "And?" he asked.

"She's going to let me know when she finds her. Seeing as Rya can't find her either, I guess we're fucked, and we have to wait."

He hummed in response but didn't move.

"Any other questions, or did you get what you came for?" I still felt irritated with him. He'd apologized for part of his actions—part—but I wasn't sure it was what I wanted. I couldn't always read him, and it made my relationship with him more complicated than the other two. Sort of. Being called Maya certainly complicated *that* relationship.

"I didn't come here to use you."

I snorted. "That makes one of you."

The amber in his eyes turned a molten gold. "What does that mean?" he rumbled.

I shook my head and sighed. "Nothing. It means nothing."

He moved forward, causing me to take a step back on instinct. Not out of fear of his presence, but to keep from falling. I stumbled slightly, and he kept walking until my back was against a hard surface and I had nowhere to go.

He put his hands on the wall behind me, boxing me in and leaning down. His heated gaze sent goosebumps across my skin.

"I will not use you, Fury. For anything. Not for answers, and not for anything else. When I come to you, it's because I want to be near you. I make my choices. I know who you are, and I don't expect you to be someone else."

He had no idea the effect those words would have on me. He didn't know what had happened last night, or how Roman had fucked my body but had Maya in his head.

I swallowed thickly. "I'm still mad at you." I cringed inside when my voice came out huskier than I intended.

His eyes flicked to my lips. "You have every right to be."

With one hand still on the wall, he used his other to graze a finger down my cheek, tracing the collarbone, then down my arm. His eyes followed his hand, and I watched him, more turned on than I wanted to admit.

"Then why are you still here?" I asked with a shaky breath.

His large hand curled around my hip, his thumb stroking the skin as he held me firmly. "If you don't want me to be here, then I'll leave." His hand stayed curved, pressed against me as he dragged it up, feeling the contours of my body. Over my hip, across my ribs, and underneath my breast.

I wanted him. Oh, I wanted him. Even if I was angry with him, I wanted him.

But I also knew that it wasn't right. Roman had hurt me, and if I let Dorian have his way with me, there could be a part of me doing it for the wrong reasons. I didn't think that was happening, but if it did, I wouldn't forgive myself for it.

I slowly grabbed his hand, taking it off my body. He didn't try to stop me, instead respecting every action of mine. Placing it back on the wall, he closed his eyes and nodded slightly. "Okay," he said softly, opening his eyes and starting to step back.

Grabbing the back of his neck before he pulled away, I said, "It's not what you think." I struggled with the right words for the moment. I wouldn't share what happened between Roman and I, but Dorian needed to know this wasn't me rejecting him. "Trust me." It was all I had.

A look of confusion appeared in his eyes before he dipped his chin once in acceptance.

My heart thundered in my chest, and I was pretty sure we both heard it in the silence that spanned between us. I hadn't told him to leave, so we stood together, my hand on the back of his neck, his hands pressed on the wall beside me, our eyes locked in a heated battle.

A knock on the door made me jump.

"Fury?" Roxanne's voice came from the other side of the door.

"Come in," I managed hoarsely.

She opened the door and came in, coming to an abrupt halt when she saw us.

She looked away. "Ezra said it's time to go unless

there's something angel business-wise that needs to keep you both here." She looked at her nails. "And he knows there isn't."

I cleared my throat, wondering how much Ezra had listened in on. "Tell them I need to change my clothes and I'll be down in less than five. And could you grab me breakfast to go, please? I'm starving." She mumbled a response, and turned on her heel, still angry with Dorian and not wanting to be around him.

"Where are you going that's so important?" Dorian asked when I moved to the drawers to find clean clothes.

"Turn around if you don't want a show." With my back to him, I took off my shirt and pulled another over my head. I bent over, changing my underwear, and shimmied my legs into some shorts. I heard a strangled groan escape his lips. He clearly hadn't turned around.

When I faced him, walking to the bathroom, I said, "I have an appointment to keep. In the meantime, I'll fill in Ezra, assuming the bastard doesn't already know. You stay here and fill in Roman and Rox. And fix things with her, Dorian. I mean it. You owe her that."

He furrowed his brows. "What kind of appointment do you have with the vampire?"

"Nothing much. Just a rapist to condition." I grinned and grabbed my boots, walking out the door.

CHAPTER 18

I picked dried blood out of my fingernails as I waited for the water to heat up. When steam billowed from the shower, I opened the glass door and stepped in.

A loud moan escaped my lips when the hot water hit my skin. I just stood there, soaking it in, letting it drench me and roll off my body. I found it a little funny that something so simple was so very much needed. It was a form of self-care for me. Sometimes it was a shower, sometimes a bath. Depended on the tub, honestly. Either way, it was my quiet space. I liked the way my muscles loosened as they started to relax. I liked the way the water sounded as they hit the tile in fat droplets. I liked the smell of shampoo and soap. If calm had a smell, it would be the scent of *clean*. Silence enveloped me and I was left with my thoughts.

Lathering my hair, my thoughts drifted to the work I'd been doing with my little vampire friend. Day three with Robert, and he wasn't that complicated of a case. It was a textbook rapist study. He wasn't a case of past abuse continuing the cycle. He was just horribly damaged. He liked power, but he liked having power over people in truly dangerous ways. He got off on it.

I smiled to myself. He sure didn't today. Today he had the roles reversed on him. When he fought back, I hit him the same way he did his victims. When he tried to get away, I'd pin him the same way he did his victims. When he'd cry, I'd laugh at him—the same way he did to his victims. It would happen like this for a long time. He did everything I'd expected, and he'd likely continue to. Oh sure, every now and then they threw me a new bone to play with. They'd eventually find more creative ways to curse me. That was always fun. I liked it when they called me more than a bitch when they were angry. It was like a milestone of sorts. We'd see how he would progress over the next few years. I'd break him like all the others. I always did. I was The Fury. In the end, I'd win.

I rinsed my hair out and then squeezed liquid soap onto a loofah, rubbing it over my body and cleaning off the blood, dirt, and grime.

My thoughts strayed to the guys and the potential of my extended stay. What if Hades and Duke didn't find a way for me to get back to the Afterlife? Ever? Earth would be my home. *Again.* It wasn't that bad this time around, though. The food was better than it was back then, and the company had significantly improved. I felt a little torn. I missed Duke. I missed aspects of my Afterlife. I missed being someone there. I had damn well earned that. But even if it scared me a little, the idea of having to say goodbye permanently to Roxanne, Dorian, Ezra, and Roman hurt more than I wanted to admit. Even though tension with Roman was at its peak, they'd grown on me, and that would be hard to let go of.

Houston was as close to Hell as anything else. For now, I

was here. I wanted to make the best of it. Rehabilitation work wasn't quite the same as it was in the Afterlife, but it was definitely nice to be back at it. For weeks I'd felt like I was floundering in my existence. I was the best of the best, and I was sent to Earth to do a job, but it felt like I was just fudging it up six ways from Sunday.

Meet guys? Check. Find out they're your mates. Erm. Not exactly part of the plan. Okay, moving on. Find out someone is after me. Seems weird. Ezra reads minds? Great. That doesn't get awkward when you're sent to rehabilitate them. Get called Sunny when someone tries to kill me—not even sure how that was possible. Get bit by some dickhead shifter then have all your mates change you in an effort to save your afterlife. Find out angels are sabotaging you somehow. Ugh.

In what world was that part of any plan? I grumbled audibly. I had one job. And I couldn't do it. I huffed out loud in frustration. The poltergeists had one job and look how much they screwed the pooch on that. Useless, they were. I wasn't useless, and I fucking knew it. I was being set up. It took a conversation with Rox to shove me in the right direction. Until that moment, I hadn't been able to figure out what finally set off the so-called bomb. Now I suspected it had to be me.

One of the many things that didn't make sense were the factors leading up to it. How in the world was I part of the prophecy? And if I were indeed the spark that would light the proverbial flame, did that mean I could in fact die? It wasn't exactly something I could test out.

And Lyra. Talk about not expecting that piece. I understood why Dorian kept it a secret. It didn't change the fact that I was pissed with him for it. It was information we needed to know.

Angels. Lyra. Imminent death and world destruction. Also, maybe, my imminent death and destruction . . .

All of these questions and no answers.

I finished rinsing off and turned off the shower. I stepped out, grabbing a towel to dry off. After I wrapped it around my body and tucked it under my arm, I went to the mirror to wipe off the steam.

As the glass was cleared, a face that wasn't mine popped in front of me.

"What's up, my demon?"

I screamed at her unexpected appearance as I jumped back, clutching my chest and dropping my towel. "Jeeeesus, Jules! You scared the shit out of me!"

She chortled, her shoulders shaking as she did so. "I'd say I'm sorry, but I'm really not."

I tried to slow my racing heart while I glared at her. "No, I don't imagine you would be sorry." I breathed in and out, convincing my blood pressure to calm down and not test the 'do I die or not' question that had been swirling around in my head.

Jules was the only poltergeist in the mirror realm. It was all her own. For that very reason, I'd never had anyone pop into existence in a mirror I was looking at. So yes, apparently *The* Fury could get scared and jump out of her skin like a kid at a horror film.

She shrugged. "When you're as old as I am, you have to get your kicks somehow."

"I'm sure you're out of practice, but that's not exactly how you make friends," I said, bending down to grab my towel off the floor.

"Is that what we are?" she asked. The tone of her voice shifted slightly. Almost hopeful.

I stood up, arching my eyebrow at her, and then started

to wring out the water in my hair. "We could be, yes. Why not? You seem unsure about the prospect."

Jules shifted her posture, crossing her arms. "I don't really have friends. People want things from me. That's why you called, wasn't it? Because you wanted something from me. Not because you wanted girl chat."

"That's fair. I did call you because I needed something, yeah. I wasn't sure you would answer me. Or be willing to help in my cause. That doesn't mean I'm opposed to building a friendship. How do you think friends meet each other?" I asked, setting the towel down and picking up a wet brush for my hair.

She looked stumped. "I . . . I don't know. I didn't have friends when I was alive. And the Afterlife proved to be a joke," she huffed.

I laughed with her. "Well, you won't hear an argument from me. But to answer that question, people meet over work stuff, or they bump into each other at a place of interest. Sometimes they meet someone by asking them for help, or a favor. Sometimes you strike up a fun conversation and they try to kill you later with spicy tacos." She tilted her head in confusion. "Never mind, the point is that anyone you meet can become your friend if that's something you both want." I left it open-ended, waiting to see what she said.

A small smile crept up on her lips and she gave a single dip of her chin. "Okay . . . friend."

I smiled in return. "Something to know about friendships, though. It's not one-sided. Don't let anyone use you. If you try to be there for them and they are never there for you, that isn't your friend. There's give and take in every relationship, including friendships. Don't always be the giver, okay?"

I meant every word of it. I wouldn't use Jules for my gain and harm her in the process. People too often tried to be good for the wrong reasons, like there was some sheet being marked with all the good deeds they'd done in life. You either wanted to treat people kindly, or you didn't. Forget about who you think was watching you; it was always what was in your heart. And there were entirely too many hearts filled with hatred and ugliness. I knew all too well. I didn't want her to get hurt.

"All right," I said after she nodded in acknowledgement. "So what do I owe the pleasure of this unexpected visit where you almost sent me to another early grave?" I tugged at the tangles, then switched to the other side. "Or did you just want to see me naked?"

She threw her head back and laughed. "Well, I have seen my fair share of boobs since I escaped into the mirrors, and I must say, yours are quite nice. But that isn't the reason for my call."

I held a hand up. "I know we had an agreement, and I want to hear what you have to say, but I don't have a bloody mary with me. I told you I would keep them coming."

She waved me off. "Oh I know you'll pay up. We're friends, right?" She winked. "And if we weren't, believe me when I say I know how to get paid. You think that little appearance scared you? I can make your life a living hell if you fuck me over."

I silently stared at her for a second, realizing she was dead serious, but still in a joking way. But not really. "I have no doubts that's true."

She scrunched her nose in a quick and cute smile before continuing. "I found Lyra."

I dropped the brush and slapped my hands on the counter. "You what?" I said in shock. "Already?"

"Please." She flicked her hair over her shoulder. "Look, I know it was your second question. Your first is going to take time. That one is harder than you think. So I decided to make your second request my first priority. At the end of the day, it really is the more pressing issue, is it not?"

I frowned. I still wanted to know if there was anyone like me. Knowing Rava was a hybrid, and that there were many others like that, was helpful, but I just wanted to know more. Almost reluctantly, I agreed. "It is."

She twisted her lips. "I thought so."

"So where is she?"

"The Vatican."

I blinked several times, not saying a word. Finally, all that came out was, "I'm sorry, what?"

She creased her brows and tilted her head. "The Vatican," she said slowly, looking at me like I was stupid. "You know, the Pope's house?"

"I know what the Vatican is," I deadpanned. "I just . . . the irony is something I can't get past at the moment."

"I know, right?" she said. "Angels are so egotistical; it didn't take me long to find them. If you were a giant narcissist with a power trip, where would you go if you wanted to see how you've been portrayed and revered for a couple of millennia? It's their favorite place to talk about. Running joke and all that the guys there are in for a big surprise when they all kick the bucket."

I snorted. She wasn't wrong. But to think our mystery angel was hiding there with Lyra? Wow. I blew out a breath. "Okay. Okay. . ." I started thinking, my mind racing at an impossible speed.

"Stop thinking so hard. I can see smoke coming out of your ears. Don't worry. I have eyes on her."

That caught my attention. "What does that mean?"

I saw a mischievous twinkle in her eye, but she kept her lips sealed.

"Hmmm," I said in response. "We're not there yet. Fair enough." I grabbed my clothes off the counter and started dressing. "I need to update everyone. Will you find me and let me know if anything changes?"

"Of course. If you're near a mirror, I can always find you."

I smiled at her. "Thanks. I owe you that bloody mary."

"Damn right you do. I won't say no to cookies either."

I laughed, and when I looked back at the mirror, she was already gone. Shaking my fingers through my hair, I left the bathroom to go find Ezra.

And there he stood, the eavesdropping motherfucker.

"I already know," he said.

I narrowed my eyes, glaring daggers at him.

He held his hands up before I could rip him a new one for it. "In my defense, you screamed in the bathroom. What was I supposed to do? I listened in. You were okay. But I heard what your new friend, Jules, had to say."

I took in a deep breath, fully annoyed—even if I understood. Count to ten. Breathe out.

"Fine. But we need to get to Dorian and Roman and tell them now."

That's when I saw it. There was a look of shame in his eyes. It was a tiny speck of a moment, but it was there, and that's when I knew.

"You already told them, didn't you?"

"I've briefed them, yes."

I pushed past him, smacking his arm with my shoulder as I did. "Take me back to Roman's," I said.

"Fury, I—"

"*Now.*" I wanted to scream at him. "If you're as smart as you think you are, you'll know not to piss me off right now. And so help me, if I find out you're reading my mind, I will end you."

He opened his mouth to say something, but I held my hand up. "And don't talk to me either or I'll cut out your tongue."

Empty threats?

Yes.

The full force of my anger made abundantly clear?

Also yes.

I slouched in an armchair in Roman's living room, staring at the ceiling and twirling a lock of my hair. The guys argued back and forth, back and forth—around and around in circles. It was enough to make my eyes cross.

Rya pinched the bridge of her nose and released a deep sigh. She appeared just as annoyed as I was. I'd met her the day she'd arrived with Dorian. She seemed nice enough. I figured if he trusted her, that spoke volumes of her character and worthiness. Dorian didn't trust many people, as evidenced by his omission of Lyra.

Each of the guys thought they needed to go after Lyra. Dorian felt confident now that he had Rya again. Roman was just heated and thinking emotionally. Ezra wasn't that different from Roman if I were being honest. They both figured Dorian knew what he was doing when it came to his daughter, and I was surprised they were all on the same page for once. Did one of them ask me what my thoughts were? Or Rya's for that matter? Of course not. If they had, they would know I thought they were all dumbasses.

I raised my hand like a child and waved it in the air, waiting for someone to notice me. When they didn't even bother to look, I reached over to the glass of water on the end table next to me. I drank what was left, then took it and threw it down on the ground.

It shattered, and all the conversation around me came to a screeching halt.

"You about done?" I asked.

Three pairs of eyes stared at me when Ezra spoke. "Tantrum much?"

I shrugged. "Not one of you have asked what Rya or I think about this. Not one of you have spoken to us, and not one of you paid any mind only moments ago when I tried to get your attention." Glancing at each of them, it was clear they were finally listening. "So if you'd let the ladies in the room have a turn, we'd tell you that you're all a bunch of morons and you need to sit back and wait this out."

Rya's lips curved upwards, and the smile almost reached her eyes. Picking up her teacup, she took a sip and hummed into it. She was letting me have the floor.

Dorian was hard to read. His features were like stone, and when he spoke, his voice was flat. "Would you care to tell us why you think that?"

"I would, thank you." I straightened my posture, sitting in an upright position in the chair, and crisscrossing my legs. "I don't think you're thinking this through. Yes, we know where she is. That's great. You don't have a plan."

"That's what we've been—"

I held my hand up to Roman and shot him a look.

"Don't interrupt and mansplain to me the conversation

I've just been listening to for the last half hour." Roman furrowed his brows and pressed his lips together. When I was satisfied he'd keep his mouth shut, I went on. "This isn't the same as last time. Lyra likes games, right? She's playing a new one now, but you're stuck in the past thinking it's just round two. It's not. There's an angel involved, and that changes the entire board. What do we know about it? Jack all, that's what. We don't know who the angel is or why they woke her up, or why they are after me. What we do know is that he's given her an amulet to protect her from supernatural magic. So tell me, what is your plan to get past that? Your magic won't work against her. Rya's magic won't work against her. She's untouchable right now. And you want to waltz up to the front door of the Vatican, bang on it, and piss her off? Leave it alone right now. We hold the cards, and you don't realize it. They don't know that we know where she is. They don't know we have someone on our side that can watch her for us."

Dorian raised his hand the same way I had. Did he see me do that earlier? Had he just *ignored* me? Now wasn't the time to address that. I needed them to hear me. I nodded my head toward him and asked, "Yes?"

"How do we know we can trust your friend, Jules? We've not met her. We know nothing about her. What if she's playing both sides?"

"She's not."

Dorian had been standing by the fireplace, but he came and sat in the armchair next to mine. "Ezra said she told you she could make your life a living hell if she didn't get what she wanted."

"Really?" I shot Ezra a dirty look before returning my attention to Dorian. "That was taken out of context." I sighed. "Look, Jules escaped the Afterlife. The only reason they haven't exterminated her in retaliation is they can't. We talked about this. They can't reach her in the mirror realm. It's her domain. It's her brand of magic. My magic isn't demon magic. It's unique to me. That's hers. She isn't going back; she isn't working both sides. She has no reason to. This may be hard for you, but you're going to have to trust me on this. Jules is on our side."

"So we're supposed to sit here and wait for her to attack you again?" Roman asked.

I shook my head. "No. We know where she is. We need to find out what we can in the meantime. We don't have a way to defeat her yet. Jules hasn't seen the angel she's with, so we don't know the motive or anything more than that just yet. Duke and Hades are working on finding out what they can too. We must play our pieces carefully. Moving too quickly on this will only end up hurting people."

"She's right, you know," Rya interjected. We all looked at her, surprised that she was finally weighing in. "I do think you're a bunch of morons. You aren't thinking ahead. Everything she said is correct, Dorian. This is a new game. One you and I don't know how to play just yet. We need more information before we can put her back in stasis. What if you and I aren't enough this time? What if we need more?" She turned her head to look out the wall of windows. The lake was calm and serene. You'd never know it felt like a sauna of death outside. "No. We play this safe. We may only have one shot at this. I agree with Fury, and you'd all do well to listen to her."

I grinned and held out my hand for a fist-bump. She looked at my extended offer and considered it. She tilted her head as though she was giving in for my sake. She fist-bumped me back. I turned to the guys and raised my eyebrows expectantly. "Well?"

Dorian took a deep breath. "Okay. We'll do this your way."

Roman and Ezra nodded silently in agreement.

"All right, then. Recon is already in place. Now I need to find out what's happening on the other side of the veil." I looked out the window, searching the trees. "Where's that pigeon when I need him?"

CHAPTER 19

The sun was setting while I waited on the deck overlooking the water. Roman's lake house was quiet. Each of the guys had a home that was appealing. I couldn't say much for Avalon as a location, but Dorian's castle was fascinating and his mansion in Houston wasn't half bad either. That bathtub in my room was something else. Ezra's penthouse was stunning. The pool, the view; it was next to everything you could need, but so high up you still somehow felt alone. Roman's house though . . . the quiet was comforting most of the time. I closed my eyes and listened carefully. I could hear the shuffling of feet at other cabins. The pack. Not all of them lived here, but many of them chose to.

Even Roxanne had moved into a small cabin nearby. She slept in the main house just down the hall from me, but she had her own place when she wanted space from everyone. Her house south of the city was left for now, cared for by someone she paid to keep it up. As she'd said it, her place was here with me and her brother.

A breeze lifted my hair, flinging strands into my face

and along my neck. That's when I heard it. A flapping of wings.

I opened my eyes and squinted them, putting a hand over my brows to shield the sunlight from blinding me as I searched the skies.

A familiar black dot came into view, quickly flying toward me.

I stepped back from the railing and let him land. He shook his body, then tucked his wings to his side.

"Trouble is stirring up," he said.

I frowned. "Nice to see you too." I crossed my arms. "What kind of trouble?"

"Oh, you know. Risk witches throwing out more prophecies, foreseeing doom and gloom. Upper Management is pissed you haven't done your job yet."

I threw my hands up. "For fuck's sake. Number one, my job takes time. Even if all this—I don't know, we'll call it weirdness—hadn't happened, I still wouldn't have finished. But the rest of it? Come on. It's not my fault. I can't control what's going on here. I was damn well set up. Mates. An angel sending assassins. Did the risk witches say anything about that?"

"You know they didn't."

"Did they see me in the prophecy this time at least?"

He pinned me with his stare and shook his head slowly. I cursed.

"Duke thinks we're on our own one hundred percent. He doesn't trust anyone right now. We're not sure if they're lying about the prophecies, or if something is missing and you aren't what sets them off."

I turned, gripping the edge of the railing. "What do you think?"

He tilted his head in confusion. "Are you asking my

opinion?" I nodded. "I think it's still too early to tell, but I personally think you're the missing puzzle piece. You talk to them more than me, but I see them with you, and I watch from afar. Mates are a tricky thing. The Afterlife often over-looks what being mated and bonded truly means. It's not our way, so it's not taken seriously. Only fools write off what they don't understand."

Scratching at the deck with my fingernail, I considered his words. "Some humans experience it. They just don't realize it," I said quietly.

"How so?"

"Having a child. That bond is beyond the concept of love. Not all of them experience it. You and I have watched plenty of people harm their children, sell their children, or cast them out for being different. We've watched them disown them when they find out they're gay. We've seen them curse them and damn them in the name of their reli-gion. For a hundred years I've seen it. I don't even know how old you are or how much you've seen, but I do know there are parents out there that have the epitome of uncon-ditional love. We've seen that too. They'd walk through fire to save them, and if something happened to their child, they'd destroy everything in their grief and their rage if they were capable of it. Thankfully, they aren't."

He looked at me thoughtfully. "I believe you're right in that. I've seen all the things you speak of, and worse, and I've seen the bond too." He walked on the railing to be closer to me as he looked out at the lake. "Interesting that you're the first one to make that connection."

I shrugged. "I chose to be a demon because I was angry at my lot in life. I suppose I'm different because I'm not necessarily angry at my core. There's beauty in the world, and it makes me happy when I see it. Gives me a smidge of hope for humanity." I nudged him with my hand. "Don't go telling anyone, though. You'll ruin my reputation."

"Right. Dark and scary. Skulls and bubble baths. That's you," he said mockingly.

"Don't forget it. I'm not above plucking out your feathers when you piss me off," I added, and he chuckled. I smacked my hand down on the wood. "All right, all right. Moving on. We need to step up our game. I had a chat with Jules today."

I filled him in on my conversation with our favorite poltergeist and asked what he and Duke found out on their end.

"Duke started researching angels under the guise of looking into your hybrid status just in case he is being watched. That talisman makes this tricky." He sighed. "It's good that Jules can tell us where she is, but the fact that an angel is protecting her and the angel itself is protected, it just presents so many problems."

I pursed and twisted my lips, tapping my fingers against the wood as I thought. Hades was right. The shield that the amulet provided wasn't just for her. It was for the angel too. And for some reason, it was all connected. Angels, talismans, and prophecies, oh my . . . How could we fight that? What in the world could even—

I had it.

"I think I know what you need to look for." He perked up in attention, waiting for me to go on. "The amulet that angels use originally came from Earth."

He cocked his head and bounced around on his feet a little bit. "How do you know this?"

"Because I'm an anti-social introvert who has spent the last one hundred years being angry, punishing people, and reading both current events *and* history." I grinned, proud of myself. "Those talismans came from a supernatural source in order to protect them from supernatural magic. Like magnets. Magnets of the same pole reject each other. That's how these objects protect the user. By repelling supernatural magic."

"And you're saying we have to find . . ."

"The opposite pole."

"And we do that by . . ."

"Well, that's a bit trickier."

He narrowed his eyes at me. "Elaborate."

"We're going to need a source of magic from the After-life. That should cancel out the talisman's power, or at least weaken it. Earth magic doesn't hold a candle to our magic."

"I'm not sure I follow. I get the idea, but what is it you're suggesting? Where do we find this magic source in the Afterlife?"

I blew out my cheeks and answered quickly. "Jake's office."

He jumped back and flapped his wings. "What? Are you out of your mind?"

I held my hands up. "Hear me out."

"I'm still here, aren't I?" he said, the annoyance in his voice was clear.

"Jake is Afterlife Resources, but more than that, when you die, you end up dumped into the Afterlife with your resource officer's assistant in the waiting room, sort of unsure what exactly is happening. Jake was the one I met. He told me how I died. He told me how the Afterlife worked. He offered me the jobs that seemed to suit my personality, but he gave me options." I took a deep breath and kept talking, silently thankful that Hades was listening. "Up until the point you pick something, you're just dead. Not like a zombie, but you know, useless. When you decide what your job will be, Jake gives you your powers essentially. When I arrived, I was just a dead girl sitting in a chair. When I left, I was a demon, and I had powers. If that's not a source of Afterlife magic, I don't know what is. What we need is the object he uses to change you." I grinned awkwardly and fanned myself, trying to get a reprieve from the oppressive heat.

He blinked at me, staring wordlessly for what felt like an extremely long time before speaking. "You want me to break into Jake's office, steal from him, and smuggle *a thing* out of the Afterlife and bring it to you? Is that what you just said?"

I crossed my arms tightly. "Yeah, pretty much."

He shook his head and looked at the ground. Finally, he asked, "What is it I'm looking for?"

"Silver. About this big." I made a circle with my fingers, indicating its size. "It looks like a pocket watch, but it can be confused with a compass."

"Which one is it?" he asked.

I smiled. "Both. Time and direction are needed when you change into your Afterlife."

We sat in silence as he contemplated my request. "Fury, I—"

"Trust me, Hades. I wouldn't ask you to do this if I thought I was wrong. I know it's risky." I pleaded with him, knowing I probably sounded whiny, but my head was starting to throb a little, and the ache made me feel woozy. I tried to push the discomfort aside, needing him to agree with me before I went inside and cooled off.

He looked at me skeptically, then the tension in his body released. "You'd better be right," he said, and he started to take off.

"Be careful," I shouted as he flew away. He cawed in

response, and it sounded louder than usual. Annoyed, probably.

I watched him fade into the distance as a lightheadedness swept over me. Texas heat was no joke. Maybe it wouldn't be some snakebite to take me out. It'd be heatstroke.

My vision warbled, and I knew it was past time for me to go inside. I turned, but the colors of the world started to swim around me in circles. I held the railing tight, waiting for the wave of dizziness to pass.

It didn't.

This wasn't the heat.

My mouth started to ache and my ears popped as the world spun harder. A cold, clammy feeling washed over my skin as a warm gush came out my nose.

Not again.

I reached up to my face, my hand coming away with blood.

Spots filled my spinning vision, and I tried to go down to my knees and call for help, but I felt myself falling and I heard a loud smack as pain radiated through my face as the world faded to black.

MY EYELIDS FLUTTERED OPEN, and my head pounded in time with my heartbeat. My vision wasn't swimming, but it was far from clear. There was a slight ringing in my ears that I hoped would stop soon. Reaching up, I checked to see if there was still blood on my face, but it had been cleaned off.

I'd been moved inside the house, and everyone was around me, just as concerned as they were the last time this happened.

The fact that it had happened twice now was troubling, though I didn't want to admit that out loud, especially to the alphas. Maybe it was also somewhat alarming considering if it happened at the wrong time, I'd be fair game to anyone trying to kill me.

"Welcome back," Rox said, using a cold washcloth to wipe my forehead. I winced. There was a knot or something there that needed to heal a bit more. "You landed on your face again."

I swallowed, smacking my lips, and moving my tongue around trying to spread the moisture. It felt like I ate sand. "Go big or go home," I mumbled.

I tried to sit up, but she put her hand on my shoulder, putting just enough pressure to keep me down. "Give it a second. You bled a lot. It was your nose and your ears again." She frowned, then added, "And it came out your mouth too."

I groaned, realizing there was a metallic taste in there.

I tried to focus past the tinnitus to listen to the voices in the room that were talking about yours truly. Filtering out the distinct tones, I realized there was a person there I didn't expect. Rava argued passionately with the guys, moving her hands, and gesturing while she spoke.

"Are you certain? It seems odd that this would be the indication," Dorian said, scratching at the side of his temple.

I watched Rava give him a deadpan look. "What about her *doesn't* seem odd to you?"

I cleared my throat. "An indication of what?" I asked weakly. Rox handed me a glass of water with a straw. I gave her a smile in thanks and took a sip.

"That you need to bite someone," she answered.

My stomach roiled at the thought of blood in my

mouth, and I shook my head. "Nope, mmm hmm, no—gross. That sounds terrible."

"I don't think it needs to happen after you've bled out. Your blood smells stale when this particular event occurs. That means it's past time to do something about it. I think when you feel this coming on, the bite needs to happen," Rava explained.

"This comes on and I have thirty seconds tops before I faceplant where I'm standing. There's no time," I said.

She frowned and looked at the guys. "When was the first time this happened?"

"Five days ago," Ezra said, running his tongue over his fang and looking at his watch. "Five and a half if we consider the time of day. Either way, vampires don't do . . . whatever this is. There's a thirst."

Rava rolled her eyes. "I know. I counsel hybrids, remember? Hybrids often present their powers and magic a little differently. Some don't. It's not exactly a science we can study."

Roman crossed his arms. "So what do you suggest?"

She paced the room, deep in thought. I closed my eyes and laid in silence while everyone else watched her. When the footsteps suddenly stopped, I opened them. "If it took five and a half days between these two episodes, let's assume we have that much time before another one. I'd say bite someone the day before, or maybe first thing in the morning. Both times this has occurred it's been in the afternoon. Let's cut it off at the pass and get ahead of it. She doesn't need to feed right now, especially not if the idea of blood is making her green in the face. Give her body time to recover, and it'll tell us when she's ready."

The alphas exchanged looks of doubt between them.

"She's right, you know," Rya said, walking down the

stairs. Her skirt flowed behind her, draping over the stairs, and falling on the steps behind her as she descended.

"About?" Ezra asked.

"All of it," she said simply. When no one spoke, she sighed. "Rava and I have been talking. She knows hybrids. This is her job. You've created a hybrid the world has never seen before, at least not that any of us know of. Dorian and I are quite old, and this is an unknown to us. A demon-shifter-vampire-fae. She was *dead*. A creature from another realm. Be realistic. How do you expect any of this to go according to your expectations of your supernatural species?"

Ezra opened his mouth to answer, but she held up a hand. "No, no, dear. Please don't interrupt when I'm asking rhetorical questions."

I snorted my laugh while Dorian cracked a small smile. Ezra didn't seem pleased.

"As I was saying, Rava's specialty is helping those dual species learn to harness and cope with both forms. We all fit solidly into our powers, as we should. Rava's clients don't, and they never will. Rava knows this experience intimately. You're all incredibly lucky she had teachings on both sides and that she's dedicated her life to helping those like her. She's going to be the best bet you have in understanding Fury at this time, and you'd do well to listen to her. You're all smarter than this. I'm not entirely sure why you are pushing back to begin with."

"Because it involves our mate." Dorian let out a frustrated breath. Turning to Rava, he said, "Out of all of us here, you're the subject matter expert. You're saying the bleeding is due to her vampire nature, then that's the best we have."

Rava cocked her head. "It's the only thing you have,"

she said smugly. "You guys didn't have a clue what this could mean."

Ezra was put out. "How can you be so sure?"

"I'm not. I'm about eighty-five percent, but it's certainly not going to hurt anything. Doing nothing will. You can't just sit around and wait for her to start bleeding and pass out again."

"So by your estimate, she has less than six days before she needs to bite someone." Dorian's gaze shifted from Ezra to me, and his amber eyes darkened slightly. A shared moment between us from earlier in the week flashed in my mind. Me pressed against the wall, him towering in front of me. I shifted my position. "I'll take her with me, and we'll work on her fae magic until then. She needs to control her sifting. We know she can sift, so let's use the time to work on it." His lips curled slightly as he looked at me.

I finally felt a little better, and I sat up. The bump on my head didn't continue to throb, so at least that had healed enough for it to not be painful anymore.

"The full moon is coming up," Roman said. He tried to meet my gaze, but an instant irritation shot through me. I was still so hurt and furious with him all at the same time. How could you long for someone's touch while simultaneously wanting to throttle them and scream at them? I still didn't want to address any of those emotions, and I purposefully looked away.

"Fury said she hasn't felt her wolf yet," Dorian pointed out.

Rava shrugged. "That doesn't really mean anything. Fury and I have spoken about this. I didn't feel my wolf until I actually shifted. There was no indication I even had one, and then I just did. It'll happen when it happens. In the meantime, I think you need to work on your other powers."

"I concur," Rya added. "Not that anyone asked me, but if we have Lyra on watch, then Fury should be focusing on her fae magic before she needs to feed and before she needs to shift. Now is as good a time as any."

Dorian, Roman, and Ezra watched me. I raised my eyebrows and looked around, wondering why everyone had gone silent. Rox nudged me and gave a look that said, 'your turn'. Then I realized they were waiting on me to say what I thought of their plan. I shrugged. "Yeah, sure. Why not."

"It's settled then." Dorian strode across the room and wrapped his arm around my waist, scooping me up from the couch. I didn't have a chance to gain my footing as he leaned down and whispered in my ear, "You're mine for five days." Then the room disappeared.

CHAPTER 20

My brow scrunched in concentration. The faint scent of smoke from the fireplace and the crisp chill coming through the stone walls nipped at my senses. I squeezed my fists, feeling the slight bite of my nails push against the fleshy part of my palm.

Despite all the concentration in the world, I couldn't sift.

"If you hadn't done it already, I'd think you weren't capable," Dorian said. I opened my eyes to glare at him, the tension draining from my body.

"Maybe you're just not that good of a teacher," I huffed. "We've been at it for hours, and I haven't moved two inches."

"We've been at it for thirty minutes," he corrected. Huh. Well, it *felt* like hours. "But perhaps there is something to be said about you needing more motivation."

His amber eyes took on a dangerous glint.

"My motivation is just fine, thank you—" I didn't get to finish the sentence before he appeared before me. He clasped his hand around my waist, pulling me against him.

In the next second, I felt the world turn upside down as he took me with him. My stomach hollowed as our feet touched solid ground once more, but the world kept spinning. My knees buckled, but instead of holding me upright —Dorian stepped away.

My shins slammed into hard stone. A frigid wind whipped through my hair, filling me with a truly bitter cold. I took a quick breath, calming my motion sickness, before looking around.

"Why are we outside?" The cocky look on his face and the arched eyebrow told me I didn't want to know.

"Motivation," Dorian said simply. "If you want to go back to the castle, all you need to do is sift yourself inside."

With that, he disappeared, leaving me to Avalon's gray skies and harsh winds.

I was going to kill him. He may not be able to die, but it wouldn't stop me from trying. Nope.

With great effort, I pushed myself off the steps and focused hard on moving myself from the extreme elements outside to the comfortable interior of the castle. Dorian said it was all about manifesting my own reality. As long as I'd been there before, all I had to do was envision myself there, and I should be able to do it.

So far this supposedly simple magic was proving extremely hard to grasp. And by hard, I meant impossible.

A tremble shook me as the glacial temperatures cut through my clothes, making it hard to concentrate. Dressed in high-waisted white pants and a tight long-sleeved shirt Dorian put me in when we came here, I was equipped for the cold inside the castle. Out here was another story.

I rubbed my hands together, trying to build some friction between them to stop the stiffness settling in my joints. I just wanted to warm up next to the fireplace. Motivation. My eyes narrowed on the set of double doors before me.

Inside, I told myself, imagining my body appearing on the other side.

My teeth clenched when nothing happened.

Inside, I repeated the exercise.

A sharp wind slammed into me from the front, knocking me back on my ass as if laughing at me. I slapped my hands against the ground, growling under my breath.

Inside. Inside. Inside—

The fire I'd been thinking about appeared before me. Burning logs and embers that only stayed that way for a moment were snuffed out from the winds barreling through.

Faint orange glowed from the coals at the bottom of the pile, while ashes and soot sprayed across my front. I frowned.

Not for a second did I believe Dorian sent the fire to me. Which meant I brought it to myself. Reframing my mind on that piece of information, I thought about Dorian's fae wine he sipped while attempting to 'teach me'.

Copying the same mentality, I imagined myself going to it.

Glass shattered before me, spraying my white pants with liquid.

My eyes snapped open, focusing on the plum-colored splatters now staining my outfit. It seeped into the cracks of the stone and pooled around me, dispersing faster while the wind whipped it across the ground.

A moment later, Dorian appeared. He didn't look amused.

Arms crossed, his eyes flicked toward the broken decanter, then back to me.

"How?" he demanded.

"I don't know what you're talking about," I replied, wrapping my arms around myself while I shivered.

"First the fire, then my wine," he answered. Taking a step forward, his boots crunched on the glass as he towered over me. He reached out, grabbing my chin between his index finger and thumb. "Now answer me, how did you manage to sift objects?"

"Take me inside and I'll tell you."

Dorian studied me for a moment. "Fine."

Turning on his heel, he strode to the double doors and pushed them open with a firm shove. My lips parted in shock. "They were open this whole time?"

His slight smirk was my answer.

I took the stairs two at a time, all too eager to get out of the cold. Once inside, he shut the doors firmly behind us.

"Where is everyone?" I asked, noticing the lack of fae soldiers and servants running around for once. The great hall was utterly empty.

Dorian narrowed his eyes, pointedly not answering. I sighed, running my hands over my arms, trying to warm them faster. "I was focused on sifting to somewhere warm. Preferably in front of the fire. Then it appeared in front of me. Knowing you're not a kind soul that would send it, I tried again, this time thinking about sifting to your wine. Once again, it appeared in front of me."

Dorian's expression remained cool as he ran his thumb over his bottom lip in contemplation. "Fae can't sift objects. Only themselves and anything touching them."

"Except I'm not fae. Not fully, anyhow."

"Indeed," he murmured, falling deeper into thought.

"You going to tell me where everyone is now?" I asked,

dropping my hands to my side now that the worst of the chills had passed.

"Sent them away," he answered, still seeming to pay attention only partially.

I frowned. "Why would you do that?"

"Lyra," he answered quietly, the fog clearing as he focused on me once more. "She and the angel know this place. How to get in and out. We reinforced the wards, but my general wanted to double our troops and protect all entry points. We did at first, but I thought my people would be safer if they dispersed for the time being. Besides, it's not like there's anything left here to guard."

"That's probably for the best," I said. "Angels aren't all-knowing. While they're good at finding out what they want, unless they're specifically looking for your people, they're probably safer away from this whole mess. Until we have a way to capture Lyra and deal with the angel, that is."

Dorian nodded, letting out a heavy sigh. "Enough about the angel for now. Until Hades gets back or Jules reports something new, we should focus on you, and help you learn your magic."

I twisted my lips, scrunching my nose. "We've established I can sift, but not when I'm trying, and I have better luck bringing objects to me rather than the other way around."

"So it seems," he agreed. "I'll want to test this more. Most fae struggle with sifting to some extent. Not as much as this, but I suspect you'll be able to sift on command, given time. We need to see if you have any other abilities."

"Such as?"

"Glamour, changing clothes, persuasion . . ."

I lifted both eyebrows on the last word, not recognizing it as a standard power the fae possessed.

"Both Lyra and I have the ability to take away free will. We can make someone do anything and everything we want—except you, it seems."

I took a step closer, hearing an undercurrent of something in his voice, though I couldn't tell what.

"Do you wish I wasn't the exception?"

"No," he said instantly. "While it would be nice to keep you from breaking rules left and right, I'd never want you at Lyra's mercy. It's a relief to me she can't persuade you."

I tilted my chin, noticing how he pointedly referred to being under her control, but spoke nothing of his.

"And you?" I asked quietly. "Would you want me at your mercy?"

His eyes darkened with lust. The tension between us came to the forefront at the sharp inhale of his breath. When he didn't immediately answer, I lifted a hand to run my fingers over his chest. His heart beat heavily, though his features remained stoic. "Well?" I prompted. "Would you?"

"You wouldn't survive my mercy," he said eventually.

I cocked my head, wanting a better answer from him. "Why do you say that?"

Dorian reached out, clasping a hand around my throat, not to choke me, but in a show of possession. His thumb skimmed my jaw softly, but the strength of his grip was anything but gentle.

"I'm not a soft lover. I want to find your limits and push you to the edge of them because I can." Heat pooled between my legs as I imagined what those words meant. "Because you'll trust me to. It won't be casual. When I take a lover, I'm committed, and when I take a mate—when I take you, I'll never let you go. I can't."

"Never let me go," I repeated, leaving it open-ended in question.

"Back," he answered. "To the Afterlife. Ezra and Roman will accept the present while hoping for more—but not me. I'm incapable of giving into this without taking everything in return."

My mouth parted, and he ran his thumb under my bottom lip, drawing conflicted emotions in me. "You don't want me to leave," I said softly.

"We should get back to training," he replied, taking a step back. His hand loosened, and I stepped into him.

"Stop it," I said. "We're talking about this."

"There's nothing to talk about, Fury. I know what I need from you, and if I didn't know better, I'd look the other way and take it. Take you. But you're not staying, and you won't—"

"You don't know that," I interrupted.

"Would you stay?" he asked, point-blank. "Would you agree to never return? To stay even if you found a way back? To remain on Earth even when your mission is finished, and the angel is gone, and Lyra is back in stasis?"

I licked my lips. "It's not that simple—"

"There it is," he said, smiling without joy. "I thought so."

"If there is a way, they may not *let* me stay. Hell, even if there's not—" I stopped abruptly, not wanting to finish the sentence or acknowledge the truth. The dangerous flash in his eyes told me I was too late for that.

"If there's not?" he prompted. I knew he knew, but he was going to make me say it.

"No one gets a free pass. The dead are meant to stay that way," I said quietly.

"They'd kill you if they couldn't drag you back." It wasn't a question, but I still felt like I had to answer.

"Probably," I said. "And because I've now got supe magic, it would be the end for me. The real end."

"This is what you want to return to?" he asked. "Why do you even want to?"

"I never said that——"

"But you do," he replied before I could continue. Dorian twisted so my back was to a tapestry and pushed me back against it. His arms rested against the wall on either side of my head. "You've made it very clear that if you can find a way back, you'll take it. Why? So you can live behind the pearly gates? Retire up in the clouds, leaving the rest of us here? Rox. Ezra. Roman. Me." I swallowed hard, not so sure now if I truly wanted this conversation. Perhaps he was right. I bit off more than I could chew with him, but damn me if a growing part of myself didn't want it. "You're willing to spend eternity away from your mates and condemn us to the same, for what? Retirement? Not needing to work?" He shook his head, letting out a callous laugh. "You wouldn't need to work another day in your life here. I'd take care of you. You could live anywhere in the world you wanted, have anything you wanted, and all you'd have to do is stay."

"And if I chose to stay, but they still came for me?" I asked, knowing it would show a card I hadn't revealed to the others yet.

"I'm not the same man I was when Morvain died. If they tried to take you—" He stopped suddenly, his eyes dilating sharply.

We stared at each other in silence.

He got it. He understood.

"You're the reason," he whispered.

I nodded, letting the truth sink in.

His head fell forward into the crook of my neck. "Fuck," he growled.

Fuck indeed.

"Do the others know?" he asked, lifting his head.

"I don't think so."

"How does Ezra not know yet?"

"I'm not sure," I admitted. "I try to shove some things away and not think about it when he's near me. I just thought it best not to say anything for the moment. We've got enough to worry about right now."

"Lying by omission?" Instead of looking judgmental, he seemed amused.

"Knowing doesn't change it," I said. "All it would do is cause more anxiety. I can't stop it if it's going to happen."

"It won't," he said, utterly serious.

"You can't know that."

"I won't let it," he replied. "If that means spending every waking hour you have making sure you can use your fae magic, then I will. If someone comes for you, whether it's the angel, the Afterlife, Lyra—you'll be able to sift."

I snorted. "That's a bold claim considering the last hour."

"Motivation," he said. "All I have to do is find yours."

I lifted an eyebrow. "What did you have in mind?"

CHAPTER 21

B ribing didn't work. Not even for alcohol.

Dropping me in extreme temperatures didn't do shit either.

After a day of trying and not getting anywhere—except for stealing objects out of thin air—I collapsed in Dorian's wingback chair, dead tired and wanting to sleep.

"Get up," Dorian said.

"No."

"Fury," he rumbled, his voice dark with intent. I didn't care.

"Fuck off. I'm exhausted." I kicked my legs up on the edge of the coffee table and tilted my head back, closing my eyes.

Cold water hit my face.

I gasped, sitting up in a flash.

"What the hell—" I growled, coming face-to-face with the fae bastard as he leaned over me, holding the sides of the chair, and boxing me in.

"We're not done here," he said sternly. "You can do this the easy way, or the hard. It makes no difference to me—

but you *will* be able to sift by the time we have to go back to Houston."

I narrowed my eyes at him. "I'm not going to sift if I die of sleep deprivation."

Dorian scoffed. "You're hardly sleep deprived. I think you can put in the extra ten percent."

"Bite me," I snapped, crossing my arms and tilting my head back.

The scent of frost, mint, and fae wine registered vaguely—then a sharp pain in my bottom lip.

I opened my mouth to protest as his tongue grazed over it—soothing the pain and replacing it with something else entirely.

I leaned forward, slanting my mouth against his. Dorian didn't waste any time invading my senses. His tongue toyed with mine; devouring me, licking the inside of my mouth, and sucking my lip. The kiss lasted forever and yet only a blink when he started to pull back.

I reached for him on instinct. My hands knotted in his hair, pulling it tight.

A rough growl escaped his throat. He knocked my legs off the table, manipulating them to either side of him before grabbing my waist and hauling me up. I gasped at the feel of our bodies against each other. His chest to mine. Hands slipping to my ass and squeezing. His thick erection pressed into my belly.

My eyes slanted open as he started moving.

"Where are we going?" I asked.

"My chambers." His lips were back on me, even as he walked. The slight movement of his body caused me to sway back and forth, rubbing against him.

Somewhere in the back of my mind, I registered that something was off—but after weeks of wanting him and denying myself—it would seem we were both feeling a bit weak-willed. Perhaps the day of training wore me down, but I wasn't in the mood to fight it anymore.

Right when I was running out of air and needing to breathe, my back hit something hard. Dorian used the opportunity to rock into me, creating delicious friction between my thighs. I tilted my head back and moaned.

His lips trailed over my jaw and down to my ear, where he whispered, "If you have limits, tell me now."

My brain scrambled, but I managed to get the words out in a semi-intelligible manner. "No hitting. No spanking. I'm not big on pain. I'll snap."

He kissed my neck, still working his hips into mine. If I could have spread my legs any wider, I would have. "That all?"

"No daddy kink," I added.

He chuckled against my throat. Without replying, one of his hands left me for a brief second. The hard barrier behind me moved. Door, I realized. Must have been a sturdy one to not rattle with how hard he was moving against me.

Dorian's fangs scraped the column of my throat, making my blood heat and my breath stutter.

"If I wanted to mark you, would you let me?" he asked.

I hummed my agreement, slipping one hand from his hair to his shoulder, letting my nails dig in.

"And if I want your mouth?" he continued.

"Make me come and it's yours."

The breath hissed between his teeth. Fangs pressing harder against my skin as he sucked on a patch of skin.

"What about your ass?"

"It's been a few decades. You'll need to go slow, but I'm down."

"Being tied up?" he asked tentatively.

"As long as there's no hitting, I'm open for it."

"Fuck," he murmured against me. "You're going to make it hard to control myself."

"Then don't," I moaned as my back hit something soft, certain it was a bed. "I just gave you permission to fuck me whatever way you want."

Dorian sighed. He reached behind him to grab my hands, pinning them above my head. I let him.

Cold shackles clicked shut around both wrists at the same time. My eyes opened, distrust running through me for the first time.

"What are you doing?"

"Shh," Dorian said, moving backwards on the bed. "We're going to play a game." He reached down to the left side of the bed and grabbed another cuff, putting it around my ankle. My heart hammered. He cuffed the second foot, leaving my legs spread and my arms pulled taut over my head.

"What kind of game?" I asked, suspicion bleeding into my voice.

His gaze was burning with lust and dark desire as he kneeled between my legs. My clothes vanished in an instant, but he didn't lower his eyes from my face.

Not even when he ran his fingertips over my stomach, down the curve of my hip, or the inner edge of my thigh. My chest rose and fell rapidly, waiting with anticipation for his next move.

His fingers skimmed over my pussy, and he lowered one blunt tip in between my folds, running from my wet center up to my throbbing clit.

I bucked against the chains.

Dorian didn't stop, nor did he speed up. Using only the tip of his finger, he ran it around my sensitive nerve bundle, agonizingly slow.

"Please," I muttered. I tried to break the chains, and they groaned under the pressure, but not even my own demonic strength would do.

"It won't work," he said, continuing his deliberate torture. "Once I learned you were stronger than me, I had them made from Tungsten. So is the bed frame. There's only two ways out of those chains."

I lifted my head to look at him. It was erotic to watch him—fully clothed, between my legs—playing with me, his amber eyes filled with such need and dark desire. "Either I let you out , or you sift."

Motherfucker.

"Please, Dorian," I moaned, trying to rock my body into him. Just a little more pressure and I'd get there.

"Please what, little demon?" he asked, voice husky.

"Let me out. Make me come."

"Which one?"

"Both," I said. He tutted.

"I told you, Fury, I'm not a soft lover. I take everything." As he spoke, my thighs began to tremble. The continued stimulation was getting to me. I was so close—

And then he stopped.

"I've offered you everything," I countered.

"Not true," he said softly. "But that's not the point right now. You need to learn to sift, and I think I finally found your motivation."

I growled, throwing my head up and down on the bed.

Motherfucker was becoming a mantra in my head.

"If you won't fuck me because I can't promise to stay, whatever, but this is just cruel," I snapped.

"I am cruel," he countered. Dorian crawled up my body. His legs straddled over my chest, he reached for my breast, lightly pinching a nipple. "But for this to work, you need proper motivation. The mating call will help. Your body doesn't want to deny me. That said, you need a reward. Escape the chains and I'll make you come, Fury. If you don't want to come, just say 'I give up' and I'll let you out."

"You're a bastard," I growled.

"I am," he agreed. "But in this case, it'll be just as hard for me as it is for you."

"I sincerely doubt that," I quipped. He twisted my nipple sharply, making me gasp. With a quick tug on his pants, he undid the front and released his cock. Hard and heavy for me, it jutted out of his boxers, the very tip touching between my breasts.

He lifted his hips, moving back and forth to run the tip over my sternum, between the valley of my breasts. Dorian grunted, a single drop of pre-cum welling at the tip.

"As you were saying," he said, releasing my breasts to shuffle off me and out of bed entirely. Seeing him only inches from my face and aching turned me on harder. Dorian walked around the bed and flashed me a cold smile. At the very end, he leaned over, beginning his ministrations to my clit once more.

This was going to be a very long night.

CHAPTER 22

DORIAN

She cussed at me. Called me a sadist. Threatened that she'd find a way to end me.

For all her cursing, begging, and writhing, she never told me to let her go—she never said 'I give up'—and I didn't yield.

She had to learn to sift, and we both knew this was the way.

I enjoyed torturing her like this. God, I did. The struggle for me was seeing her splayed open, crying in near ecstasy, begging for my cock. It made me want to take her like nothing else. I couldn't. Wouldn't. If the inevitable came— if she left us—I'd at least have this time with her. I wouldn't waste it.

After three hours of still not sifting, she started to drift, stuck between truly needing rest now and the mindless haze of being edged for three hours.

I backed off, giving her just enough reprieve to sleep before starting again. I waited, admiring her while she slept. The curves of her body. The slight rise and fall of her chest as she gently breathed. I wanted to burn the image in my mind. Her pussy was still glistening when moonlight filtered in the window, casting its glow on her form. It was time.

I woke her up with two fingers rubbing her clit, and Fury stirred on the brink of orgasm, moaning.

I stopped once more.

"You'll be lucky if I don't cut your dick off for this," she ground out in a husky voice.

"You won't," I said, completely assured as I switched to kneading her breasts, flicking my thumb over her sensitive nipple.

"I've done it before," she replied. "And because you can't die, you'd just be cockless and forced to watch while I fuck my other two mates."

Under different circumstances, I would've fucked her mouth. Considering the threat, I'd pass.

"It'd grow back—and I'd chain your ass up here and fuck you for good measure if you ever tried it."

"I'm chained now, and you won't even fuck me," she complained as I took her nipple in my mouth.

She liked this game. Loved it. While my little mate wasn't about pain, per se, she didn't seem to mind bites as long as I sucked them afterward.

I'd done it so much, her nipples would have been bruised if not for her advanced healing. That pleased me. Much as I wanted to mark her, bruises weren't the kind of marks I liked.

"I'd eat your pussy and lick you clean if you'd sift," I replied with her breast in my mouth, releasing it with a pop.

She groaned. Her eyebrows scrunched in concentration. She'd done it a hundred times now, attempting to sift.

Occasionally she brought objects to the bed. Knives mostly. I didn't question where her thoughts were when that happened. I'd move them to the nightstand and then continue, though I did find it amusing.

This time, covered in sweat, breathing hard, her legs shaking, and her center dripping wet for me—she scrunched her face in real concentration.

I moved away from the bed, over to the decanter of fae wine that sat on a credenza.

"Sift for me, little demon. I want to watch you come. I want it as much as you do." I poured myself a glass of wine, turning my back on the bed for only a moment.

A damp hand grabbed my shoulder, turning me.

My surprise registered as Fury stood before me, raging mad. Her yellow eyes glowed near golden as she stared shrewdly.

She took the glass from my hand and drained the wine in one go before throwing it across the room.

"Get on your knees," she commanded, voice hoarse from all the screaming and cursing.

Yes. A rush of euphoric hunger shot through me. I smiled, satisfied, and eager to finish her off.

I grabbed her waist, spinning her body and switching our positions, pushing her backside against the furniture to prop her up. She was going to need it. I dropped onto the antique rug without question. She lifted one leg, slipping it over my shoulder—then grabbed a rough handful of my hair. While I normally wasn't the one in this position, for her—for this—I would gladly.

"Suck," she demanded as I grabbed her ass, pulling her closer to my face.

I parted the lips of her pussy with my tongue and wasted no time taking her clit between my lips. I pushed two fingers in her, filling that void. Fury's hand tightened in my hair and she held onto the side of the credenza with her other, leaning her head back, moaning low and long.

"Don't stop," she said with a shaky breath.

I whorled my tongue around her clit, then sucked sharply. She gasped, her channel clenching around my fingers.

"I need more," she begged, her breathing picking up. Giving her what she asked for, I added a third finger, sliding it in with ease as she coated my hand. Fury rocked against my face, both her legs shaking from the sheer exertion of what was coming.

I twisted my hand inside her, pressing my fingers together, adding my pinky as I fucked her hard with my hand. I kept my tongue pressed against her clit as I groaned against her.

Her hips jerked and her legs quaked. The hand in my hair pulled tight, sending pain scattering across my scalp. Her other hand dug into my shoulder, clawing at me as she came violently, pouring into my hand and down my arm.

Mouth open, she screamed. Her muscles contracted and spasmed while her orgasm tore through her, drawing out the pleasure and leaving ripples of aftershocks in their wake.

Her hand in my hair loosened, turning more affectionate as she ran her fingers through the strands.

The leg over my shoulder slipped off to the side, and she quickly lost all balance. I grasped her hips to steady her, using the furniture behind her to give stability.

"I don't think I've ever come that hard," she said in a raspy voice.

I glanced at the clock on the wall. "I edged you for over four hours."

Her lips pressed together. "I'm still pissed about that."

I arched an eyebrow, pointing at her wobbly legs and the wetness covering her thighs. "Mmm, I see that." I chuckled, ignoring the heaviness of my cock while I watched her secure her footing and test the strength of her legs. She stretched her arms and arched her back in a big yawn.

I took a towel from a nearby table, wiping her down and drying off what moisture still coated her. She remained silent and unmoving, letting me care for her. Lifting her up, I carried her to a lounge chair and set her down.

"I'll get you a bath ready. Does that sound like something you'd like?" I asked.

She hummed in agreement, still in her post-orgasm euphoria haze, and a small smile of relief appeared on her face.

"Anything else?" I offered. She appraised me, considering her options.

"Anything I want?" Fury traced the fabric on the chaise, but I wasn't sure what she'd ask for.

"Within reason, I'll give you whatever you want."

"Cheese fries?" she asked tentatively.

"I can do that," I replied with a small laugh. It wasn't what I expected. "We'll get you cleaned up and fed, then you need rest."

"And I want you to stay with me. Keep me company," she said, rolling to her side. "Where's the tub?"

"In there." I pointed to a door she hadn't noticed before. I bent down, sliding one arm under her legs and cradling her back with my other.

I walked to the bathroom, intent on making sure she recovered from a very long, very intense session. She needed to feel clean. She needed to be cared for. Worshipped. And she would be.

She also needed as much rest as I could give her. She didn't know what I had in store for the rest of our time together.

We'd only just begun.

CHAPTER 23

Crystal clear water tumbled from the cracks between the rocks and into the eight-foot stone basin that was the tub. I let out a low whistle, taking in the natural cut of the gray stone that revealed veins of silver and gold. A giant stained-glass window was centered over the space, melding the view of the island below in the blue, red, and purple panes of the design.

"This must have cost a fortune," I said, slowly stepping toward the tub.

Dorian shrugged as if it were nothing. "There's a cave on the island filled with several geothermal pools. Hot springs. My favorite looks similar to what you see here. It's actually a favorite amongst many of the fae on Avalon. I wanted one for my own private use, so I had it recreated."

"Not big on sharing?" I commented as I approached it. My own distorted reflection looked back.

"No."

I bent at the waist to grip the edge and slowly climb into the steaming waters. The first heated touch made me tense. The pool was fairly deep, coming up to mid-thigh. I stepped forward, wading through the clear water, and then lowered myself in, relaxing. A blissful sigh escaped me.

"That's a shame," I said, picking up our conversation again. While I wasn't looking at him, I sensed his eyes on me. "Sharing is caring."

"I can't say either of those are on the list of my better qualities."

"Are you good at sharing anything?" I asked, searching his face for a reaction.

He pinned me with an intense stare. "I'm possessive, so not particularly, no."

I snorted, reclining back in the bath. The hot water made my breathing slow and even, but heavy, making it difficult to float properly.

"How would you even handle it, then? If I stayed?" I posed the question nonchalantly while I stared at the rock ceiling.

"I would get over it this one and only time. You need your mates. After losing my own . . . I wouldn't try to separate you from them. But that doesn't mean I'm living with either of them. We all have separate lives. For you, we come together—but that's where the commonalities end."

"Hmm," I murmured as I thought about what that meant. "And what would my life look like? Bonded with three mates who don't care for one another?"

The whole idea was more theoretical than anything. The way humans would talk about what they'd do if they won the lottery. A dream so far off I could imagine it, but I couldn't actually imagine *living* it. After all, with a rogue angel, a crazy fae princess, and the Afterlife's own code—my chances of any future here were slim to none. That didn't stop me from thinking about it, pointless as it may have been.

"I imagine we'd find something similar but more permanent than what we have now. You'd spend time with each of us and our people, and at times we'd come together for you." He kept his hands in his pockets, turning to look at the images on the stained glass. "Why do you ask?"

I shrugged lightly. "I'm not sure. I think it's because I like to picture it. Play it through my head, like a movie. The dreams and ideas I have for my life. It's what . . ." I trailed off, realizing that I was coming uncomfortably close to rehashing the past.

"It's what you've done since your first life," he finished for me. "It's comforting."

I met his gaze, and in his eyes, I didn't see pity. I saw a hint of empathy. Understanding. I blinked, and it was gone, but I nodded slowly in response. "Yes."

"I think many of us do it. As much as you may feel like you are, you aren't alone."

I raised an eyebrow, surprised that he somewhat admitted to a vulnerability. I had the option to press on it, but I figured it would push him away if I did. For now, we were talking, and that was more than he usually gave.

"I've been alone my entire existence. I'm used to it. This," I gestured to him and then waved my hand about, "is new to me. I'm not entirely sure what to do with it all, but it's nice to think about, even if it sounds like you want to split custody with them when it comes to spending time with me." I splashed water at him, and he took a step back when it wet his pants.

"It's more complicated than that," he said, shaking his head. "Beyond basic personalities, we're different, Roman, Ezra, and I. Our species, our age, our histories, what we can give our mate. Could you see us all living in one house? No matter the size, it wouldn't work."

"Okay, fair point. No, I can't picture it." I huffed a laugh just at the mere idea of living under one roof. "What do you mean, though, about what you can give your mate?"

He considered me, tilting his head as he thought. "Roman and Roxanne could give you a family within their pack. It's what they are, and it's what they value. Ezra has made no attempts to hide that he's trying to mold you into a clan enforcer. You'd work without a set of rules or regulations the other vampires are forced to abide by."

"And you?" I prompted. "What would you give?"

"Whatever life you want," he said, walking toward the tub. His footsteps were soft, but sure. "We could live anywhere in the world at the drop of a hat. Go anywhere. See everything. The fae aren't affectionate in the same way shifters are, nor do I think you'd easily find a job you'd enjoy among my people—but we would have everything else."

I swallowed hard, my head bobbing below the water. I sat up, bumping into smooth rock beneath me.

"Material things," I murmured.

"Experiences and companionship. They're quite different. I'm not going to profess love or write you poetry. It's not who I am. But I will find what pleases you and give it to you, because in the end, it would please me too." I looked up at him. Dark, moody, his arms crossed over his chest as he leaned against the rock wall, watching me. He was shirtless, and across the ridges of his muscles, his pale skin reflected some of the light coming from the window and pool. Eyes burning, he stared with an intensity that rivaled the sun, despite his stoic face. "At least I would, if you stayed."

If I stayed . . .

Here we were again.

My heart pounded, and I could feel it in my head. I knew he heard it, but the conversation had taken a turn into something more serious than I'd anticipated.

"Well, let's focus on keeping me alive first," I said, backpcdaling into more familiar territory. Dorian's eyes shuttered, putting me at a distance. I didn't blame him.

"Everything you'll need should be on that shelf," he said, pointing to the opposite side of the tub where a larger niche housed several bottles with white labels on the bottom. I nodded once.

"You're not staying?"

"I believe you were promised cheese fries," he said. A good excuse, even if it was just that. I went along with it.

"I wouldn't say no to a beer either. Or more of that fae wine," I suggested.

His lips thinned, not amused. "You need hydration after that session."

"I'm a supe now, right? I doubt dehydration could kill me."

"That's not an excuse to test it," he said.

"Or is it?" I drifted over to the shelf, plucking one labeled *shampoo*. "You said so yourself; you wanted to find my limits." Popping the cap open, I took a whiff. Oh, that was nice. Pouring a decent amount in my palm, I lathered it between my hands before moving to my hair.

"I'm not going to justify that with a reply," he said.

"You just did."

Dorian vanished, sifting out before I could push him any further.

I sighed to myself, taking my time to wash and rinse my hair, soaking for a bit longer until my fingers started to wrinkle. When I was just getting out of the tub, he reappeared with a Styrofoam container and a chilled bottle of water.

I pursed my lips, fishing the towel off a hook on the wall and wiping down my body.

Once I finished drying myself, I wrapped my hair in the towel and walked out into the bedroom once more. Dorian said nothing, setting my food on one of the small tables.

"You were gone a long time for cheese fries," I remarked, taking a seat. The cool air felt nice after such a warm bath.

"Fae or not, I still have to wait in line."

I cracked the lid, my stomach letting out a low rumble as the smell hit me.

It was perfection. The right amount of cheese spread over crispy fries and topped with bacon and chives.

The first bite had me moaning in a way that clearly did things to him. He reached down and readjusted himself, taking a seat across from me.

I lifted an eyebrow. "I'm surprised you haven't taken care of that."

"I did," he said. "Twice. While you were sleeping."

I swallowed thickly, and it had nothing to do with the ooey gooey goodness that coated my tongue.

"How is it?" he asked, changing the subject. Probably for the best. Orgasms versus greasy cheese fries was a tough call, and right now, my hunger for actual food was winning.

"Delicious. Incredible, really. Where'd you get them from?"

"A food truck in Austin. They're good, but wait another month for the Fort Bend County Fair," he said. "James dragged me to it a few years back. He insisted they had the best french fries."

"If they're better than this, I'll be shocked. This is to die for," I said around a mouthful. Dorian inclined his head. "Gotta say, I'm confused as to how James managed to drag you to anything. You're not exactly the dragging type."

He cracked the smallest hint of a smile. "Every now and then I can be obliging. He caught me on a good day."

"You have good days?" I feigned mock surprise. "Will you make sure I get to see you on one of these alleged good days, or is it like an annual allowance and you only have so many to spare?"

"It's a centennial allowance, not annual, and I'm afraid I've used up my allotted time for the current century," he quipped.

"Ugh." I snapped my fingers in disappointment. "So close."

A small laugh escaped him before he cleared his throat and schooled his features.

I chewed silently, thinking about seeing Dorian at a county fair filled with children, cotton candy, and shitty games. What did this guy look like? I couldn't picture it. To be honest, there was a lot I couldn't picture about him.

"So going to county fairs isn't exactly on the list of things you like to do in your free time. What is?"

He furrowed his brows in confusion, clearly wondering why I was asking.

"I mean, don't answer if you don't want to," I said, sticking more fries in my mouth. "You can ask me questions too. I won't promise I'll answer them, which I imagine goes both ways."

"Fair enough." Dorian crossed his legs, leaning back in his chair. "I like art and I like to read."

"Solitary things," I said, nodding along. "I understand that. Any particular art or era?"

"I'm fifteen hundred years old. I've lived through the

eras. What I enjoy is the evolution of art and what makes an artist. Even if I don't like the work, I can appreciate it. The brushstrokes. The methods. The technique. Art is created from emotion, and it's meant to evoke an emotion from its audience," he explained, gesturing to different pieces he had on the wall of his room. "Art speaks differently to everyone. I find pleasure in that."

I finished chewing my bite, licking the cheese off my fingers. When I started to ask another question, he held a finger up and wagged it at me. I snapped my mouth shut and held my hand out to tell him it was his turn.

"What is available to you in the Afterlife in terms of entertainment?" he asked.

"A lot of what is here, in a way," I said, wiping my hands on a napkin. I opened the bottle of water and took a drink. "Definitely more limited, though. We still socialize in the Afterlife. There are sex clubs and movie theaters; libraries and places to gather and eat. We have neighborhoods and pools; we can have pets if we want them." I shrugged. "We don't travel, though. It's the Afterlife. You are where you are."

"And what did you do with your free time?"

"I went to work, then I went home. I borrowed movies and shows. Television and film were such a great invention. The storytelling possibilities feel endless. I like reading too. Humans found a system for writing nearly fifty-five hundred years ago. It gives me a lot to read up on. Languages to learn. But on your point of emotion, I like music. The way you view art? That's music to me. That's what I collected."

"Collected?" he asked.

"Well, yeah. We had places where we lived. Possessions. I kept it small and uncomplicated, but I did allow myself to splurge on music. I didn't socialize much. I did sometimes, of course. The sex clubs were weird when I ran into co-workers, so that was an ick factor I couldn't burn out of my mind, but I got laid elsewhere. Never anything—" I stopped talking when I saw a possessive shadow cast over Dorian's face.

"Is there someone in the Afterlife?" he asked carefully.

I took a shaky breath, intrigued by the look in his eye. "Never anything serious was what I was going to say. And no. There is no 'someone' waiting for me."

"Good." He reached into his pocket and pulled out his phone. After he tapped on it for a minute, I heard the slight sound of speakers crackle as they came on, waiting for a song to play. A cello's dark timbre filled the room.

I smiled. "Bach." Dorian dipped his head in acknowl-edgement, then looked at a grandfather clock in the corner of the room.

"It's been a long day. You should rest," he said, turning the volume down.

I wouldn't argue. A yawn crept its way up and I covered my mouth with the back of my hand. "Will you leave the music on?" I asked. I drank the rest of the water and stood up, taking the towel off my head, and shaking out my hair. I ran my fingers through it and tried to separate some tangles while I walked across the room.

Flopping down on the giant bed, I stretched my arms over my head and then wrapped them around myself. After a warm bath, good food, and far too much exertion—my mind drifted quickly, sleep closing in fast.

I felt the bed dip beside me. A strong arm wrapped around my waist, pulling me in close. His lips pressed against my temple and the last of my consciousness fled.

For the first time in a long while, I slept without dreaming. No nightmares plagued me. No death or prophesized apocalypse. No fires and fear. Just quiet and calm bliss.

I was completely and utterly content.

I stirred when a cold shackle touched my wrist. I frowned in my sleep, mumbling that I needed five more minutes.

The clank of another one closing, this time around my ankle, brought me to. I blinked, trying to sit up. But I couldn't. My hands were trapped above my head and Dorian stood at my feet, securing my other ankle.

My heart started to pound, already knowing exactly where it was going.

"I'd say I'm sorry, but I'm not."

I tilted my chin as far forward as I could, my chest already heaving from the anticipation. "When I get out of these, I'm going to sit on your face."

Dorian smiled, equal parts playful and cruel. "I look forward to it."

His thumbs parted the lips of my pussy as he leaned forward and took a long, hard lick.

"You have three hours. After that I'm going to come on you and leave it there until you get out to clean yourself."

It was dirty. Disgusting. And hot enough to make me groan as liquid flooded between my thighs.

"Challenge accepted."

CHAPTER 24

D orian sat on the edge of the cast iron clawfoot tub while I soaked in my bubble bath. Instead of his lavish hot spring replica, I'd opted for the en suite attached to what he said was my room.

My room.

He'd given it to me, telling me it was my space. I could do whatever I wanted with it. A place for escape and rest if I chose not to be with him. He understood what leading a solitary life meant. I couldn't always find comfort with other people. Sometimes I needed to be by myself. I was grateful for it. I hadn't even asked him for a place of my own, but somehow, he knew to give me that.

I sighed in contentment. The soapy water came up to my neck, my entire body submerged in its glorious warmth. I had my hair pinned up in a messy bun and my head rested against the soft pillow while he watched me quietly.

I found it almost fascinating how much he could say without using words. I liked to watch the details of his face as he thought, or reacted, or even as he spoke. Each little line that creased on his flawless skin. Each little twitch near his eye or around his mouth. His breathing and sounds would change as he considered something.

He didn't have to say much. He clearly held himself up well in conversation, but he was just as content with silence. I could see how after fifteen hundred years. I would probably like silence a lot too. I sort of already did, but that came more from my history and inability to trust people. I imagine a similar situation played a part for him, but also the amount of time he'd been on Earth. What did one really have to talk about after all that time?

I lifted my leg, poking my toes out of the water and nudging him.

"Penny for your thoughts," I said.

He hummed lightly. "Nothing in particular. Enjoying the silence with you before we head back."

I adjusted myself in the tub, and the water sloshed around, echoing in the bathroom. "I would say that five days went by quickly, but that would be a lie. You knew how to drag it out," I said, raising an eyebrow at him.

He raised the corner of his lips ever-so-slightly. "I know." He clasped his hands in his lap, keeping his thumbs out as he tapped them together. "Though I don't recall you actually complaining. Threatening me and telling me you hated me, perhaps, but no true grievances. You seemed more than content to learn magic."

I laughed. "Yes. Learning magic. That's what we'll call it. The long, drawn-out orgasms played no part in my will-ingness." Placing my hands on the side of the tub, I pulled myself to a seated position, the water level just below my breasts. I watched him carefully, and his eyes didn't stray, keeping his focus on me.

"You learned to sift, didn't you?" he asked with a wry smile.

"That I did." I nodded. I may not have tried long distances yet, but I could finally control it. I could do it at will and to any location in the house. Even sifting one room to the next was a huge step. All things considered, learning how to do that in five days was quite the accomplishment for me. This wasn't my world, nor was it my magic. It was now, but everything was still raw and new.

I watched him for a moment, looking for the little movements on his face to see if I could figure out what he was thinking, but nothing came. I blew out a breath. It would take time to learn it all. If he got his way, we would have nothing but time. I had no way of knowing what would happen, but I didn't have high hopes. I hated having that conversation with him. The passion and the intensity in his voice when he talked about it was evident. He was a man that liked to have answers and be in control. Sometimes I wondered how much he teetered on the edge between control and chaos.

"Well," I said, "I have reached optimal pruning. We need to get ready to go." I moved to stand up, the water falling in cascades off my skin and splashing back into the tub. Dorian handed me a towel as his eyes roamed the length of my body. Stepping over the sides, I took it from him and smacked his hand away playfully as I walked to the mirror and took down my hair. "You've had enough. I need to be able to walk later, thank you."

Hunger flashed in his eyes, and he looked at me with a salacious smile. "Pity." Then he winked.

I stood there momentarily shocked. Did Dorian just . . . flirt with me? Did Dorian ever flirt? Did he know how to flirt?

His face was stoic again and it would have appeared the

moment was gone, but I could see the twinkle of something there.

I opened my mouth to ask him about it, but the words were lost. In the blink of an eye, my towel was gone, and I was wearing linen pants and a light sweater over a camisole. "Really?" I deadpanned. "You have absolutely no patience."

He shrugged. "It's wasting valuable time."

Grumbling, I walked out of the bathroom while I ran a brush through my hair. I shook it out, trying to give it some volume.

When I entered the bedroom, I saw some packages left on the bed that hadn't been there before. I looked at him and he gestured for me to go on.

I tore off the pristine cream wrapping paper, opening a box that contained what looked like a smaller version of my phone. I heard his footsteps behind me as he came to a stop. Facing him, I asked, "What's this?"

"Turn it on and see," he answered, reaching for it, and pressing the button until the screen lit up. "It's for your music." He opened a tiny box with earbuds and handed them to me. "Keep those for when you travel, but when you're here with me in Avalon, it's connected to speakers in your room, as well as mine." He touched play and Saint-Saens' "The Swan" played softly in the background.

I scrolled through the library on the iPod and my mouth hung open. It was impressive. He had music from each decade, all categorized, each one filled with musicians, artists, and bands I liked. Everything from classical to 1920s jazz to 1960s funk to 1990s industrial metal.

"You have a rather extensive range in the types of music you appreciate, and there's plenty of storage space for you to add more. If it gets full, we'll get another, and another.

You said you collected music in the Afterlife, so I wanted to give you that here too." He turned around and held his arm out, gesturing to a record player and a gramophone on the credenza. "The quality isn't the same, but I imagine it's more nostalgic to listen to certain artists the way you had originally in your first life."

I was speechless. As the days had passed—when I wasn't tied up and being edged, orgasming until I nearly passed out—we continued to talk. He showed me art he liked, and I played music I liked. Every emotion on the spectrum could be conveyed with both, I'd come to see. We were more alike than we often realized.

When I was alone by choice or by circumstance, I always had music. It was my one constant. Art was his.

I looked around at everything in the room, thankful for Dorian's gesture, but feelings of worry and disappointment were taking hold.

I silently made my way to the chairs by a large window, and I sat down.

"I've done something wrong," he said, not at all trying to hide the confusion in his tone.

I shook my head. "No, this is . . . this is really special." I swallowed.

"But?"

I put my hands in my lap and sighed. I would've much rather stared at my pants and picked at some imaginary thread there. Instead, I met his gaze. "My room. The claw-foot tub. This." I held up the device in my hand. "These are material possessions, Dorian. There's a lot that's out of my control right now, but when we talked about it, you said experiences and companionship. I can't help but wonder if . . ." I trailed off, not really wanting to say the rest of what I was thinking.

"Go on," he said flatly.

"Are you trying to buy my affection so I want to stay here?"

His mood darkened instantly. Shit. Nope. I'd misread this.

"That isn't what I'm doing." He went to the window and looked out over the moor. "They might be things, yes, but they are things you find comfort in. It's different."

"Oh," I whispered. I couldn't think of anything to say to him. I'd just accused him of trying to buy me, and I was way off.

"It isn't about making you want to choose me, or us," he started, coming to sit in the chair across from mine. "Whether or not you stay remains to be seen." The tone of his voice deepened as he considered what that meant. "Regardless, you're here now. You had built something in your afterlife, and for one hundred and three years, you've been set in your ways. The music you collected, the places you went, the solitude after a long day—it's all gone. While it was never our intent, all of it was ripped away from you. It's my desire to give some of that back to you. It's more than giving you gifts or buying material things for you. It's giving you a piece of what you left behind. You can have those things here too."

I sat in silence and considered his words. He was right. Remarkably so. None of these things held the same value to Rox, or Rava, or Caitlin. They were all things that were valuable to me. Yes, they cost money. Yes, it was tangible. But it *meant* something.

Thinking back to what he'd said they could all give me; I could see it more clearly. They were each trying in their own way. Dorian may have thought Ezra was just trying to make me a clan enforcer, but I could see his reasoning behind it now. I had a job in the Afterlife. A purpose. He was giving that to me because it would make me happy. If I stayed, he wanted me to do what I felt I was good at. It's what he had to offer me.

Roman could give me stability. A family. Something I had never known. Rox was already like a sister to me. If only Roman could just let go of his past, I could feel more like I was part of his pack.

And Dorian . . . I saw it now. It went beyond comfort. He was giving me the gift of security. In his own weird way, he was trying to give me a space to be myself. To be alone and to feel safe. To show me that if I stayed, I could still be who I was. I don't know that many would understand the gesture —could see beyond the monetary value—but it was powerful.

"Thank you," I breathed. "That means more to me than you know."

"I'm glad," he said quietly. After a few moments, he cleared his throat. "We have an hour before I have to drop you off at Roman's."

"Say no more," I said, getting up and scrolling through my new iPod library of treasures. Finding what I was looking for, I pressed play and Gershwin filtered through the speakers. I turned around and put my hands on my hips. "I'm going to get a drink, and you are going to dance with me."

He raised his brows in surprise. "Dance?"

I strolled to the credenza and opened a small door, pulling out a decanter and two glasses. Setting them on top, I looked into the mirror as I poured myself a drink. I held it up and offered him one. In the reflection, I watched as he declined. I shrugged, bringing the crystal to my lips, and tilting my head back for a big swallow.

"FURY!" Jules' voice screamed and her image appeared in front of me.

I inhaled in surprise, breathing in, and choking on whiskey. The heat of the liquor made my throat tighten as I coughed and spluttered, spewing it all over the mirror and the furniture.

"Fuck, Jules," I managed to say through a strained and hoarse voice, wiping my chin with the back of my hand and looking at the spilled drink down the front of my clothes. "Stop doing that."

"It's Lyra," she said in panic.

I snapped my head up, freezing at the urgency in her voice.

Dorian was beside me in an instant. "Where?" he asked darkly.

There was no time for introductions. I stared at Jules' wide eyes and my heart almost stopped when she spoke. "Roman's."

CHAPTER 25

I swayed on my feet, recovering faster from sifting with Dorian than I probably ever had before. Adrenaline can do that to you.

On the shifter compound, everything was utter chaos, and yet nothing like the attack on the summit. People weren't outright brawling, but instead *running*. I followed the direction they were coming from, and my heart stilled at the sight of lavender hair.

Rava.

"I need to find Lyra," Dorian said, scanning the area.

"Don't try to face the angel alone if he's with her," I said quietly.

After a short pause, Dorian nodded. I wasn't sure if he would truly honor that, but I didn't have time to get caught up in our trust issues right then.

I took off in the direction shifters were coming from. It seemed to center around the cabin I knew to be Caitlin's. The she-wolf and Roxanne stood at the front, attempting to hold their ground and discourage people from interfering while a tense-looking Rava hulked out.

I didn't have a better way to describe it when she grabbed the railing of her own house, ripped it clean off, and used it as a spear to throw at Rox—who narrowly missed being impaled.

Fuck.

"What happened?" I called out, approaching the scene.

"Don't know," Rox said. "She came home early from work and started destroying the compound and attacking anyone she saw."

As if irritated by their presence, Rava narrowed her glowing purple eyes, and turned to heave a rocking chair over her head. Roxanne tried to push in front of me and shield me from the throw, but I stood my ground—letting her aim straight for me before catching the chair in my right hand. It was an awkward angle and uncomfortable at best. I dropped it to the ground immediately and kicked it to the side with my foot.

While we weren't sure how much I could survive, I think she and the others often forgot that first and foremost, I was a demon. My strength trumps all.

"You," Rava said in a visceral growl. Claws grew from her nails, long and lethal as she partially shifted. "This is your fault."

I was on my guard and didn't let the surprise show on my face. It was obvious she was out of her right mind. While not as blank as some of the others Lyra had influenced, the flat rage that seemed to consume her was all too familiar.

"Mine?" I asked, pointing at myself. "Pray tell, what did I do this time?"

She let out an outraged shriek as she launched herself at me.

"Rava!" Caitlin screamed, torn between interfering and

not wanting to hurt her mate. It didn't escape my notice she already had blood on her and was limping.

"Get her out of here, Rox," I ground out, sidestepping the fae shifter.

"And leave you here with her—"

"Yes," I said in a hard voice. "You forget. I'm stronger than anything that walks this Earth, and I've been facing off demons for over a century. I can handle her." With that, I grasped the railing Rava had used as a spear and pulled it from where it was embedded in the ground.

It came free easily. Wielding it in one hand, I stared down my hybrid friend with grim determination.

"Don't kill her," Caitlin pleaded as Rox grabbed her around the waist and started hauling her away.

"I won't," I swore. That didn't mean I wouldn't hurt her. I didn't want to, but if she gave me no choice, I'd have to incapacitate her somehow.

"You are the cause," Rava hissed as she got to her feet once more. "The effect. The reason."

Her voice took on an eerie quality, making my skin prickle.

"For?" I prompted.

"*Everything.*"

A shudder snuck its way up my spine as she lunged again. Faster than me, but not enough to disarm. She closed the space between us and swung her leg in a powerful roundhouse kick. Rather than taking the hit, I flipped the railing vertical to intercept. Her shin smacked into the wood, and it instantly splintered.

I grimaced as the chunks of it littered the yard.

"You're really going to regret this when you come to," I muttered, swinging the section of wood I still had like a baseball bat. When she wheeled back around for another kick, I stepped into it, swinging the railing straight into her thigh.

It hit like a boom of thunder, cracking through the compound.

Rava let out a strangled sound, falling forward.

I dropped the wood, catching her shoulders.

She stiffened, pulling back her lips in a snarl as she peered up at me.

"Angelus venit," she uttered like a curse.

Her incisors lengthened. She surged forward, snapping her teeth at my neck.

If not for my hands on her shoulders, she would've taken a nice chunk out of me, but I pushed her away.

She stumbled back several feet. Cold resolve hardened in her expression.

"The angel is coming," I repeated back to her. While rusty, my Latin was passable and downright flawless compared to people from the modern age. I spent a lot of time learning other languages in the Afterlife. The language of the dead being one of them. It was fitting. "Where's Lyra?"

I didn't expect an answer out of her. Not really. But the flat voice she used to reply left me chilled to the core.

"Hunting."

She lurched forward, swiping a clawed hand through the air, aiming for my jugular. I ducked—taking a knee to my chest. The air left me as I slammed into the ground, wood chunks digging painfully into my back. Her booted foot came down on my chest, holding me there.

She leaned over to pick up the railing off the ground where I'd dropped it.

My heart stuttered in my chest.

Just past her, on the roof of another building, I caught

sight of a woman with flowing white hair. Lyra stood on the edge of the gable, deftly evading both Dorian and Roman.

Terror shot through me, because if Roman had the chance—he'd try to end her.

Rava lifting the rail over her head drew my attention back to my current predicament.

Sweat dotted her forehead as she looked down at me, the wood suspended above her, ready to pierce my chest any moment.

I grabbed her ankle, prepared to throw her off me the moment that railing moved. But the concentration in her brow made me hesitate.

"Rava," I said slowly. "It's not your fault. You can fight it."

"I—can't—ahh!" She gasped, the blank rage falling over her once more as she tried to slam it through my chest. I squeezed her ankle, crushing the bone beneath my fingers.

It cracked then popped, and I rolled sideways, throwing her leg outward.

The railing buried itself in the ground where my chest had been only a second before. Rava screamed in pain as she sprawled out beside me.

I crawled on top of her body, taking advantage of her disoriented state.

She looked up at me confused and yet conflicted, as if wavering in between the persuasion driving her and her own free will.

I gave her a sad smile. "I'm really sorry about this."

Then I slammed the side of my fist into the junction below her ear that connected her neck, skull, and jaw.

Pop.

The hit rattled through me as Rava lost consciousness.

I really hoped she woke free of Lyra's influence, but the

only way to guarantee that was to get her away from here. I glanced up at the roof where they were still battling—if you could call it that. Dorian was trying to reason with her while Roman was aiming killing blows.

She evaded them both, dancing on a willowy frame that was utterly ethereal.

Gritting my teeth, I stared at the spot I wanted to be.

My stomach flipped as I sifted on the spot—directly in front of Roman's outstretched claws.

On instinct I jumped back, dodging a blow that wasn't meant for me.

"Fury, no!" Dorian shouted. The last thing I saw were his golden eyes blown wide with fear.

Then a soft hand grabbed my shoulder. My stomach flipped. I knew it was Lyra.

I didn't have time to respond as she sifted us out.

The world went black.

CHAPTER 26

ROMAN

She sifted in front of me. I'd damn near hit her, and then she was gone.

Disappeared.

Taken.

By Lyra.

And I couldn't stop it.

My world started to spiral out of control. Not again. I couldn't lose another mate.

"Where the hell is she, Dorian?" I roared, demanding an answer I knew deep down he didn't have.

Dorian grabbed his head, gripping his hair through his hands as he bent at the waist and let out a scream filled with fear and rage so intense it rivaled my own emotion. "Fuuuuuuuuuuck!" The sound carried over the lake, disturbing the birds and causing them to fly off and leave their trees.

When he stood up, I could see that his eyes were glowing. His chest heaved as he took in short breaths in panic.

I clenched my fists, opening them and then tightening

them again, trying to get the monster inside me under control.

"Dorian. Where. Is. She?" I asked through gritted teeth.

"I don't know," he said in a loud whisper. "We aren't going to find her up here."

He sifted, appearing on the ground below us and walking toward Caitlin and Rava's cabin. I jumped down, landing with a fist and a knee on the soft earth.

Roxanne came running out of the house, her eyes wide with fear. She'd heard Dorian. Every soul on this lake heard him. Still, she asked the question. "Where's Fury?"

I shook my head, unable to say the words. Every fiber in my being wanted to break down. I wanted to destroy everything. Everyone. But my sister grabbed my face, staring deeply into my eyes, speaking to me softly. "Roman, tell me where she is."

"Lyra took her," Dorian said from behind her.

Roxanne spun around, her mouth falling open slightly. Rya came running out of the main house and anger coursed through my veins. *The witch.*

"Where were you?" I growled, storming toward her. "Where the fuck were you when Lyra was here? Where were you while we fought her? Where were you when she sifted and took Fury with her?" Each question, my voice grew louder, echoing in the surrounding trees.

The witch straightened her shoulders and crossed her arms, unmoving. With narrowed eyes, she said coolly, "I don't answer to you, shifter."

Roxanne jumped in front of me, slamming her hands into my chest. "Stop it, Roman. Your fight isn't with her."

My sister's strength matched my own. She was my equal in that, and not many knew it. They all assumed I had the power, but the truth of it was she did too, with the exception of immortality. She was a better leader. More level-headed, more compassionate, less temperamental. She should have been my second, but it wasn't something she ever wanted.

She shoved me back, my foot sliding in the dirt as she pushed me. The rage I felt vibrated in my chest as I stared Roxanne down. "*No,* brother," she said, a stern and forceful tone taking over.

"Rya came with me," a voice called out. "I brought her here." My gaze shifted to Tristan. He came out of the house, pulling a sword, daring to challenge me on my own land. He didn't stand a chance. My wolf was breaking through. Fur erupted, covering my skin, my body shook, my bones popping and changing—

Crack.

Roxanne's fist made contact with my jaw, breaking it. My head swung around, pain radiating through my face, healing what was broken and damaged as quickly as it had happened.

"Get him under control, Roman," she yelled. "Do it for me."

Dorian held his hand up, calling to his second. "Stand down, Tristan."

"Caitlin is asleep. I cast a spell to calm her. Her mate was under Lyra's influence, and she was losing control. I can see that's common around here," Rya said, looking at her nails.

"Enough," a weak voice said, breaking through the chaos.

We all turned to see Rava, sitting up in a crouched position, her elbows resting on her knees as she held her head.

Rya strode past all of us, coming to her side, but at that moment, Roxanne grabbed my shoulders. "Look at me," she whispered. "I want my brother back. Get your-self together. Fight it. Whatever is taking over right now will not help Fury. It won't. *You* are the alpha, not the wolf."

My partial shift rescinded, the fur disappearing. I reached up and held her wrists that pressed against my upper body, closing my eyes. I exhaled through my nose harshly and nodded. When I opened them, she searched my features, seeking my wolf. When she didn't see him, she let go, walking past me to get to Rava.

I met Tristan's gaze, dipping my chin, and he sheathed his sword.

I cursed myself for what I'd almost done. Rya. Tristan. I was going to kill them, and anyone that got in my way. This wasn't their fault.

We surrounded Rava while the witch tended to her, placing her glowing hands over her head and her ankle. When the light faded, she stopped.

"I'm not the healer my sister is, but that should do it," Rya told her. "You've healed quite a bit on your own already."

"What happened?" Roxanne said, kneeling beside her.

Dropping her knees, she crisscrossed her legs, then looked up to Dorian. "Lyra happened." She suddenly real-ized one of us was missing as she searched behind us. "Did she . . ." Rava started, trailing off.

Roxanne nodded softly. "Yeah. She took Fury."

"I need you to tell me what you know," Dorian said to her, but my sister looked up to him.

"How are you in control right now?" Rox asked him, narrowing her eyes and searching his body language for signs. "Roman is about to lose control to a part of him that no one wants to see. I heard your scream. We all did."

He crossed his arms. "Lyra won't kill her. That's the only thing I know for sure right now."

"How do you know that?" I asked him.

He sighed. "Because Lyra likes to play games. If she wanted Fury dead, she would've tried to kill her. She had the opportunity when Fury sifted between you and Lyra, but she didn't take it. She used Rava as bait to bring us all here. She wants her alive."

"I want to find comfort in that, but forgive me if I don't share your assessment," I muttered.

"I think he's right," Rava said, putting herself back in the conversation. I raised my eyebrows to her in question, urging her to go on. "Lyra came to me at the clinic."

"She what?" Dorian's voice was soft. Confused.

Rava shifted on the ground, throwing her arm out for someone to help her up. I caught it, pulling her to her feet. She leaned over, dusting herself off before standing upright. "I had a new patient appointment today. Claimed she was a shifter-fae hybrid. Took me all of two seconds to figure out who she was, though I can't say she was hiding it much. She just needed to get close to me, and that was the easiest way to do it."

"Why not just sift and take you just like she did Fury?" Roxanne asked.

"That's not how the game is played," Rya answered. "Just taking Rava away isn't enough of a mind fuck."

"Bingo," Rava said, pointing at the witch.

"What did she say? I need to know everything," Dorian said.

She blew out a harsh breath. "I called her out on not being a hybrid. I figured I knew who she was. Rya and I have been working on figuring out Fury's situation, and she's also filled in the blanks about Lyra, so it was pretty obvious when the patient lifted her cloak and I saw her hair and eyes. The murderous grin was a big hint too." She ran her hands down her face. "I called her by name. I asked her what she wanted. She teetered between laughter and tears. There's a weird internal struggle there. It was hard to read." She looked at Dorian with sad eyes, but he remained unresponsive and unfeeling.

Roxanne put her hand on his arm and motioned for Rava to continue.

"She told me she wanted to play a game, and I said I would. I thought I could get some answers from her. I got some, but none of it made sense. She said some things in Latin I don't know. I think it was Latin. I can't remember what words they were. She said 'his voice. It plagues me.'"

His voice. I made a mental note, knowing Dorian was doing the same. My wolf stirred violently, furious and on edge with each passing moment.

"Lyra said the light was blinding, then she started laughing. It was madness. High-pitched and, well, crazy, for lack of a better word. It sent chills over my entire body. Then she disappeared."

"That's it?" I asked. Rava had lost her mind and attacked people, destroying everything in her path. There had to be more.

She shook her head. "No," she whispered. "I felt a gentle touch on my temple, and then I heard her in my head. She took control. Told me what to do." Her eyes welled up, tears sitting on the edge waiting to spill over. "I tried to fight her off."

Roxanne wrapped her arms around Rava, comforting her and soothing her worry. "This isn't your fault."

I looked away. Rox was right, but it didn't stop me from putting blame on Rava. She should've known better. She shouldn't have taken on Lyra by herself. She shouldn't have tried to talk to her. She should have called . . . should have . . .

I sighed, releasing some of the tension in my shoulders. Should have *what*? I asked myself. What could Rava have possibly done? Run away? Pretended she didn't know who Lyra was? Tried to stop her? None of it mattered. Lyra had a plan, and whether or not Rava called her out on it, she was going to manipulate and control her. She was going to use her. That was her purpose in going to the clinic. There wasn't a damn thing Rava could have done. I knew that, even if my baser instinct wanted to blame her, it wasn't her fault. My sister was right, even if my wolf didn't agree.

I met Rava's gaze, and her eyes were filled with guilt. She questioned if her alpha placed that weight on her shoulders too. "Roman?" she asked, her voice trembling.

"This isn't on you, Rava. Lyra is . . ." I trailed off, thinking of what I could say that would relieve her of the burden she was feeling. "Lyra is more powerful than any of us. I don't blame you for any of this."

She closed her eyes, letting the tears fall while Roxanne stroked her head.

"What did she say in your head?" Dorian asked.

Rava let go, removing herself from the embrace as she wiped her eyes and cleared her throat. "She blamed Fury for everything. She said she was the reason this was all happening. Her words came out of my mouth when I faced off with Fury, but they didn't make sense. Lyra was so angry. I've never felt a rage that strong, and it took over. I had no control of my actions, but I fought it as best I could. I almost came through, but her strength . . . the hold she had over me was too much. She was hunting, but I didn't know what for. She said the angel was coming, and then Fury knocked me out."

Dorian paced, scrubbing his hands down his face. When he stopped, he looked to Rya. "I know she has the talisman but try again. Just to see if you can find her. Try both of them. Rox, take her to Fury's room. She's going to need something Fury has touched. Clothes, a hairbrush, anything." They both nodded, turning on a heel and rushing into the house.

My arms stayed crossed, and I stared at the ground, my chin pressing into my chest. A thought occurred to me, and my head snapped up. "Does anyone know how to reach Bloody Mary?"

Dorian pointed at me in agreement. "Not the way Fury calls her, but there's the legend-way, right?" he asked.

"Yeah, saying the name thirteen times in front of a mirror or something like that."

"Tristan," he said, facing his second. "Look it up. Find out the way people normally do it. Her real name is Jules. Try to contact her. You're a friend of Fury's. She should help."

Tristan gave a single dip of his head and sifted.

"Where's Ezra?" I asked. I needed some good news. Anything to placate the storm flaring inside me. To calm the wolf's desire for blood and revenge, even if only a little.

"Right here," he said from behind me.

I turned, seeing him and James, Dorian's butler.

"Tell me you have something," I said, the desperation in my voice leaking through.

Ezra's eyes were haunted as he confirmed my fear. "I can't reach her. I can't make a connection to figure out where she is. She's blocked, or asleep, or . . ." he trailed off.

"Don't finish that sentence," I growled, red clouding my vision.

I couldn't take it. I couldn't bear the thought of it. I stormed off, ignoring them as they called for me. I heard Dorian tell him to let me go. It was in their best interests to leave me.

My feet pounded the forest floor, pine needles crunching and twigs snapping while I headed to nowhere.

The fear ate at my insides, tearing apart the little of me that was left. The nightmares were real. Foreshadowing what was to come. Fury being taken away. Of my failure. Of losing my mate. All of it rippled through me. I wasn't worthy of all that I'd been given. Earned. What I was born into. None of it. If I couldn't protect my mate.

I stopped, looking at my axe embedded in the thick trunk when I chopped wood.

Memories came flooding back to me.

I turned, seeing the tree where we'd been not that long ago. Where I'd claimed her as mine, marking her neck, thrusting into her with her back pressed into the rough bark.

Where I realized Maya was gone, not forgotten, and Fury had taken her place.

Where I somehow said Maya's name out loud while I was accepting the past and embracing the future.

Where I made Fury think she wasn't what I wanted . . . that she was second place and always would be . . . that I didn't love her . . .

That was the last thing she felt from me.

My body vibrated in a partial shift as I tried to contain it. Push it down. Not let him take over.

I clenched my teeth, stomping toward the tree, pulled my fist back, and smashed it into the trunk. I screamed, letting all my emotion come out in a feral roar as I hit it again and again.

The wood split, creaking as it tipped. I threw a punch into it once more, sending it over. The tree slammed to the soft earth, sending dirt and debris flying up in a cloud. A ferocious resounding crack went through the forest, mirroring the emotional turmoil that raged inside me.

CHAPTER 27

Cold was the first thing that registered.

Being shoved to the ground, the second.

I took a quick glance at my surroundings, surprised to find myself standing on the cliffs of Avalon again. The castle where I'd spent the last five days learning to sift was right behind me, but instead of Dorian for company, I was stuck with Lyra.

"Why are we here?" I asked, rolling to the side, and coming back up in a crouch.

I expected her to be positioning herself to strike. Perhaps preparing to toy with me. She'd been on the hunt after all, according to Rava.

Instead she hissed, looking away. "Capture Fury," she said in a lilting voice. "Play with Fury. Hunt Fury—but never kill."

Her neck twisted in a strange motion that wasn't natural.

"Why not kill?" I asked, seeing if I could penetrate the madness clearly eating at her.

Lyra lifted her head, eyes focused on me with more

clarity than I thought she possessed. "Because then the angel would get mad, and bad things happen when I make him mad." She dropped her chin and started pacing. The billowy white dress flowed around her, sleeveless and light. It certainly wasn't enough to fight the chill, not that she seemed to notice.

"Why are we here, Lyra?" I asked again, hoping she might give me more.

"This is my home," she whispered. Lifting her chin, she looked out over the cliffs, her eyes beautifully and horribly sad. "But the angel's my home," she added, slipping back into her insanity. "The light. Look into the light . . ."

My chest constricted.

Look into the light.

Dorian's brief explanation of his daughter's descent into madness whispered in my mind. I had a horrible, awful feeling about what happened to her that might've caused her to change. To become what she was.

"Did the angel kill your mom, Lyra?" I asked, slowly standing up. I didn't wander closer, careful to avoid setting off her fight-or-flight response.

Her eyebrows furrowed together. She trembled.

"Mother," she whispered in Gaelic, a language I'd briefly studied and only knew enough for small talk. "Look into the light," she repeated in a shaky voice. Her features smoothed as if the phrase settled something within her.

I recognized the response for what it was.

Conditioning.

"What did he do to you?" I said, unable to help myself.

Her chin turned, and she regarded me with furious eyes.

"He saved me," she said, in a hauntingly eerie voice that was childlike and yet not. "Took away the pain. No"—she frowned at herself, hands curling and uncurling like a cat pawing at its tail—"he was the pain. He . . ." she trailed off as she struggled with words.

"Did he punish you for seeing him?" I asked her. "Did he tell you to look into the light?"

I wanted to go to her. To help. To piece together the shattered remnants of her mind and find out what truly happened to her—by who, and why.

But whoever this angel was, he clearly did a number.

"It's your fault," Lyra said without looking at me. "I slept. I was asleep, peacefully and blissfully asleep, and he woke me—*for you*. To play with *you*." Her head turned without her body moving an inch. "I'm his doll. A marionette. A puppet for him to play with . . . but you're mine."

Lyra sifted and the hairs on my arms stood on end.

"He won't let me go because of you," she said from behind me. I whipped around, but she was already gone.

"You're wrong," I called out. "It's not because of me."

She reappeared a few feet away and then sifted right in front of me, inches from my face. "Why?" she asked, her white eyebrows drawn together in concentration. "Why?" she repeated. "Why? Why? *Why?*" she said, raising her voice with each punctuation.

"Because he's a sick fuck that's hiding behind you—just like he hid behind the supes who died when they kidnapped me the night he woke you."

She blinked, like she was struggling to process what I'd just told her.

"Died," she murmured.

"Yeah. That's what happens to people he uses."

A cold wind whipped over the cliffs. That wasn't strange for Avalon by any means, but the chilling laugh that followed froze me more than the Isle of Glass ever could.

"*Lyra*," a charismatic voice said.

I stared up into the sky where a pair of ink black wings blotted out what little of the sun there was. He wore a cloak that flapped in the wind around him while keeping his face obscured in shadows.

"Finally," I huffed. "Why are you here? What have I ever done to you for you to fuck with my life like this? Not to mention the mission—"

A hand locked around my throat, squeezing.

Lyra had moved when I looked away. That was my mistake; forgetting she was still a very real threat even if she wasn't the one pulling the strings.

"We don't talk to him like that," she said as if she were scolding a child. "Ask for forgiveness."

"Over my dead body," I uttered hoarsely.

Her head tilted to the side. "You're a difficult one." Almost unbothered, she added, "No matter. There are other ways to make you behave."

Her hand tightened, threatening to crush my windpipe.

I struck out, slamming the side of my closed fist into her elbow. She hissed in pain, loosening her grip enough that I could sift away.

I reappeared on the castle roof. Swallowing hard, I thought of the knife I knew to be sitting on Dorian's nightstand and I sifted it to me. It appeared in front of my face, and I caught it.

The wind blew harder, making it more difficult to keep my balance at an elevated position on the battlement. I'd chosen the spot closer to danger—closer to the angel— hoping I could have the element of surprise. Or at least get in a good throw before he retaliated.

If I could get the angel out of the air, I knew I could take him. Getting him out of the air, that was another matter.

"Hey fuckface," I called over the wind. Both Lyra and the angel turned to me at once.

I threw the knife, aiming for a wing instead of his body.

He swerved midair trying to dodge my throw, and the knife nicked the edge of his hood.

Fabric tore right as another body barreled into mine. Lyra crashed into me and sifted us back down to the cliff. I pushed her off me just long enough to get to my feet, but she kept coming.

A rabid savageness seeming to consume her.

"We—" She slashed.

"Don't—" I ducked.

"Hurt—" She brought her knee up.

"The—" I used my forearm to stop it, punching her stomach.

"Angel," she growled in pain.

"He's controlling you," I said over the roar of waves crashing into the rocks below us. "Using you. He has you brainwashed—"

"It's no use," the angel called out, making the hairs on my neck stand on end because I'd heard that charismatic voice before. "Lyra's mine. My puppet. My pet. Her only desire is to please me."

I don't know how I didn't notice it the first time he spoke, but with every word he uttered now, it was a battle ram to the iron bars I'd kept around the bad dreams threatening to suffocate me. A key opening a lock on a safe I long since sealed shut, trying so desperately to never open it again.

I stopped without a single regard for the woman before me and stared at the figure in the sky.

The face that looked back at me was my worst nightmare. My greatest tormentor.

It was my ex-husband.

"That's impossible," I said. "I killed you. I—"

"You're as ill-mannered as you were in life, but far less breakable now." His lapis-colored eyes travelled my sweater-clad body, hungrily devouring it with a mere look.

My stomach twisted. Bile rose in my throat. I'd rather drown in the ocean than watch this.

It appeared I might get my wish.

"Punish her, Lyra. Be my good girl."

I didn't see it coming, but I could honestly say I wouldn't have stopped it if I had.

I was utterly and completely frozen in my spot as her bare foot came up and slammed into my chest.

The air left my lungs.

I went sailing through the air . . . but I never landed.

The angel's cruel, smiling face disappeared over the edge of the cliff, and only then did I realize I was falling.

CHAPTER 28

Down.
    Down.
Down.

My heart thumped rapidly against my ribs as my inevitable end loomed near.

Who would've thought I'd be Sparta-kicked off a cliff?

Not me. At least it was far more dramatic than being bit by a rogue shifter. Not that I wanted to die. Just the opposite in fact. I'd only just learned how to live. Learned that I *could*.

And now, somehow, a monster from my past was back to haunt me.

Or end me, it would seem.

Black feathers appeared in my periphery. I flinched away, assuming it to be the angel—but the squawk of protest and talons that gripped my arm were anything but.

"Sift, Fury! SIFT," Hades yelled. "You lazy, good-for-nothing demon!"

His talons split the skin on my forearm as he tried and failed to pull me up.

The idea was endearing, really, and it didn't even hurt with all the adrenaline coursing through me. Then again, the pain wouldn't catch up. Not where I was headed.

The sound of the roaring waves grew louder in the space between one heartbeat and the next. I knew with some kind of certainty this would be it.

Death.

The apocalypse.

The end of everything.

Because my fucking ex.

Anger coursed through me. A fury, one might say if they were so inclined. It was the sort of anger that drove a woman to murder—or to changing her name to Fury.

It was a shade of red so vibrant and deep, your transgressions could never be wiped clean.

I was so pissed that I didn't realize I should have died already.

The fall wasn't that long.

I twisted midair and Hades' claws grabbed me again, only this time it worked.

My descent had slowed, and instead of crashing into the wicked-looking rocks below, I was being pulled away from them.

I turned my head, trying to grasp what was going on. Why there were white feathers everywhere—

"You need to lay off the beer and cheese fries," pigeon grumbled as he hefted me up and over the edge of a rock and dropped me unceremoniously. "Better yet, don't let yourself get kicked off a cliff."

I opened my mouth to snap back with something snarky and completely rude given he'd just saved my ass— but when I lifted my arm to get up, a white *wing* appeared.

What the actual fuck.

"Hades . . ." I said his name, but it didn't come out like I expected. A sort of growled croak sounded around me instead, echoing back. "What am I?"

"Not a wolf, that's for sure."

Blood rushed to my head. A sudden exhaustion hit that weighed me down. I just managed to angle away from the ocean spray that was misting around me when the darkness closed in.

And in the black abyss of my mind, the nightmares came.

CHAPTER 29

EZRA

I heard a tree crash in the distance. Roman was losing it. I listened in on his thoughts every now and then, checking to see when he'd explode. None of them knew just how close he was to the edge of insanity.

I'd learned quite a bit about him and Fury and what they'd shared. I'd learned his part of it. She had no idea what the truth was. If I'd made her feel that way . . . if that was our last encounter before this, I can't say I'd be much different from him.

He'd be back soon, though not even he knew why he was returning.

Dorian paced by the windows, quiet and stewing in frustration. This was out of his control, and for a fae alpha like Dorian, that wouldn't do. He managed to keep relatively calm, and I didn't know how or why. If only I could have read him.

Rya and Roxanne came up empty-handed in their task. It was a stretch, and we all knew it, but we still hoped she'd find a tendril of Fury to latch on to. They sat on the couch. Rya rested, exhausted from multiple attempts to locate her.

She wouldn't give up. Roxanne stared at the floor, chewing her thumbnail, deep in thought.

Tristan had called the poltergeist, successfully summoning her. She had nothing, but she was searching. Every few moments I glanced at a mirror hanging on the wall by the stairs, waiting to see if she had returned with news. It was futile. She'd speak if she arrived, but it didn't stop me. I needed something to do.

I kept feeling for that connection. Reaching desperately for that tendril that linked my mind with Fury's. Anything to tell me where she was. Something. But I couldn't feel her. I couldn't hear her. I could read the mind of almost anyone, but something felt different with her. My mate. And that feeling was gone. It absolutely terrified me.

We were on the verge of cracking. The clock ticked and tocked, each moment that passed sent a spike of anxiety through me.

The door slammed open, Roman quietly seething and stomping through the house until he made it to the kitchen. He took a bottle of water, then returned, sitting in his chair and draining the water. His eyes looked like the blue of an iceberg, and just as dangerous as one.

Another tick.

Another tock.

Another glance at the empty mirror.

Another reach for that lost tether, finding nothing but silence.

A loud caw echoed over the lake, and each of us snapped our heads up.

"Hades," Roxanne shouted, jumping off the couch. "Open the door, the window, open it." Her scrambled words came out at a furious speed while Dorian wrenched the sliding door to let the crow fly into the room.

All of us were on our feet, looking at the bird as he landed on the back of a chair.

"Where's Fury?"

"Is she okay?"

"Is she hurt?"

"Where's Lyra?"

Everyone started shouting questions to him at the same time, myself included. Rava stuck her fingers in her mouth, letting out an ear-piercing whistle no shifter had the right to make. We all grabbed our ears as the sound ripped through us.

"Thank you," Hades said when the sound died down, dipping his head to her. "Fury's alive. She's shifted. Needs your help. Let's go."

"Where is she?" Dorian and I asked in unison.

"Avalon," he answered.

Adrenaline pumped through me. Alive. Shifted. But alive.

"You left her on Avalon with Lyra?" Roman growled, taking a step forward. "You left her to die?"

Hades flapped his wings, preparing to take flight if Roman attacked him. "Ease up, shifter. First of all, Lyra left. The angel showed up and 'poof' they disappeared. Second, what was it that you wanted me to do if Lyra was still there? I'm a *bird*. Want me to claw her eyes out? Pretty sure if you, the vampire, and Fury couldn't take her down, I'm shit out of luck in a one-on-one with señorita psycho. I came to get you three. That's what I should be doing, and I did it, and you're bloody welcome for it."

"So let's go," I said, looking at Dorian and Roman.

"I'm going too," Rava and Roxanne said.

Roman turned to them. "No. Stay here. That's an order." His eyes flashed. An alpha command. I'd not seen him speak to his sister that way. A crease formed between her brows, incensed he was holding that position over her. I had a feeling she could defy him if she wanted to, and I couldn't sense a lick of fear, but she didn't fight it. I listened in for a brief moment. She was doing it for Fury. No one else. She wanted her safe, and the sooner that happened, the better.

I wanted them to hurry the fuck up so we could get to my mate.

Rava surprised me, stepping forward, addressing Roman with both confidence and caution. "With all due respect, I can help. She's shifted. She's scared. This is what I do, alpha. I can help her through this. We all can."

Rava's thoughts were screaming for me to listen. She still felt somewhat responsible. A measure of guilt. But she knew Roman may be too emotional to help Fury shift. I couldn't, and neither could Dorian. If Roman didn't succeed, Rava would be there.

I took a risk, stepping in when I truly had no right to. I'd be pissed if someone stepped in and tried to make a decision for my clan. But this involved Fury. It was different. And I just wanted to go. "Bring her, Roman. She's earned it."

He turned his head slightly, glaring at me over his shoulder from the corner of his eye. He grunted, giving her permission.

"To Avalon," he said.

Dorian put his hand on Roman's shoulder, and Rava held her arm out for Hades to land on her. She reached her open palm to me, and I took it.

I felt like the ground was pulled out from under me, but then dropped from above, landing on the cold, hard earth.

A brutal wind cut through my thin T-shirt, freezing my

skin. My teeth clattered together, and I crossed my arms, rubbing them for friction and warmth. "Well, this is a fucking nightmare," I said. "No wonder Dorian lives here."

He ignored my comment, staring at the castle. "She's not in the castle. I can sense her, but I don't know where," he growled, looking at me for answers.

"I haven't felt a connection yet. I can't find her," I said through chattering teeth.

Hades cawed, hovering over the edge of the cliff.

My heart dropped into the pit of my stomach. I think it did for all of us. We darted toward the edge, dropping to our hands and knees to peer over the edge, fearing what we'd see.

But we saw nothing. The face of the steep cliff led down to a rocky base where explosive waves collided with the stone. And we saw nothing.

No wolf.

No body.

No Fury.

"Where is she?" Roman called over the wind.

I pointed to Hades as he flew down the cliffside, taking a sharp turn and entering what had to be a cave.

"You've got to be kidding me," Rava groaned.

I turned to her. "What's the problem? Just sift us there."

"It's not that simple," Dorian answered. "We don't know where we're sifting. We haven't seen the location. We don't know what to visualize. We could sift into the rock," he explained, speaking loudly so we could hear him over the water crashing below us.

"*Into* the rock?" I repeated. "As in, we'd get stuck inside the rock for however long until we could break out or just live encased in it for fucking eternity?"

"Yes, that, except Rava would die since she's not like us," Dorian answered.

Roman's body trembled, and I doubted it was the cold.

Rava cursed, pinching the bridge of her nose, walking away from the cliff, further inland.

Dorian ran to her and grabbed Rava's shoulders. "I have an idea. You won't like it."

"Well, we're already on a winning streak with things I don't like, so no need to stop now."

"I need you to think of sifting to Fury. Not her location," he said, squinting his eyes, wondering if she understood what he was asking of her.

"That won't work." She shook her head when he tried to argue with her. "No, it won't. Listen to me. She's shifted. It's not her body. It's her wolf, and we don't know what her wolf looks like. We can't imagine shifting to her because if I think of her hand, it's not her hand. It's her paw. We don't even know the color of her fur."

I saw what he was getting at, which said a lot considering I knew nothing of sifting, but her point was valid. None of us knew what she looked like. Only Hades.

Hades.

"Sift to Hades," I blurted out.

"Holy shit," Roman said, his eyes getting wide, turning to Rava. "What he said. Do that."

"How do you know it'll work?" she asked Dorian, worry and doubt filling her voice.

"It's something Fury can do," he said. "It's how she started to sift. Thinking about objects and about what she wanted to be *next to*, rather than where she wanted to be. You're both hybrids. I believe you can do it too."

She frowned. "Maybe . . ."

I heard her fear. What if she screwed up? What if she failed? Fury needed us. What if she wasn't enough?

This shifter needed to get in line with those thoughts. We had the same things running through our heads. We were in good company.

Dorian put his hands on her shoulders and turned her around, facing away from us. He gestured for me to keep walking in the opposite direction, so I did. Leaning to her ear, he said, "Close your eyes. Picture Ezra. You don't know him as well as Roman, so choose him. Picture his black hair. Think about the tattoos on his arms. Visualize his green eyes. Picture him. He is your location." He paused, waiting several moments until she took a shaky breath and nodded quickly. "Now, sift."

She disappeared, and I slowed my steps, then she reappeared right in front of me. She peeked one eye open and saw me, realizing I had moved from the spot she'd last seen me. She shouted a brief whoop of excitement and relief. I didn't quite share the same enthusiasm, but I wanted to get to my mate.

"Do it again," he said. "Focus on Hades."

She blew her cheeks out. "Okay. Okay," she said, psyching herself up. She grabbed my hand, and Roman rested his on Dorian's shoulders.

God, I hope I don't fuck this up and end up in a rock, Rava thought so loudly I didn't need to listen in to hear her.

"What?" I said, and my eyes shot open right as the ground was pulled out from under me.

CHAPTER 30

I opened my eyes, blinking several times and wincing at the pounding in my head.

Ugh. What happened?

I didn't know where I was. I needed to get my bearings, but my body protested, feeling lighter and weak all over.

My vision started to clear, and I could see things with an unusual clarity. Images were sharper. Focused. I was in a cave, I thought. I laid there, staring at the minute detail of the stone walls. The veining in the rock. The condensation dripping down the sides.

I lifted my hand to my face . . . and saw feathers. Bold, white feathers.

This isn't real. This can't be real.

Flashes of falling and seeing a white wing entered my mind.

I tried to sit, but tiling my head forward only allowed me to see small, black stick-like legs. Legs with three pointed toes. And claws.

There's really only one appropriate thing you can do when you see that instead of your own feet.

So that's what I did.

I screamed.

Except it came out in a loud honking squawk.

"That's the worst raven call I've ever heard," Hades said, laughing and snorting through his beak. The wheezing kazoo sound filled the cave. I turned and saw him standing nearby.

"I'm a *what*?" I said in panic. No, no, no, no, no, no. This wasn't happening.

"You're a raven," he chortled. "Oh my god . . . this is pure gold. It's everything I could have ever wanted. You're a *bird*." He dragged out the last word, losing the final enunciation to a fit of laughter. He tipped over, falling on his side. His wings flapped around while he got his entertainment at my expense.

"How am I a raven? What happened? How did it happen?" I blurted.

"Well, it happened when Lyra kicked you in the chest, right off the side of a cliff," he explained, getting himself up and finding a boulder to stand on. He kicked out a leg, making a 'hiyah' sound. "Then this was you, except with arms." He flailed his wings and yelled, looking like a right idiot. "You were screaming, 'save me, save me!' Then I came, you're welcome by the way, and I told you to sift." He puffed his body out quickly, looking like he swallowed a balloon, sending small feathers flying out. "And imagine my surprise when you shifted instead, and into a white raven no less."

Fractured memories came back to me. The Sparta-kick. Falling. Hades showing up. I was supposed to be a wolf.

Right? I was a part shifter. Part wolf. But . . . I wasn't. I was a damned bird.

"A white raven," he said quietly, chuckling. "Talk about getting the fuzzy end of a lollipop. Your camouflage sucks."

A spike of anger ran through me.

"I'm going to wring your neck," I shouted, thrashing around, and flipping my body over upright. I wobbled at first, unsure about my center of balance.

"Gonna need hands for that, pigeon," he mocked, moving to a standing position, and flying up to sit on a rock. "You'll need to shift back for that."

I took a few steps, feeling far braver than I had any right to. "Ravens are bigger than crows," I reminded him. "When I catch you—"

"Fly up, then," he said. "C'mon. I'm right here."

"I . . . I . . ." My voice trailed off. I *what*? I had nothing. I didn't know what to do. I wasn't even mad at Hades, though him laughing at me didn't help things. In a way, I probably deserved it. I was woman enough to admit it. I was now a bird. Out of my element. In a cave, and I didn't really recall all of what had happened. I sighed, letting all the bravado melt away. "I need help," I finished.

"I know," he said. "I went to get your mates." He looked at the cave entrance. "Not sure what is taking them so long. They're up on the cliff right now."

"Thank you," I whispered. "For helping me not die. And for getting the guys."

"I'm sorry, what was that? I couldn't hear you," Hades said, lifting a wing to the side of his head where his ears would be if I could see them. "Waves are loud out there, crashing on the rocks."

I glared at him. "I said, thank you," I grumbled. "You don't have to rub it in right now."

"You're welcome, and I most certainly do have to rub it in. Don't tell me you wouldn't do the same. You're many things, but a liar isn't one of them."

"Fine," I admitted. "I'd one hundred percent be giving you shit."

At that moment, Ezra and Rava landed on the cave floor in a heaping pile. Dorian and Roman appeared, landing on a boulder, and tumbling off, grunting as they hit the ground.

Rava rolled off Ezra and looked around. A huge smile graced her face, and she whooped, slapping her palms on the ground. "I did it!"

Did what, I wasn't sure, but I'd never been so happy to see all of them.

Roman and Dorian pushed themselves up, wiping off their clothes; Ezra and Rava did the same.

"Where is she?" Dorian said to Hades. "You said she was here."

"I'm right here," I said. But no one paid any attention to me.

Hades turned his gaze from the group and looked directly at me. "She's right there. Look down," he said, gesturing with his wing. Then he laughed again, snorting.

I narrowed my eyes at him, then turned my attention back to the guys. "I don't know how to shift back," I told them.

But they stared at me. They didn't answer me. They just said nothing.

Ezra blinked repeatedly. "I can't hear her thoughts."

Roman's mouth gaped open slightly, and Rava hid a small smile behind her hand. "She's beautiful," she breathed. "I've never seen a white raven before."

"How . . ." Dorian started, but he didn't finish his thought.

"Can we talk about this later?" I asked. "I'm a bird. I'd like to be a person again."

"They can't hear you," Hades told me.

"She's talking?" Roman asked, surprise lighting up his face. "Nothing is coming through. Why can't I hear her?" There was a panic in his tone that wasn't at all comforting.

"Because she's not a wolf," Rava answered. "That's the best guess I have. But Hades seems to understand her just fine. Can you understand us, Fury?"

Disappointment was an understatement.

This is so humiliating, Hades.

I really had no way to respond. So what did I do? I bobbed my head.

And I squawked, wincing at the terrible sound I made.

"Or incredibly entertaining, depending on your perspective. Don't worry. We'll work on your caws and croak. That sound you make is horrific," Hades said to me before looking at the others. "And yes, she can understand you. She doesn't know how to shift back. She'll need your help, Rava. Roman looks unwell. I don't shift, so I can't talk her through this."

I huffed in annoyance.

What had happened? I couldn't sift right. I'd just turned into a bloody raven. What next? I needed to drink harpy blood to survive? Or maybe some terribly endangered, hard-to-find rainforest critter the size of a shrew. That'd be my luck.

What a clusterfuck.

Rava kneeled in front of me, inspecting my bird form. "Hey, Fury," she said, smiling warmly at me. I lifted a wing in an awkward bird-wave. "I need to walk you through this, but I've never been a bird, so I assume this is all going to be the same basic mechanics of shifting."

I tapped my feet a little bit, trying to let her know I was listening and ready to go.

"Okay," she breathed. "How did you shift when you turned into a raven?" She looked at Hades, waiting for him to relay my answer.

"She says she doesn't know. She was falling off a cliff, and she was angry she was about to die," Hades said.

Rava frowned, twisting her lips in thought while I patiently—not really—waited for her to tell me what to do.

She exhaled loudly, then looked at me again. "I need you to visualize being your human form again. Demon-hybrid form. However you view and define yourself, I need you to focus on that. Remind yourself that you're safe right now."

Visualize . . . myself. How did I define myself?

That was a great question, really, and that would've been better to understand and work on *before* I had shifted into a bird. Now didn't feel like the best time for a therapy session on self-discovery. I didn't know what the hell I was.

But apparently I needed to call it something right now.

Demon. I'd been one longer than anything else. Now I was a hybrid too, but I didn't know how to relate to my hybrid self at all. I was just starting to figure it out. I sighed.

"Stop overthinking this," Hades interrupted. "You're Fury. *The* Fury. Start acting like it."

How the hell did he know what I was thinking, anyway? I snapped my beak at him. "Shut up," I said.

But he was right. Once a human, then a demon, now a hybrid. I was still Fury. I pictured myself. That was it.

I nodded my head to Rava.

"You need to tell your body and mind to become that form again," she said.

Okay.

Shift.

I am Fury.

Shift into Fury.

Shift.

Nothing happened.

"She looks constipated," Hades said, laughing loudly again.

"Could you stop being an asshole for one minute? I am trying to concentrate!" I shouted at him. He shook his head, chuckling and making a high-pitched wheezing through his beak.

I closed my eyes, taking a deep breath.

Fury. I am Fury. I have red hair. Great tits. I'm *THE* Fury. I am the best demon the Afterlife has ever seen.

One, two, three, SHIFT.

Nothing.

Nooooow. . . SHIFT.

Crickets.

SHIFT, DAMN IT.

. . .

I flapped my wings in frustration.

Roman growled in frustration. "What's wrong?" he asked Rava, then looked at Ezra. "Why isn't she shifting?"

Ezra shrugged his shoulders. "I have no idea."

"I'm not sure," Rava whispered. "It's hard not being able to properly coax her through it while she struggles on the emotional side of it."

"Oh my god, I'm going to be a bird forever," I moaned, throwing my head back and letting out an incredibly pitiful sound.

"Stop bitching," Hades chastised.

I turned my head sharply in his direction. "Easy for you to say," I said, feeling my frustration rise. "You have no idea what I am going through. You're always a bird."

"I am. And if you don't get your shit together, you will be too," he retorted.

"NOT helping," I yelled at him.

Rava and my mates stopped making suggestions and stared at us while we had a conversation, and they only got one side of it.

"Ease up," Dorian said to him. "She's clearly struggling—"

"No," Hades snapped at him. "She's being a pussy. And she's whining."

Roman growled, baring his teeth, but Ezra put a hand over his chest.

"I'm trying, you stupid—" I said to Hades before he interrupted me.

"You're not trying hard enough. If you want to be a bird forever, then give up. Fine. But don't whine about it."

"I don't want to be a bird," I shouted.

"Then SHIFT and be your peachy demon self again or shut up and accept that you have only me to talk to for the rest of your fucking life." He threw his wings out, challenging me.

That. Son. Of. A. Bitch.

He was being a giant asshole and everyone in the room was just letting him.

My chest heaved with anger.

Rava leaned toward me, speaking in low tones. "C'mon, Fury. He's calling you out."

"She can't shift. She'll fail her mission. Just as useless as the poltergeists. The world will end, and it will all be because she's too—"

I was going to kill him.

Adrenaline shot through me, and my joints popped. I felt a gush of wind over my body as I screamed.

Then I heard it.

My scream, a real one, echoed in the cave, reverberating off the walls while little pebbles vibrated on the floor.

"Fury!" Rava cried out, throwing her arms around me while my mates let out a collective sigh of relief.

My contentment was short-lived when I saw Hades standing on the boulder.

I reached out and took a step, stumbling. I felt weak and tired, cold and completely uncoordinated. "You little fucker! I'm going to—"

Rava held me. "Don't, Fury. He helped you shift," she said quickly.

"I—what?" I furrowed my brows.

"You're welcome. Again," Hades said, taking a bow.

"I caught on to what he was doing. Ezra heard me and shared it with Roman and Dorian," she explained, releasing me only slightly. "You'd said you were angry when you shifted during your fall. He made you angry so you could fuel the shift back to yourself. It was worth a shot, and it turned out to be the right thing. We'll work on it more later, but for now, we have you back."

I looked at Hades with an apologetic smile. He tilted his head to the side, and I was pretty sure he knew that was my way of acknowledging what he'd done. Had he not been there, I would've died—if I could die. We still didn't know.

She let me go and I tried to steady myself. A burst of cold registered in my mind. I looked down. I shifted. I was myself. And I was also butt-naked. My nipples were hardened, and goosebumps pebbled my skin. I rubbed my hands over my arms and looked at Dorian.

"Right, of course," he said. "Sorry."

In an instant I had clothes. I breathed a sigh of relief. The guys moved toward me, but I held my hand up to them. "I'm fine, honestly. But give me a second to get acclimated."

"What happened?" Dorian and Roman said in unison.

"Did Lyra bring you here right after she took you?" Dorian asked.

I nodded. "Yeah. Not the cave, obviously, but Avalon. Outside the castle, near the cliffs."

"What happened? What did she say?" he pressed.

Fractured pieces of our cliffside standoff put themselves back together, playing like a film in my mind.

Her madness.

Her blame.

That voice . . .

My dead husband's face flashed in my memories.

A tremor shook my body.

The angel.

It was impossible.

"Tell them," Ezra said quietly, looking at the ground with his arms crossed.

I shot a glare at him, a spike of anger coursing through me before I let it go.

"Tell us what?" Dorian asked.

I looked at Dorian and I felt so much sadness. I didn't know where to start, but the beginning was probably the best place. "She's being used, Dorian. The angel controls her. Manipulates her. Maybe even the same way she does with her victims."

"Did she say that?" Roman asked, taking a step closer to me, his anxiety spiking.

"Not in so many words, but basically, yeah." I looked away. "It gets worse," I whispered. "I think . . . she kept talking about a light. Looking into a light. I think after the angel killed her mother, he punished her for it. It wasn't seeing her mother killed that sent her over the edge. It was him. And he's conditioned her to think he's taking away her agony, but he tormented her then and he's doing it now."

A darkness flashed through Dorian's amber eyes and a low rumble sounded in his chest.

Being clothed again warmed my body quickly, but I put my hands in my pockets anyway, rocking on my feet a little. It was an awkward feeling to pass on the news about his daughter being tortured. "She had moments of lucidity, though. It was extremely brief. Like she's still in there, but she's in an incredible amount of emotional pain and that outweighs everything."

Rava shuddered, clearly remembering something similar, though I didn't know what. "I tried to fight her control when she was inside my head. Maybe she's fighting the angel too?"

"You did," I told her, recalling the moment she'd broken through in our fight. "And I think you're right. If he's been at this for a long time, if it was him who started it, who knows how shattered her mind is."

Roman crossed his arms. "Why, though? Her downfall into . . . what happened a thousand years ago has nothing to do with right now. It has nothing to do with Fury."

I sighed. "The first event has nothing to do with me, but him bringing her back? That's one hundred percent for me." I relayed her message to me, trying to remember each and every word she said.

Dorian ran his fingers through his hair, pacing and

grumbling. "This doesn't make any sense. Why? What does this angel want?"

I met Ezra's gaze and straightened my shoulders. I wanted nothing more than to pretend that never happened, but he already knew it.

"The angel showed up," I said.

All eyes pinned me with concern, anger, anxiety, possessiveness—you name it.

"And?" Roman said through gritted teeth.

"And he's making himself appear like my husband. Ex-husband. We didn't really divorce since he killed me, but I like to think of him as my ex," I answered.

Dorian and Roman froze. Even Hades didn't move. Roman's eyes didn't bother flickering. They just went straight to icy blue as he tried to suppress his response. The veins in his neck bulged, and the muscles beneath his shirt were taut as his body shook.

A cloud of something terrifying washed over Dorian. For the first time, his eyes took on a different amber hue. Gone were the warm shades of gold. An amber red circled his iris, eliciting a shiver to crawl across my skin. I'd watched his face. I saw the jaw tense. The eyelid twitch slightly.

Dorian moved a step closer to me but still kept his distance. Whether it was to give me space or control his emotions, I didn't know. "You said he's making himself appear to be. How do you know it's not him?"

I shook my head, reaching out to take his hand in mine. I held it firmly, meeting his swirling, violent eyes. "It can't be. John Adams was extinguished."

"He's playing a hell of a card in this game, then," Ezra said. "You froze when you heard his voice. Saw his face. He'll do it again to catch you off guard."

"Yes, thank you for that," I said with a clenched jaw. Annoyed as I was with him for reading my mind, he was right. No matter how much I knew the piece of shit was dead, the trauma . . . the history . . . it was always there. That moment I saw his face, it scared the hell out of me, and as much as I hated to admit it, hearing his voice sent fear through me that I'd thought was long gone. Turns out I was wrong.

Rava cleared her throat. "If this angel is the one that did this all to Lyra, is there a way we can reverse it?"

I smiled at her, ever the caring counselor. She didn't want to harm her. She wanted to fix her. We were on the same side in that. This wasn't Lyra's fault. It was the angel's. I didn't want Dorian to suffer the loss of his daughter. Roman and Ezra would respect that because that was what I wanted, and if they didn't, they'd hate the consequences. Hurting her would hurt Dorian, and that would hurt me. I flashed my vampire a look, making sure he heard every thought, and my threat. He blinked once slowly, audibly exhaling through his nose. I watched Roman's body language tense, and the muscle in his jaw tightened further. Ezra passed it on. Good.

"I don't know, but I plan on figuring it out," I admitted, answering Rava's question. "If I'm right and angel magic fucked with her head, maybe demon magic can fix it."

Dorian squeezed my hand back, silently thanking me.

"How do we do that?" Roman spoke carefully, testing the water to see how much input he had. I appreciated that he was at least trying to see my side. "I don't want to start off with the defeatist attitude here, but we can't capture her. We don't know where she is right now, and we don't have a way to subdue her."

"Jules can help us find her again. That's no problem. I'll

have Roxanne whip me up a bloody mary, and we'll summon her." I shrugged and waved a hand. That part was easy.

"And the rest?" he asked.

I grinned, quickly glancing at the crow who had waited patiently. "Hades?"

"Oh, I found what you wanted. Stole it too," he answered.

I explained my theory on the amulets in Jake's office and the one protecting Lyra. No one argued with me, and why should they? It was better than anything else we had so far. I had confidence. I was rarely wrong with stuff like this.

"There's more to this thing than you knew," Hades added. I raised my eyebrows in surprise and gestured for him to go on. "If I'm correct—and when have I not been—this not only bears magic from the Afterlife, but it might be able to trap magic *from* the Afterlife."

For the first time in a while, I felt a huge wave of excitement. I wanted to know more. I had so many questions. How did he find that out? Was Jake in on this? Did he know? Did Duke tell him about it? How could we test it?

Before I could give voice to any of the thoughts running through my mind, exhaustion slammed into me. Any energy I had escaped me instantly, and even though I hadn't moved, I lost my balance. Dorian held me up. I raised my hand to the side of my head, trying to stop the room from moving.

"We need to get her out of here now," Rava said, holding her arm up for Hades to land on her. "She's going to pass out."

"No, I'm not," I mumbled incoherently. "M'mm just . . ."

Ezra and Dorian stood beside me, and Roman touched Rava's back.

"My place," Ezra said.

A rush of wind blew over me as I teetered on the edge of consciousness and my vision blurred.

Hold on, kitten. We're taking you home.

Home . . .

CHAPTER 31

Dorian sifted us to Ezra's place. The impact jarred my already weak body, and I canted forward. Ezra caught me around the front and Dorian grabbed my shoulders.

"I got it," my vampire said.

"She needs water and rest," Dorian said without releasing me. "Don't give her alcohol." I groaned. They both ignored me.

"You do realize I am almost two-hundred, right? I think I can handle our mate for a few hours." His green eyes flashed with annoyance. While age was a sore subject between them all, Ezra and Dorian seemed to go at each other on this subject quite a lot.

"Never mind that your mate is a hundred and twenty-six and doesn't need 'handling'," I griped. Sure, my weak knees disagreed, but once I laid down for a bit I'd be right as rain.

"No sex either," Dorian added, still ignoring me. "She doesn't need to be getting so worked up right after her first shift."

I might have called him a cockblock if not for the sudden wave of dizziness. My head lolled forward, and Ezra snatched me up, pulling my front firmly against him, before bending to pick me up.

"No shit, Dorian," Ezra snapped. "Now if you'll excuse us—I need to lay her down."

I saw Dorian nod out of the corner of my eye, then sift out. Ezra walked through the penthouse, carrying me to his bedroom.

The bed dipped under me as he placed me gently under the covers and then crawled in behind me. Despite laying still, the dizziness intensified. My head spun as my face grew warm.

"Ezra," I murmured. "I don't think this is from shifting."

Before I could even finish, I felt my canines sharpen, my mouth turning sore.

"Shit," he cursed. "The bleeding. You need to bite me."

I rolled over and opened my mouth to object when spots appeared in my vision. Ezra looped an arm around my waist and pulled me in, placing the crook of his neck where my mouth was.

"Bite," he commanded "Now."

Giving in, I braced myself for the bleeding to come. My lips peeled back as I pressed my fangs into him. His skin gave way with a pop, and Ezra tensed.

Then the strangest thing happened.

The pressure in my head *subsided.*

I wasn't drinking his blood by any means. It was more like everything building up in me released *into* him.

Ezra rolled, pulling me on top of him. I straddled his waist, locking my arms around his neck. He groaned then sat up, shuffling us both until his back was against the wall.

His cock hardened beneath me.

While biting him was helping me feel better, the taste of our combined blood on my tongue was not sexy. I lifted my hips so I wasn't pressing into him, and Ezra skated his fingers up my spine, soothing me and kneading the muscle.

"That's right, kitten," he murmured. His voice reverberated through him where my lips pressed to the column of his throat. "Get it all out."

He must've been able to tell from the lack of suction that I wasn't drinking either.

It made no sense. A vampire that didn't *drink* blood, but instead *gave* it.

Would violently expel it, apparently, if not given.

I would have shaken my head at my own conundrum if it wouldn't have resulted in ripping a chunk of his flesh out. Ezra chuckled. "Much appreciated."

I let his obvious mind reading slip, at least this time. It had been a *long* afternoon, full of revelations and anxiety. Topped off with me needing to bite him so I didn't pass out and start bleeding out all my orifices.

Man, I really was a freak.

"Focus on the positives, Fury. We now have a solution to your predicament, and your animal has surfaced. You completed your first shift—"

I released his neck when the pressure completely faded, and my fangs started retracting. "Almost dying in the process," I added.

Ezra knotted his fingers in my hair and brought my mouth to his. He sucked on my bottom lip before licking my fangs clean of any traces of blood. While the blood giving wasn't a turn on for me, him licking me clean most definitely was.

I lowered my body down on him, rocking my hips

against his. The bulge between my thighs twitched. My hand slipped from his neck, down his chest to the edge of his slacks. He grabbed my hand from between us, linking our fingers and pulling it away.

I frowned, leaning away from the kiss.

Ezra sighed. "Dorian is right. Your body has been through a lot. As much as I would love to fuck you and see how long it takes to break this bed—you need rest."

I narrowed my eyes at him. "I feel much better. Besides," I scooted back, a devious smile cracking through the frown, "I owe you for eating me out in front of Kendrick."

I dropped my other hand to the front of his pants, rubbing my palm over his thick length. Ezra groaned, tilting his head back against the headboard.

"You're wicked," he said. "Utterly evil."

I slipped my fingers just over the hem of his pants and pulled. They ripped down the center. "Well, I am a demon." I smirked, wrapping my fist around his cock. My fingers couldn't completely wrap around, but the strong pump I gave had him stiffening.

"Fucking hell. I'll never live it down if they find out—"

His protest turned to a groan as I bent at the waist, taking him in my mouth.

Ezra released my hand and knotted it in my hair. I half expected him to pull me back, but instead he pulled me forward, thrusting upward. I gagged on his cock as the head penetrated the tight barrier of my throat.

He rocked in and out in shallow thrusts until I couldn't breathe.

Bringing me back to the shallow end, he yanked upward, and I followed.

"You sure you're up for this, kitten?"

I licked my lips, feeling the first inklings of my crow outside my shift. While not truly invasive, it was like having a set of emotions that weren't my own and yet it also drove me.

And right now? She was feeling possessive over Ezra. He'd pleased her when he had me bite him. Now she wanted to own him.

In that, we were in agreement.

"I won't tell if you won't."

In hindsight, I might have listened if I knew how much he liked being deep-throated. I was tuckered out. After a nap, then a bath, I sat at the kitchen bar while Ezra made me a bag of popcorn. Made was a bit of a stretch given he used the microwave, but I was still feeling boneless and not at all ready for the upcoming meeting. Hopefully, Jules could find Lyra again—and they could come up with a plan to capture her.

Not to mention the angel.

I really didn't want to rehash that again.

A bowl of popcorn appeared in front of me. I took a handful of buttery-goodness, munching on it idly while I worked through my thoughts.

"There's something we need to talk about," Ezra said. He crossed his arms over his chest, leaning back against the counter facing me.

I lifted an eyebrow, waiting for him to speak.

"Roman."

I tensed instantly. "What about him?"

Ezra sighed. "We need to talk about what happened the night of the burning ceremony."

My lips pursed. "You said you wouldn't come between me and my other mates."

"I'm not, actually. The opposite, in fact."

"Fine. What about it?" I asked stiffly.

"It's not what you thought it was," he said. "He wasn't calling you Maya. He was thinking about how what he feels for you is eclipsing her."

My mouth parted, not sure how to process the information.

"What do you mean by eclipsing her?"

Ezra ran a hand through his ink black hair, the dragon tattoo that wrapped around his chest moving as his muscles flexed. "It's not my place to say more, but you need to talk to him. You haven't given him the chance to explain. I know it hurt you, what you thought he was saying, but you don't want that conversation to be the last thing between you guys as we go into this." He motioned about, and I knew what he meant. This. The angel. Lyra. The inevitable fight that was coming, not including the Afterlife and their impatience with me for not having finished the mission.

"No, I don't," I agreed. A smidge of guilt ran through me for being unwilling to listen to him that night, and for avoiding him just about any other time we were near each other, but how else was I supposed to take it when he said another woman's name after claiming me? Especially the name of his deceased mate?

"Don't beat yourself up too much," Ezra said quietly.

"I won't." He gave me a look. "I mean it. I've got a lot on my plate right now, and I'm happy that's not what he meant—really—but I'm not going to lose sleep over it when we've got things to deal with that are way more important than my love life."

"I'd say that's debatable."

"Not really—"

"The angel," Ezra said. "He looked like your ex. Sounded like him."

I tilted my chin back, looking at the ceiling. "It's not possible," I said eventually.

"If it looks like a duck and quacks like a duck—"

"Not this time," I said. "There's got to be something I'm missing here, but it's truly *not possible* that it was my ex-husband."

Ezra narrowed his eyes, striding forward. "How do you know for certain?"

"Because—"

The clock ticked as it hit seven o'clock. Dorian sifted in instantly, followed by Tristan with Rya. Next came Rava with Roman, who dropped him off and then went back for Caitlin and Roxanne.

Ezra clapped his hands together, rubbing them in anticipation.

"It's a full house tonight," he said. "Feel free to help yourselves to food and drinks, but heads up, there's no alcohol in the apartment. Roxanne is only bringing what's necessary for Jules."

"Good," Dorian commented. "She doesn't need it." He looked pointedly at me. I stuck my tongue out in reply. I know, very mature.

"Why do you think I don't have any?" Ezra responded, surprising the hell out of me.

I turned my affronted face on him, and he winked, not giving a solitary fuck.

I was definitely regretting that blow job right now.

I should've bitten his dick instead.

Ezra choked on a laugh, clearly hearing my train of thought. I flipped him off as I slid over the edge of the stool. Roman stood off to the side, surveying the situation with stormy blue eyes and hunched shoulders.

He appraised me as I walked up to him and angled my head toward the hallway. Getting the gist, he followed me out of the room. I escorted him down the hall, away from prying eyes and ears even though it would be impossible to escape them all.

My room is soundproof, Ezra said telepathically.

Thanks for that.

I took Roman to the bedroom, hoping he couldn't smell what happened earlier. If he could, his face gave nothing away. He stood at the far end of the bed, watching me as I closed the door.

"We should talk about what happened . . . that night," I started. "I recently realized that I might have been hasty in refusing to listen to you."

"Ezra told you," he said, clearly not thrilled about the idea.

I bit the inside of my cheek and nodded. "Only a little bit. He told me it wasn't what I thought, and that I needed to come to you about it."

Roman sighed, his shoulders sagging, but whether it was from relief or feeling defeated, I wasn't sure. "Normally I'd want to rip his fangs out for interfering in our relationship." He scratched the back of his head, rolling his neck. "In this case, I should probably thank the bastard."

I gave him a wry smile. "What happened that night, Roman? Why did you call me Maya—or at the very least— why did you say her name when you were still *inside me*?"

His expression changed, dropping in shame, but he didn't look away or back down.

"I never meant to say her name. I wasn't thinking of her in that way, or imagining you were Maya. I just—we mated. Fully. I marked you. I fucked you—and it was everything that I never thought I'd have or feel again. It was *more*. What I feel for you is different from what I felt for Maya, but not any less. If anything, I felt guilty because these feelings I have for you are possessive and territorial and bestial in a way I wasn't with her." He exhaled a heavy breath. "I loved Maya, but it was the kind of love you have from being raised with someone and falling in love with them for the first time. I don't want to call it puppy love, because that disrespects her memory and the life we shared—but I can't help but feel like I didn't love her the way she truly deserved—the way I love you."

My mouth fully dropped open.

Speechless.

That was my name.

"You don't have to say it back. I'd rather you didn't until you feel it too. I just want you to understand what happened that night wasn't regret or me using you to replace her. I was caught up in all the emotions of being mated again and the realizations I was only just starting to piece together for myself."

Still struggling with how to respond but not wanting him to feel rejected, I walked up and pressed my lips to his. Roman melted beneath my touch. His rough hands grasped me around the waist, lifting me clear off the ground so he could kiss the hell out of me.

I wrapped my legs around his body and a chuckle slid from his beautiful lips.

"As sexy as you are, and as much as I've missed you—I

can smell what you and Ezra were up to. I'm not interested in a quickie or fucking you on the same bed."

"Maybe one day you'll both fuck me in the same bed," I murmured playfully against his lips. His breath hitched, and I smirked. "But you're right. The others are probably here by now."

He slid me down his body until my feet touched the floor. While the wounds were still healing—for both of us it would seem—he'd managed to renew my fragile trust in him and make it even stronger than it was before.

Voices from the living room washed over me as soon as we opened the door, and the scent of the bloody mary Roxanne made for Jules reached my nose. Most everyone was seated on or around the giant sectional. A mirror leaned over the flat screen, balancing on the mantelpiece, and bracing against the wall.

I walked around to the front and kneeled to grab the drink off the coffee table. Roman took a seat between Roxanne and Caitlin, Rava making room for him by sitting on her partner's lap.

"Okay, I'm going to call Jules and we can see if she's found Lyra. If she has, we come up with a plan to separate her from the—"

The air shifted around me, and I stopped.

Everyone bristled with hostility, jumping up in reaction to whatever was behind me. I followed their gazes to just over my shoulder and slowly turned around.

The drink slipped from my fingers. Glass shattered and the bloody mary pooled around our feet like blood.

Duke stood before me, his friendly smile lighting up the room.

"How's it going, kiddo?"

I threw my arms around him, blinking rapidly to stop

the water that was building up in my tear ducts from falling down my face. Elated as I might be, I had a reputation to protect.

Clearly. I sniffed.

Duke hugged me back, letting out a boisterous laugh. When I released him, the tension in the room eased, but it wasn't exactly what I'd call friendly.

"Ummm, Fury, who's this?" Roxanne asked.

"This," I turned back to them, "is Duke. He's my oldest and dearest friend."

Duke snorted, slinging his arm around my shoulder. "We died a half second apart. Fury here kept me company until my beautiful wife and daughters passed on many years later." Roman and Dorian visibly relaxed upon seeing that we were very much in the only-friends category, despite being close.

"I'm happy to meet you. Fury's unintentionally told me quite a bit," Ezra said, sticking his hand out.

Duke took it, giving him a firm shake. "You must be Ezra. Your telepathy definitely threw the Afterlife for a loop. I've been saying for years the poltergeists have gotten lax."

"You're telling me," I huffed. Fucking useless was more like it.

"We've heard all about the poltergeists and issues with Fury's mission. I have to say, it almost seems like someone in the Afterlife wanted her to fail with all the things we've encountered," Dorian said slowly.

Duke nodded, his jovial expression turning muted. "You're not the only one who thought so. That's actually why I'm here. I started looking into things. The prophecy. Why Fury was chosen. Her history. Whatever I could get my hands on to try to see if she'd ever unintentionally had encounters with an angel."

My chest thundered. "And?"

He shook his head. "It's not good, kid. Upper Management has kept *a lot* of shit under wraps—"

"The angel," I said, gripping his forearm. "Tell me about him. Who is he? Why is he after me?"

Duke gave me a sad fucking smile that made my stomach bottom out.

"You might want to sit down for this one—"

"Tell me," I insisted.

"Azrael," Duke said softly. "The archangel of death. The wearer of a thousand faces."

I frowned. "I've never met Azrael. Not once—"

"But you have," Duke said softly. "You were married to him."

I reeled back, feeling the color leach from my face. "No-no—that can't—I extinguished him," I said in an angry whisper. Anxiety and adrenaline raced through me. "I watched the records. He died of a heart attack at fifty-two. They were going to let him in. He wasn't even going to be punished. I—I killed his soul, Duke. There's no coming back from that. For anyone."

Duke shook his head slowly. "Baby girl, you killed the wrong man. You married John Adams, but Azrael took John's place over most of the time you two were married."

Sound warbled in and out. I'd killed the wrong . . . *no*. It couldn't be . . .

"I don't understand," I muttered. "I . . . why?"

He placed his hand over mine as I held onto his arm firmly. "Azrael was sent to kill you. He deviated from his mission, but Upper Management had been turning a blind eye to his exploits for centuries. Until you got pregnant with his child . . . children from the Afterlife are forbidden,

Fury. Exterminated when they're found without question or compassion."

I stumbled, reaching blindly for something to hold me up. Ezra was there. He caught me by the waist as my legs shook, threatening to give out. "I-I don't understand. Why was he sent for me? I was just a girl . . . no one. Why was he sent to kill me?"

Nothing on this world or the next could have prepared me for his next words.

"You weren't a no one. You were . . . forbidden. An abomination. A descendant of angels."

To be continued. . .

EVERYONE WANTS TO BE DIFFER-
ENT, **until they are. Take it from a true Heinz 57, being special isn't all it's cracked up to be.**

Especially when it sets off a series of events that will end the world. You know, the catastrophe I was sent to prevent in the first place.

Fate has a funny way of doing whatever it wants.

In trying to change the future, I'm now the catalyst for destruction.

I should have known it was a bad omen when I shifted into a white raven instead of a wolf.

Our enemies may be more powerful than we ever imagined, but I've got a talking crow and Bloody Mary on my side.

I have friends now—and family. Not to mention, one hell of a love life I have no intention of giving up. I would die for any of them, but that's not the plan.

It's time to see if I can stop this black swan.

Tick. Tock.

ONE CLICK BLACK SWAN NOW!

Join Kel's Newsletter: www.kelcarpenter.com

www.ingramcontent.com/pod-product-compliance
Lightning Source LLC
Chambersburg PA
CBHW060655190726

48289CB00002B/415